THE BREACH

EDWARD J. MCFADDEN III

SEVERED PRESS
HOBART TASMANIA

THE BREACH

"We cannot prevent equilibrium from producing its effects. We may brave human laws, but we cannot resist natural ones," Captain Nemo, 20,000 Leagues Under the Sea

1

Mother Nature was still undefeated.

The ninth hole tee box stood above the floodwater like an island, and trees and bushes climbed from the dark water and cast spiderlike shadows across the flooded golf course. A dinghy was tied off on the signpost, showing a diagram of the ninth hole, and the Zodiac slapped against the water as it bobbed on the temporary sea. Insects buzzed and chirped in rhythm with the distant waves, and somewhere a seagull squawked. Marine cop Nate Tanner took a pull of bourbon and thought of all the drives he'd shanked from where he sat.

The night was dark and damp and the air smelled of rot. Clouds obscured the stars, but stray beams of moonlight shined through gaps and reflected off the Great South Bay. A light fog floated just above the floodwater like a carpet, and Tanner felt like he could step off the tee box onto the plush rug and walk to the station out on Wood Point with the mist seeping between his toes. He took another pull of Jack Daniels and wiped his mouth with the back of his hand.

Four days had passed since the storm hit and most of the news vans had left the island, but the destruction remained. Hurricane Tristin was a bitch, and she had slapped Long Island harder than any storm ever had. The Category 4 nightmare that displaced half the population, knocked out all utilities, and turned large sections of the south shore into Little Venice, would take decades to fully recover from. Landfall was a direct hit, and the wind and flooding left everything east of New York City crippled.

Tristin made landfall on August 24th, 2019, at approximately 12:59PM, and Tanner recalled every detail of the harrowing night. The storm tore a quarter-mile hole in Long Island's southern barrier island, and the Atlantic Ocean poured through the breach into the Great South Bay, which was technically a lagoon. Long Island endured sustained winds of over one hundred and fifty miles per hour, and suddenly Tanner felt differently about the extra expense of hurricane strapping in home construction. Strict building codes helped save the day, and though many houses had damage, most still stood. The wind had been the worst part for Tanner. It found every crack and weak point. Wind can't be stopped, and given enough time, like water, it proved to be one of Mother Nature's most powerful weapons.

Pale light leaked from the top of the marine command tower and spilled across the floodplain that had been the third and sixth holes. The tower was manned, despite the lower level of the station being flooded. Tanner saw the dark silhouette of Kipper's head in the window. Wood Point Golf Course surrounded the station on two sides, the bay and a canal on the other two. Tanner and his crew did their best to fortify the seawalls around the station, but the storm surge had been too much. He'd retreated, though the station survived the worst beating the brick structure had ever been exposed to.

Tanner tossed back more whiskey and recalled the night his life changed. It had been almost a year—he'd shot a boy, arrested a senator, and Audrey left him, all on the same night. It was like every bad thing he'd ever done came home to roost at the same time. Then came Tristin like a bad rebound: mean, jilted, and ready to wreak havoc.

Something swam past, but he couldn't make out what it was. Most likely an odd duck out for a swim in the dark. All the animals had been acting strangely since the storm and Tanner figured their circadian clocks were off like his was because he couldn't sleep for more than five minutes at a clip. When he closed his eyes, he heard the howl of the wind and running water, and he'd wake drenched in sweat.

Tanner raked fingers through his hair, jerked his head side to side, and rolled his shoulders, trying to crack his neck. He failed, and pain shot down his spine to the tips of his toes. His chest was ice, and as he took another pull of booze, his stomach gurgled and protested the lack of food. The last four days seemed unending, and he was tired, unshaven, and in need of a shower and sleep. In the morning, he and his crew would continue the arduous task of clearing the bay of major impediments, while the coasties worked to get the buoys set and the major waterways open. The Sound led to New York Harbor, and despite the south shore of Long Island taking the brunt of the hurricane, most of the Coast Guard units worked the north shore to ensure the Sound was passable.

A high-pitched hum rose above the roar of the insects and Tanner's ears rang. It sounded like a massive cicada, except it had a dolphin-ish quality, a gentle squeak that clicked just below a rising buzz. The water around Tanner's little island rippled, and the gentle two-inch waves lapping over the grass grew to a foot. Breaking whitecaps sloshed across the tee box and rushed over his boots.

A mountain of churning whitewater rolled toward Tanner.

The smell of rotting flesh and seawater washed over him, and Tanner staggered back, his vision blurred. Trees moved and swayed, shadows danced, and the rumble of rushing water grew. Thick clouds sailed overhead, the night grew darker, and the dancing shadows disappeared like phantoms. Bay water mounded above the floodplain as if Poseidon himself climbed from the depths to remind Tanner he was the god of all waters, not just the oceans.

Tanner dropped his bottle, jumped into the dingy, and pulled the motor's starter cord. The waves grew in height as the sea advanced in a roiling knot, and the sound of the giant cicada drowned out the other insects. Pain lanced Tanner's back as he strained to start the engine. The motor sputtered as he pulled the cord harder and faster, but the engine only choked and popped.

When Tanner was a boy, his dad told him stories about the Vietnam War, and how sometimes doing nothing was the smartest thing, even when facing great danger. Take a breath, count to ten, run through your protocols, then act. He remembered telling his father how crazy that sounded. You're drowning, or being chased, and you stop to think? With the chase example, his dad admitted no, you wouldn't stop and think, but the rest of the time his advice was solid.

Tanner counted, pulled the starter cord, and the engine caught and roared to life. He untied the guide rope and slid the throttle switch to maximum. The Zodiac churned like a brick through the water, passing trees, bushes, the tops of ball washers, and signs. A fist of water trailed behind the boat, and Tanner jerked the outboard's control handle left. The boat arced right as the ten-horsepower Merc screamed and clawed at the floodwater.

The fog grew thick inland, and it was hard to avoid floating debris and low areas. The trailing mound crested, and the push of water lifted the boat and drove it forward as Tanner hunkered down. Dry land crunched beneath the boat and Tanner leapt over the gunnel onto slick grass. He slid a few feet, his arms outstretched for balance, and skidded to a halt beneath a thin oak tree. The whitewater dissipated like a bubble below the surface had burst, and floodwater rushed over the grass and around the trees.

The high-pitched clicking ended with a deep, hollow grunt that was replaced with a skittering sound that reminded Tanner of cockroaches. Thousands of crabs poured from the water, scuttling over tree roots and grass as they rushed to escape the flood. Blue claws and hermits climbed over the slower-moving horseshoe crabs and headed for the trees and dry land.

Tanner ran, hit his head on a branch, and went down like a sack of potatoes.

"You alright?" his mother asked, her face in a halo of white.

"Not really, Momma," Tanner said.

"Well, suck it up, buttercup," said his mother as she faded, and he faded with her.

2

The day was clear and cool, but a rank salty-shit breeze permeated the air like the scent of smoke after a fire. Tanner's head pounded. He had to stop getting banged up. His worn-out body just couldn't handle it. At forty-two, his binge-drinking days were behind him, but since Audrey left, he'd been trying to rekindle his love of booze and was failing miserably.

He drove slowly through the tunnel of fallen trees and debris that lined the side of the road. It brought back memories of his youth, when Gloria tore across Long Island. Tanner and his friends built an intricate fort and tunnel system through the debris piles, and he remembered how disappointed he'd been when the dump trucks came around a month later to fully clear the road and destroy all their hard work.

A commercial jet lumbered overhead, leaving a white streak and a rumble of thunder. The plane stood out; MacArthur Airport had been closed to commercial flights for four days, but now was open and a limited schedule of flights had started.

The water along the shoreline receded overnight, but not enough to make any difference because the tide had been brutal.

"Oh, shit," Tanner said. The captain's white Tahoe was parked on the grass next to two boats lying on their keels, motors up. Tanner had moved the main base of operations for the marine division to an old post office at the edge of the flooding. The red brick structure hadn't been used for years, but its sturdy mid-century construction left it standing tall amidst the destruction. It was set back off the first unflooded road to the north of the swamped golf course, and small craft could travel with ease out to where the larger boats were tethered to the PD station and its makeshift docks.

It was almost 10AM and the captain was going to give him a tongue-lashing for being late when so much needed to be done. When he saw the chief talking on his phone and pacing back and forth, he knew his day, which hadn't been anything special so far, was about to get worse. He'd decided to keep what he'd seen... what he thought he'd seen the prior night to himself. Nothing good would come of telling anyone, even if it hadn't been a whiskey-induced dream.

Tanner swung his battered Jeep in next to the boss's car and got out. "Morning, Captain. Sorry I don't have coffee ready, but I—"

"Save it," the boss said, "and open this door before I lose my shit." Tanner complied. "Where you been? Don't tell me sleeping another one off."

Tanner said nothing.

Captain Terry Quinn and Tanner went all the way back to the academy, and if it wasn't for Quinn, Tanner would have been fired long ago. The man had eyes as hard as rocks, and twice as cold. When Quinn looked at you, it was as if your mother herself was giving you the stink eye. Above his hard eyes, thick eyebrows knitted together, and a dark caterpillar mustache made his face look fat. Quinn was a good man, and a good cop. He didn't like screw-ups, and at that moment, that's what Tanner was, but something in the captain's face made Tanner think the sweet scent of opportunity might be on the air.

Once inside the old post office, they took seats around a folding table that served as Tanner's desk, atop which sat all the stuff that had come in the last couple of days that he hadn't looked at. The captain picked up a sealed envelope. "My written orders from two days ago." He held the envelope up as evidence.

"Don't you have someplace more important to be?" Tanner asked. "Half the island is underwater and you're worried about me being on time to gather driftwood? What's up?"

"What's up is you're an idiot. Why don't you answer your phone?"

"Dead battery."

Quinn sighed. "What about your radio?"

"I forgot it in the car."

"You forgot? You sound like my teenage son."

Tanner was getting pissed. "I don't have time to play wet-nurse with you today. I've—"

"Zip it," Quinn said. "Did you know three people are missing on the bay? Three separate vessels?"

That shut Tanner down. He rolled his shoulders and cracked his neck. Pain throbbed down his back, and his stomach sank like he'd just jumped from an airplane.

"What? No wiseass comment?"

Tanner said nothing.

Quinn slid a file across the table and Tanner stopped it with his palm. "Not much there," Quinn said. "Clammer's wife said he left at his normal time and never came back, and two recreational boaters scouting through the wreckage have been reported missing. Aerial has done a full overhead, and they think they spotted three debris fields, though they weren't certain on one of them. There's a lot of hurricane debris in the water. You can see in the pictures that—"

"I'll be going out there, don't need pictures yet," Tanner said.

Quinn just stared at him, breathed deep, and said, "Jurisdiction technically falls with the Coast Guard, but they're stretched so thin, boaters taking unnecessary risks won't be high on their priority list. So I think marine division should lead. But not you."

"Why?"

"You got no capital. You're an Italian bank. One step out of line and the jet-ski gang will bounce you. And what if there's something to this and your mug ends up on News 12?"

"Don't give me that shit. You were there that night also, sir, or do I need to remind the world?"

Quinn's face puckered. "Don't threaten me, dipshit, or blame me for where you are. You want to be cutting up tree branches with a hand saw? I know that's nothing next to busting the hardcore criminals out on the bay. Little girls taking seventeen-inch fluke."

Tanner laughed. It was funny. "I'm the aquatic crime scene expert. That's *one* reason I'm here. I'm not asking for special treatment, just fair treatment."

"You embarrass me on this and you're done. No more soft landings and cozy morning coffees on the bay checking fishing licenses. You will be done. Are we clear?"

Tanner nodded, but said nothing.

"Are we clear!"

"Yes!" Then in a softer tone, "Sir."

"Find out what happened. Make it fast, because you may be needed inland," Quinn said. "What's the status of the fleet?"

Tanner's eyes shifted to the floor. He didn't know. "We're still evaluating, but we have *Big Boy*, our forty-two footer, and three SAFE boats ready to power out. Two of the smaller center consoles actually floated inland and were found basically where they sit out front. We use them to go back and forth to the station."

"What's it like out there?"

Tanner shook his head. "Ain't pretty, sir. Not pretty at all. The tower is useable, but to get to it, you have to climb through a second-story window because the first floor is still flooded."

"You OK?" Quinn asked softly, now using his friendly tone.

"As well as anyone else. This one really kicked the snot out of us."

"Sure did. The cost estimates are off the charts. Our grandchildren will be picking up after this bitch."

Silence fell between them, and that's when Tanner knew something else was up, something his old buddy hadn't told him yet. Quinn could have called him about the missing persons, and usually when the small talk was done, Quinn would be back on his phone and hurrying to get someplace he didn't really need to be. Tanner let the silence hang there. Like when someone farts and everyone in the room pretends not to smell it.

Quinn coughed softly, and that's when Tanner knew it was coming. "One other matter."

"I'm getting a raise?" Tanner said.

"You've been busted down a rank for that shit you pulled with the woman over at Davis Park last year." Quinn breathed out, like a brick had been lifted from his chest.

"Bullshit."

"Not bullshit. It was all I could do to save your ass. She wanted you fired. I had to agree to bust you down a rank and give her a stack of PBA cards for her and her friends. How many petty larcenies and speeding tickets will never be now because of your bullshit? You've become a real nut-sack."

"You're a riot, Alice. A real riot."

"You grabbed her ass," Quinn said.

"She wishes."

"With the reduction in rank comes a pay cut. Stay straight and when everything blows over…bad choice of words. When everything quiets down, and Ms. Layborn forgets all about you, I'll see what I can do about getting you reinstated. Technically, Randy is in charge now, but I don't care what you two do. I think it makes sense for you to stay in command, but the official word is you've been busted down and he's in charge."

"You did all this because you love and cherish me?"

"Don't mess around. Now's not the time. Keep me appraised. I expect to hear from you by sunset at the latest."

3

The Johnson outboard gurgled and shook as the eighteen-foot Boston Whaler inched across the flooded golf course, causing a mini-tsunami that gently rolled through the trees and shrubbery not fully submerged in the floodwater. Tanner had the motor tilted up in case it got shallow, and the lower unit sucked air and struggled to take in the water needed to cool the engine. Debris floating just below the surface could damage the outboard, so he was being extra cautious in the flood area.

A line of geese flew south across the bay in a tight V-formation, trailed by seagulls and pipers. It reminded Tanner of the fall exodus that was still two months off. The scent of salt-shit faded as he left land and its troubles behind. So he'd lost some money. So what. He already lived in a trailer park...well, what was left of it, anyway. His rank? He laughed. He was heading onto the bay, and that made everything all right.

Randy Vernon stood next to Tanner, and there was no other person he trusted more. Because of his recent drop in the pecking order, Randy was now his boss. They hadn't discussed it. Both men wore jeans, blue inflatable PFDs, faded blue Suffolk County PD work shirts, and were strapped with Glock 19s. Randy had a tight crew cut, but Tanner's dark shoulder-length hair blew across his face and tickled his nose. King Quinn regularly pointed out that his hair was longer than was permitted, and Tanner would tell him to break out the tape measure.

The boat edged against the floating dock tethered to the flooded station house, and with the unspoken practiced ease of dancers who'd performed the same routine together many times, Tanner and Randy tied off the center console and shifted their gear to a twenty-two-foot SAFE boat with blue inflated pontoons and an aluminum cabin. The craft had twin two-hundred horsepower Honda four-stroke ultra-cooled outboards that ran so quiet you could whisper to your girl on a cell phone as they pulled 5000 RPMs.

The dance continued, and Tanner punched the coordinates aerial division had given him into the GPS as Randy piloted the boat out into the bay. They waved to Kip in the tower, who gave them the single finger salute. The wind was light, and the steady chop cutting northeast was minimal, small rollers that were no more than seagull farts. Randy brought the Hondas up to speed, but Tanner barely heard them. The beater he used to cruise around the bay had an old Johnson two-stroke that screamed bloody murder unless it was in its sweet spot of 2200 RPM exactly.

"Where to ca…boss?" Randy said.

"You can still call me captain of this vessel. That is unless you want the responsibility?"

"No, I'll take a pass on that if it's OK with you."

Some people lead, and some followed. "Glad that bullshit is out of the way. Everything OK at home?" Tanner asked.

"Got some water in the basement, and I might need to rip the sheetrock in the sunroom. Told you we built that bastard too low." Randy looked out at the water. "Where to first? Looks like both pleasure crafts were in inland flood areas. The clammer was over in the flats outside the breach."

"Head over to the breach," Tanner said.

Randy jerked the wheel, and the boat leaned to starboard as he avoided a patch of seaweed. Tanner saw chunks of wood and other debris floating in the tangled mass of green and brown as they passed it. A cross wind was throwing sea spray, and Tanner tasted salt on his lips and his shades dulled as a sheen of water covered the lenses. The sun was rounding ten o'clock, the green water awash with dappled sun rays. Randy pulled back on the controls, and the tone of the motors lessened.

"You gonna tell me what's got you spooked?" Randy asked.

"What shit are you rambling about?"

"I know you. What's bothering you? You lie to the captain about something just now?"

"It's what I didn't lie about," Tanner said. "When the hell did you become a detective?"

"Just know you. You usually walk around like you live on a cloud and the rest of the world grinds below you to make your life good."

"You saying I act like a god?"

Randy said nothing.

The hole in Fire Island National Seashore was a quarter-mile wide, and had become a labyrinth of sandbars, tidal pools, wave breaks, and fast-flowing channels that changed every minute with the pull of the tide and shifting weather. Breaches had opened and closed on Fire Island before, and the current one was an expansion of a prior breach. Each time one opened, the debate began about whether the Army Core of Engineers should be asked to close it, with solid evidence on both sides saying it would help or hurt marine biology and water quality. On the horizon, white waves broke across sandbars as the turbulent Atlantic Ocean pushed its way into the bay.

More birds flew south overhead, and the sonar showed a mass migration of fish and crabs heading out of the bay through the breach. Tanner thought of the crabs from the night before, how they'd fled the bay as if their lives depended on it.

"I think some strange shit happened last night," he said.

"You think?" Randy said.

"I was a bit under the weather."

"Sure. A cold, and you took some cough medicine." Randy barely contained a smile.

"Cough medicine. Yeah, that, so I may have a distorted memory of reality."

"How much cough medicine did we have?"

Tanner looked at the deck. "I felt pretty shitty."

Randy chuckled. "And? What did Alice see down the rabbit hole?"

Tanner spilled it all; the waves, the rolling sea coming at him, chasing him inland, and the crabs. He left out the part about falling like a child and hitting his head.

"Shit. Good thing you didn't tell the captain that. He might have pulled you and insisted on a psych evaluation. No way you pass that shit."

"Thanks," Tanner said.

"What's that?" Randy said, pointing.

Before them, off the port side, a gas slick glittered in the sunlight and in the middle of it a barking dog clung to a seat cushion. Randy spun the wheel, and the boat arced left across the water. Waves crashed three hundred yards to the south, and to the north a sandbar towered above the waterline.

The dog yapped and whined as Randy shut down the motors and glided through the debris field. There wasn't much left. Some pieces of wood covered in fiberglass, a cooler, pieces of lifejackets, and seat cushions. Sonar picked up a motor, but Tanner couldn't see it beneath the shifting sands. The dog growled and bared its teeth as the boat eased up beside him. It looked to be a mutt, a terrier mixed with a black Lab. He was small, with curly hair and a long snout, and Tanner plucked him off the seat cushion with a crab net and dumped him on the deck.

The animal got up, shook himself off, and wagged his tail and barked, as if to say "where's the food?" Tanner lowered his head and put out the back of his hand as he approached the animal, and as he bent down to pet the dog, the furball sprang forward and licked his face.

"You sure are a lucky shit, boy," Randy said.

"Lucky-shit," Tanner said. "I like that. How you doing, Lucky-shit?"

Lucky-shit barked and wagged his tail.

"Maybe LS. Cause of the kids and all," Randy said.

"I don't have kids."

"Yeah, but who are we kidding? This animal will eventually end up living with me."

"LS it is then," Tanner said.

Randy started the motors and piloted the boat across the debris field in a widening grid pattern. It was clear a clamming garvey made of fiberglass-covered wood had been destroyed in the breach, but the small pieces and lack of rough seas led Tanner to believe the breach hadn't destroyed the boat. If the craft had foundered in the breach, it would have rolled and broken apart. Larger pieces would be visible and there would be more floating debris. It was almost as if the boat had been put in a giant blender.

"Oy," yelled Randy.

LS ran to the front of the boat, put his front paws on the gunnel, and barked.

"I see it," Tanner said.

A boot floated on the surface at the edge of the debris field, and Tanner snagged it from the sea and dumped it on the deck as he had LS. The dog shot toward it and sniffed the open end of the large white rubber boot.

LS backed away when he got a whiff, his tail between his legs.

There was a foot in the boot.

4

Tanner and Randy sped across the bay in silence. LS lay sleeping on the deck behind the pilot bench, exhausted from being in the water for hours. The foot was on ice and carefully wrapped in a plastic evidence bag. The two mariners hadn't spoken about it. What was there to say? There weren't many hazards in the ocean that could cut your foot off clean right to the edge of a boot. It was surgical, as if a giant blade had hacked the foot from its leg with one clean slice. A freak accident was an explanation, as was a shark, but he didn't think a shark had done it. Sharks tear and rip their prey by thrashing their head back and forth, leaving a frayed mess.

Another line of geese passed overhead, moving south, but they made no noise. The splash of the bay as the SAFE boat knifed through the water and the gentle rumble of the boat's motors were the only sounds. The sun had marched past noon, and the sea was choppy with boat wake. Patches of seaweed rolled over the bay like brown polka dots on emerald fabric, and a large patch caught Tanner's eye. He directed Randy toward it as he peered through binoculars.

Randy said, "Where do you think the rest of the body is? It should've been floating, yeah?"

Tanner said nothing.

"Yup," Randy said.

They came upon what they'd thought was a large, thick seaweed patch only to discover it wasn't seaweed at all.

"What do you make of that?" Randy said.

"Looks like shrimp turds," Tanner said.

"Smells like it, too. Must be a mighty big shrimp."

Tanner knifed him with his eyes, and Randy's smile fled away from his face. "You want me to take a sample?"

"Yeah. A big one."

LS lifted his head, sniffed the air, then put his head back down and closed his eyes.

Randy broke out the plastic gloves and a baggie. "Seriously though, what do you think this stuff is?" He leaned over the gunnel and scooped some of the light brown sludge into the baggie.

"Who knows? The hurricane dredged up all kinds of crap. Maybe it's a badly decomposed whale corpse."

"It don't smell like no fish."

Tanner had no response.

Sample taken and location marked, Randy slipped off his gloves and brought the Hondas back up to speed. The next location they'd been given was at the mouth of Brown's River. Rock jetties that marked the entrance to the canal were underwater, and the beach was nowhere to be seen. The houses, restaurants, and marinas along the canal were flooded and abandoned, the dock bulkheads barely visible in the brackish water. Everything imaginable floated in the flotsam and jetsam, and it was impossible to tell if a boat had been wrecked at the location. There were no boat parts floating on the surface and the sonar screen showed a dark line on the bottom and a lot of noise above. There were several sunken boats, but most appeared to be tied within slips.

They found no sign of the lost boater, so they took pictures and moved on. Tanner wondered what the hell the whirlybird had seen that made this area stand out from the normal destruction. Maybe he should have looked at the aerial pictures.

They headed back out onto the bay, this time cutting west under the bridge toward Babylon. The Ocean Beach Parkway was flooded, and the bridge to Democratic Point was closed to commercial and civilian traffic. The wind picked up, and a dark line of clouds moved in on the horizon to the west. The last thing they needed was more rain, but it looked as though that was exactly what they'd be getting come nightfall.

Tanner spotted the third debris field easily. A large chunk of a boat's bow bobbed in the waves, and a transom with an outboard still attached stuck out of the water. Tiny white-capped waves broke over the wreckage, which slowly drifted toward shore. The gas and oil slick had mostly dissipated, but the large boat chunks had dark oil rings around them at surface level. There was no body, or any signs of one.

Tanner and Randy looked at one another, but didn't speak. Tanner knew Randy was thinking the same thing as he was. What the hell had broken the boat up into such fine pieces, same as the first one? If it had capsized after hitting a piece of garbage, the boat would still be mostly intact. If there had been an explosion, the debris would show burn marks.

"What the...?" said Randy.

Tanner followed his gaze until he saw the large pincer claw floating in the water next to half a surfboard. Tanner nodded, and Randy eased the SAFE boat through the debris field toward the claw. For a third time, Tanner used the crab net to scoop up his prey.

The claw was bigger than any he'd ever seen, measuring over a foot. It was thin, with tiny teeth, and it reminded him of the secondary pincer claws of a lobster, the ones at the end of the legs you sucked the meat out of.

"I'm getting a real bad feeling," Randy said.

"Easy, Han." Tanner walked around the claw, examining it, afraid to touch it. He grabbed a gaff and poked it, but it didn't attack him.

LS walked across the deck and sniffed the claw, then looked up at Tanner with eyes and a wagging tail that said, "What are you poodles afraid of?" Then he barked and hopped.

"Easy, Lucky-shit," Tanner said.

Tanner heard the sound first, the same low-pitched wail as the night before. When Randy heard it, he said, "Oh, shit, you weren't screwing with me."

"Turn up the gain on the sonar," Tanner said. Randy bolted to the pilothouse with Tanner on his heels.

To port, a wave crested above the whitecaps, a snowball of water that grew as it rolled toward the boat. The sonar screen darkened as if the seafloor rose from the depths, and the bay surged like a giant bubble was fighting to the surface, white-green water and seaweed rolling their way. The boat shook and listed back and forth, throwing sunglasses and coffee cups off the control dash. A stench of rotting flesh punched Tanner in the gut, and he almost threw up. The screeching cry got louder and went higher in pitch. Tanner winced and put his hands over his ears.

"Screw this," he said. Tanner ran from the pilothouse, drew down on the wave, and fired as fast as he could pull the trigger, emptying his Glock 19 into the oncoming water.

The wave crested on the starboard side and dissipated into a swirl of whitewater and seaweed. The shrill wail faded, and a small two-foot chop slapped against the boat.

Randy stood next to him. "Sonar's clear. What the hell?"

"What the hell, indeed," Tanner said.

***

Tanner really didn't want to make this particular call. The sun started its descent to the horizon and rain clouds thickened and moved in.

As he waited for the captain to come on the line, Tanner pulled his flask from a pocket and looked over his shoulder. He didn't see Randy, so he took a fast pull and put the flask away.

"How'd you make out?" Captain Quinn asked.

"We've got a situation out here." Tanner held his marine phone to his ear. "One confirmed dead via an appendage, two vessels confirmed destroyed by an unknown force, several people missing and feared dead."

"You're joking," the captain said.

"There's something in the bay. Something big. Some kind of predator."

"A shark?"

"No," Tanner said. "Not like a shark at all. Much bigger. A bottom crawler. That's why we haven't seen it."

"What are we talking about here?"

"I don't know. Something I can't explain."

Captain Quinn sighed loudly. "I don't need this right now. Things down here are beyond out of control."

"Sorry I couldn't give you the answer you wanted," Tanner said.

"What do you recommend?"

It was Tanner's turn to sigh. "We need to close the bay and beaches to commercial and civilian traffic and enforce it with the help of fire departments and regular PD foot patrols. The firemen can patrol inland flood areas; most of them have nicer boats than we do thanks to Homeland Security money. Me and my crew will search this thing out and find out what we're dealing with."

"Are you kidding? It's Labor Day weekend for shit's sake! All first responders are stretched to the breaking point. The people need a couple of days of R&R to get their minds off how screwed they are, and you want me to close the bay and the beaches? For Labor Day weekend? And take police and firemen off recovery efforts to look for…what? A sea monster?"

"Unless you want blood on your hands, yes."

"What did you see?" Captain Quinn said.

Tanner broke the connection without answering.

The sun was falling fast and soon darkness would make the search more difficult. It was time to head in and grab some food and rest. Tanner didn't know it at the time, but it would be his last night of peace for a long while.

5

Overnight, there was a sighting, but thankfully the old man called the police and not the press. Despite one confirmed dead, with a strong possibility of others, Tanner didn't know what to tell the public, and with safety precautions taken, he'd decided to tell them nothing. Closing the bay and beaches using storm flooding and debris in the water as pretenses was easy. It made sense, and everyone's attention was elsewhere. Despite this, Tanner knew it was only a matter of time before a reporter came sniffing around a story about a sea monster in the bay. Locals talked, and for a beer, they talked a lot.

Tanner hadn't slept a wink, but it wasn't for want of trying. He'd lain in bed, staring at the ceiling, only to fall asleep minutes before his alarm went off. LS had no trouble sleeping like a stone and the dog barely lifted his head when Tanner left to head to work. Lucky-shit's first day on the job as a police dog would have to wait. The poor thing was still exhausted.

The prior night's rain held off, and the floodwaters had receded a little more, inching back into the sea as slow as a relative that's overstayed their welcome. Tanner piloted *Big Boy*, and Randy kept pace in a twenty-two-foot SAFE boat. Tanner had Jane Ricky as support, and Randy had Freddy Gipp. Both were solid cops, exceptional watermen, and military vets. After the events of the prior day, all four officers were strapped with Glock 19s, and there was a rifle and shotgun stowed on each craft with extra ammo. Tanner had also stowed extra gaffs and three spear guns.

The boats cut across the windblown chop, heading east to meet with Kris Dopson, an old fisherman who claimed to have seen a giant beast in the water he called a sea scorpion. Tanner had to hear this one for himself. As they raced east, it was easy to see the mobilization of local forces had begun. The Coast Guard, along with police and fire department rescue boats, patrolled the bay and flood areas, but so far whatever lurked in the bay hadn't shown itself.

A burst of static came through the radio, and Tanner adjusted the gain.

"You there, Tanner? You copy?"

"Command, yes, I copy."

"We've got another report of someone seeing this thing. Down by the mouth of Carmans River." Kipper's static-filled voice came through the speaker in broken fragments.

"We're heading out that way," Randy said.

"We'll check it out," Tanner said.

"That's a 10-4. You can meet Mr. Jackson and his son at that small marina just inside the mouth of the river. You know the one I mean?"

"That's a 10-4. Tell them we'll be there in an hour or so."

"That's a 10-4." Static. Then silence.

The GPS led them through Patchogue Bay to where the old man waited at the end of a long dock next to a flagpole, which was nestled in a tidal estuary that flowed from Abetes Creek. The pole had a guide rope that hummed and chimed as the wind tossed it about, and the air carried the scent of smoke and salt. It was a welcome respite from the salty-shit-rot aroma. Salty-shit-rot. His new designer scent to be sold at the candle shop next to the bacon and wood smoke.

"Morning, sir," Tanner said as he stepped off the patrol boat onto the dock. He pushed the craft back, and Jane backed the boat out into deeper water. Randy jumped from the SAFE boat and he and Tanner shook Mr. Dopson's hand.

"Morning to you both. How are things out there?" the old man asked. He was bent with the weight of his years, and the cane he held in his left hand wasn't for show.

"Not bad," Tanner said. "Everyone will have to be real careful for a while. Sir, my name is Tanner, and this is Officer Vernon."

"Call me Randy."

"You boys know why you're here?" Dopson asked.

"Sure," Tanner said.

"And you don't think I'm cracked? Or drunk or high?"

"No, sir," Randy said.

Tanner's tongue had suddenly become tied.

"It's just such a strange thing…" Dopson lifted his head and looked out to sea, the Great South Bay a mess of windblown whitecaps. "It was right out there. Just lounging around like a whale playing in whitewater. For the briefest instant, I thought I saw a tall tapered spike burst from the water and then two huge claws. Water rolled around it. Only saw it there for a second, but it was shaped like a scorpion. And the sound it made. Damn near burst an eardrum."

Tanner and Randy exchanged glances.

"I saw that. You think I'm seeing things?" the old man said.

"No. I don't think you're seeing things at all," Tanner said.

"Ah. You've seen it?"

"Not really. More like experienced it. Can you be more specific about what you saw? How big was this thing? What color?"

"Color?" Dopson appeared confused. "Real big. That I can tell you."

"Bigger than that boat?" Randy asked, pointing at the SAFE boat.

"Way bigger."

Tanner and Randy exchanged glances again. Tanner said, "Bigger than the big boat there?"

"I'd say it was about that size," Dopson said.

Randy chuckled. "That boat's forty-two feet."

Dopson said nothing.

"Anything else you can tell us?" Randy said.

Dopson shook his head.

"Thank you for your time, Mr. Dopson," Tanner said.

"Be safe out there," the old man said.

Tanner and Randy boarded their vessels. Dopson's sighting had legitimized Tanner's encounters, and it was good knowing he and Randy weren't the only ones who believed the thing existed. *Big Boy*'s inboard engine hummed and the aluminum hull vibrated as Tanner pushed down on the control levers and headed back out. The bay narrowed significantly as they approached Smith Point Bridge, beyond which lay Narrow Bay and the entrance to the amusement park that is the Hamptons.

Carmans River had a large mouth that narrowed quickly, and the marina sat nestled in a small cove to the west. The Jacksons had less to offer than Mr. Dopson, except they added a deep brown color and shell-like exterior to the description, though both said they couldn't be sure because the thing never came out of the water. Their account of the sounds and smells lined up, and clearly they'd seen the creature.

The *womp womp* of a helicopter echoed across the water and a Coast Guard copter tore past. No sooner had its echoes faded than the call came in. Someone had been shot out on the bay, and Tanner ordered all marine units to the scene.

"Head out Stones Throw way," he said.

"Your town?" Jane said.

"Yeah, off Sapphire Point. Apparently, two alphas disagreed over who was more stupid, and Lenny put a bullet in a fireman's leg to subdue him. This all the speed you got, Jane?"

"What were they fighting over?"

"Who knows, probably whose booger was bigger."

"What do you make of this sea scorpion stuff?" Jane asked.

"I don't make anything of it," he said. He didn't like not knowing what was happening, confronting something unknown that couldn't be planned or prearranged.

When they arrived at the scene, Jane pushed through the knot of boats, fully taking advantage of the ship's size and rank. The vortex of the bullshit swirl was three civilian center consoles; one with Auxiliary Policeman Lenny Crimpatlon on it, and two light-duty fire rescue boats with firemen dressed in civilian clothes. The wounded fireman paced back and forth on his deck, his hand pressed against a bandage on his leg. He looked fine. Hurricane accident.

Tanner stepped off his ship onto one of the rescue boats and then continued onto the part-time police boat. He said, "Lenny, what the hell were you fighting over? And you drew down? Are you nuts?"

"He threatened me, sir, and I thought this was important, and they were messing around with it." Lenny wore a reflective vest and a whistle on a lanyard around his neck. He handed Tanner a bucket full of the brown fish turd he'd seen the prior day.

"You were fighting over fish shit?" Tanner asked. He dumped the bucket onto the deck, and said, "I'm willing to forget this bullshit if you morons apologize to each other. If not, I'll write this up and it looks like shit for everyone. Lenny, you'll lose aux status, might be brought—"

The bullhorn atop the pilothouse boomed. "Tanner, we gotta go. We're getting a distress call," Jane said. The large police boat spun in place as she turned the ship's wheel and fired the left mobility thruster.

Tanner hopped boat to boat until he was back next to Jane. The rescue boats parted much faster the second time, and when Tanner looked back, he saw that Randy and Gipp were right behind them. Jane dropped the hammer, and the boat leapt from the water, driving through the waves and spraying the front windshield.

"It's Kipper, says he's under attack," she said.

Tanner held the comm button. "Kipper, you copy? Kipper?"

"I'm here. It's coming at me, Tanner." Static. "Huge claw cut right through the hull. I'm going down. Mayday. Mayday. Help. Hurry." Help and hurry came through loud, but when Tanner tried to raise Kipper again, he couldn't get him.

There wasn't much left of the boat when Tanner got there, and the monster was long gone. Ralph Kipper's twenty-two-foot SAFE boat was crushed to nothing, its debris field barely identifiable in the green water. The crushed aluminum pilothouse stuck from the water like a forlorn tooth, but that was the only big piece. Tanner trolled through the wreckage, searching for survivors.

A blood slick drifted on the surface, undulating and rolling with the waves. Pieces of flesh and fat floated atop the blood and slowly sank below the emerald water into the deep black mud below.

6

Losing the police boat and the presumed deaths of two crew raised Tanner's investigation to fast pace status at DEFCON two, full red. The captain was getting his nuts twisted from above, though most of the press had chalked the loss of the police boat up to storm debris in the water, and the brass had done nothing to dispel that theory. The mainland was hanging on by a thread. No power, and fuel, food, and water shortages were Long Island's main concerns. Kipper and Johnson's funerals had been postponed, and Tanner was thankful for that. He didn't think he could face Judy and Laura. They were nice ladies, and each woman had to explain to young children why their daddy wasn't coming home ever again. The thought of it made him tear up.

He'd crashed from exhaustion and hadn't gotten drunk the prior night. It felt good not to be hung over. The morning wasn't such a choir and the sounds of the birds and sea eased his mind instead of driving nails into it. The moment of serenity was lost when he pulled into the mud lot next to the temporary station and saw a young woman sitting on the front step holding a pad and pen. Lois Lane had finally shown.

He hopped from the Jeep and walked past the woman without a word.

"Sir," she said. Then she yelled, "Lieutenant Tanner, may I have a word?"

He stopped and sighed, making a show of turning around slow as if she was this biggest bother since poison ivy. "No. You may not. Who are you?"

"Betsy Lindholm with the *Suffolk County News*. Can I ask you a few questions about the deaths on the bay?"

"*Suffolk County News*." He whistled. "You must have been in the top ninety percent of your class in journalism school."

She was short and petite, and very attractive in a twenty-four-year-old sort of way; firm in all the places that sagged on him, bright innocent eyes, and a block of solid granite on her shoulder. He liked her. "What have you learned about the foot you found?" she asked.

He froze and looked at her, and almost asked how she knew about the foot, but didn't. Apparently, she'd done a little better than the top ninety percent.

"Two boaters and two police officers are also missing? Do you have any comment on that? About their possible whereabouts?"

Now Tanner was pissed. "Their whereabouts? Which parts?"

Betsy's mouth fell open a crack, and she went a paler shade of white, the red blotches on her neck standing out like hickeys. "Have you seen it? What killed them?"

The conversation was getting out of hand, like a wave sucking you into darkness. "If you have questions, you need to go through the command press office. Hang out here and I'll get you their number."

"Why are Coast Guard special ops being brought in? You guys can't handle it?" she taunted.

He turned to stare her down, but had to settle for a draw. "What? Special ops?" He had to get up earlier.

"The Commandant of the Coast Guard dispatched a cutter last night. They'll be here today."

Tanner turned and unlocked the office and went inside, locking the door behind him. He instantly felt like a shit, but what was done was done, and in this situation, the press was the enemy. If they ran stories about a monster in the bay, every dumbass want-to-live-in-video-game apocalypse freak would be on the shoreline with their binoculars, serving themselves up like appetizers.

He dropped into a folding chair and it almost collapsed. The day had already beaten him. Tanner pulled out the stainless steel flask his father had given him. The Navy logo was on the front in raised brass, and he stared at it a moment before he twisted off the cap and took a nip.

The station was pumped out, though still an island, but soon they'd be able to abandon the temporary base. The floodwater continued to recede, and soon it would be too shallow to take a boat out to the station and he'd have to take the Jeep on the road through water that was still two feet deep.

Tanner had to get nasty with the captain's assistant to get Quinn on the phone. "Are you shitting me? Threatening to call FOX? I got a four alarm here in case you didn't know. What the hell do you want?"

"You got Coast Guard special ops coming?" Tanner asked. "When the hell were you going to tell me?"

Captain Quinn laughed, and it wasn't a patronizing laugh, like ha ha. It was a he might fall off his seat and break an arm laugh; full, loud, and inspiring. "Gods, I love you, brother. I'm a captain on the Suffolk County PD. Last time I checked, the Commandant of the Coast Guard outranked me, but it's sweet you think so highly of me that you believe he'd call me personally. Get your shit together and go meet the coasties. I put a whirlybird up so you know where they are."

Quinn had a way of helping Tanner put his foot in his mouth. "Thanks, Quinn."

"Make nice or you'll be scraping hulls until you die. Savvy?"

"Savvy."

"I'll see you tonight at the New Week party?"

"Lacy coming with you? I want her to meet my new little boy." Tanner always flirted with Captain Quinn's wife because she loved it and the captain didn't. Mrs. Q would love Lucky-shit.

"Screw you."

***

The Great South Bay was a choppy mess. A northeast wind blew out the two-foot waves that rolled and broke in random patterns across the bay, and a light mist that wasn't quiet fog settled over everything. Tanner helped crew *Big Boy*, which floated with the current just east of Smith Point Bridge. He had his entire operational fleet behind him, four cop boats and eight fire rescue boats, all spread out in front of the bridge. No special ops team would get into the bay without stopping to say hello to him first.

Aerial reported that the ops team broke off from the USCGC *Vigilant*, which continued to chug through the ocean along Fire Island seashore toward the breach. The ops team had to enter the bay via Moriches Inlet because there was no other way to get to the Great South Bay from the ocean that far east.

The coastie SAFE boat roared through the inlet and came toward Tanner's armada. The ship looked similar to the boats the PD used, except it had orange pontoons, and a pilothouse painted white with the Coast Guard logo on its side. A black M2 Browning .50 caliber machine gun mounted on the bow was pointed at the deck and unmanned, as were two smaller guns to port and starboard.

Six coasties stood nut to butt next to the pilothouse, three on each side. They wore full dark blue body armor and carried MK18 carbines, the shorter brother of the AR15 designed for close quarters combat. The Coast Guard boat made straight for *Big Boy*, leaving no question of its heading. The SAFE boat roared in at full speed and reversed thrust two hundred yards from *Big Boy*'s aft deck, stopping on a dime. A fine piece of piloting.

As the coastie boat inched closer, a woman in a casual dress uniform exited the wheelhouse and headed for the bow. Without breaking stride, she stepped up onto an orange pontoon and jumped onto *Big Boy*'s aft dive platform just as the two ships gently kissed amidst the rolling sea with a squeak of rubber on metal.

Tanner went to meet her, unable to stop smiling. She spied him and made straight for him. "You in charge of this blockade?" she asked. She looked immaculate in her light blue dress shirt stacked with a full salad bar, her cover cocked slightly to one side, dark hair peeking out from beneath it. Nothing looked out of place on her except a thin sheen of sweat glistening on her brown skin.

"It's a welcome party," Tanner said. It was, of a kind.

"Petty Officer First Class Belinda Jefferson. You can call me PO Jefferson. Some welcome. You're full of shit. We saw your bird."

Tanner smiled. Gorgeous, feisty, smart, and accomplished. He felt attracted to her at once. "I thought it best if we spoke before you entered my bay. So we can share information, help each other out, and avoid misunderstandings."

She laughed. "Your bay? It's funny you think you stopped me."

Tanner looked around and smiled. "I have stopped you."

"Little old me? I suppose you have. My Triton 3300 submersible that's making its way through the breach right now hasn't been stopped, and that counts, right?"

Tanner fumed. "You put a submersible in the breach? The first boat went down in there."

"That's why we're here. Now are you going to move your tubs or do I need to move them for you?"

"Easy. Easy. I'm sorry if I offended you, but we knew the guys that were killed so this is a little closer to home for us."

That cracked the ice. Jefferson looked at her shiny patent leather shoes, and said, "I'm sorry for your losses."

"So what's the plan?" he asked.

"We're going to run the sub in a grid pattern all over the bay and see if we can find this thing."

"This thing? What have you been told?"

"Not much," Jefferson said. "Just that something big has been causing all types of mayhem, and that the something definitely isn't a shark."

"That about covers it," Tanner said.

"Then let's get going before I get an alpha charlie call." Tanner said nothing, but he must have looked confused because Jefferson said, "An ass chewing. When we get there, you can join me on my boat and we'll monitor the sub together. That work for you?"

"Sure."

"Then shut your crumb catcher and let's get going."

Tanner smiled at her and she smiled back.

7

The command console on the coastie boat made Tanner's SAFE boats look like children's toys. High-end sonar, radar, communications and navigation, all controlled via touch displays set at an angle in the front of the pilothouse. There was a traditional boat wheel mounted in the center of the console, but two helmsmen controlled the vessel via touchscreens and the manual wheel rotated as if a ghost was at the helm. Tanner didn't know if he could pilot the thing because he'd first have to turn off whatever digital controls were in use, and he and computers had a destructive relationship.

One of the large displays was divided in two and showed the aft and forward views from the Triton submersible's exterior cameras. The green water was murky with particles of decaying vegetation and visibility was less than ten feet. In the lower right-hand corner of the aft video was a small punch-out showing the sub's pilot. A coastie called Sharkey sat in what looked like a dentist's chair, enclosed in a glass bubble. Sharkey slowly worked a joystick that steered the forty-six-hundred-pound sub across the sandy bottom of the breach.

Tanner and Randy stood with Jefferson and her first mate, Cuddy, behind the helmsman.

"Why they call you Cuddy?" Randy asked. "Sharkey kind of looks like a shark, so I get that, but why Cuddy?"

"Cause I was always asleep in the cuddy cabin when I was a kid. Real names PO 2nd class Dinkins, sir."

"I'm no sir," Randy said.

"Technically you are," Tanner said.

"What do you mean? He outranks you?" Jefferson said.

She'd been nice to him, and he thought they were developing a relationship, but what he saw in Jefferson's face told Tanner she didn't trust him at all. "A technicality. Randy is kind of filling in, but he doesn't really do the job, so, you know, duty and all that."

"Didn't have anything to do with an obnoxious ass grab, now did it?" Jefferson said.

"Not true," Tanner said.

"Really? You didn't get in trouble for grabbing a woman's ass?"

"Where do you get your information? I'm offended."

"I got my file from the FBI. Heard of them?" Jefferson adjusted the communication levels and called to Sharkey. "How you doing, cowboy? We got a deep bench if you need to come up."

"That's a 10-4, but let me finish up the breach, and Danny can go trolling through the mud."

"That's a 10-4. Out."

"Now wait a minute," Tanner said. "I don't get to explain myself?"

"Why do you care what I think?" Jefferson didn't even try to hide her smirk anymore.

"I don't know. I just do."

"I read your statement. Either way, you're kind of a pig."

"Maybe, but I don't put my hands on a woman who doesn't want me to, so excuse me if I'm getting a little pissy about the distinction."

"Fair enough," Jefferson said.

"Look, there's a New Week party tonight at Randy's house. Why don't you come by and I can explain myself."

"What's a New Week party?" she asked.

"It's a tradition in these parts to have a party one week after a major hurricane. It goes back to the storm of 1938. People were living in tents, and many had died, but they stopped to celebrate living through the week and starting a new week."

She said nothing, and Tanner thought he heard one helmsman snicker.

The aft camera was obscured by bubbles as Sharkey engaged the maneuvering thrusters. The breach was clear, but Tanner knew that meant nothing. Whatever they were hunting was at home in mud, burrowed beneath the slime, and if it didn't want to be found, it wouldn't be.

Two whirlybirds skated across the sky, coming at them from opposite directions. One was from the cutter and the other from aerial division, and the sound of their rotors echoed like approaching thunder. Both crafts flew low, and as they got closer, bubbles obscured both of the sub's exterior views.

Sharkey's voice crackled from the comm, "What's happening up there?"

Jefferson's eyebrows knitted and Tanner shrugged.

A deep humming sound competed with the pounding of the helicopter rotors, rising in pitch and resonance until the sound filled Tanner's head. A deep swirl of water developed off the port bow, a giant eddying mass that looked as though it might become a cyclone.

"Get the sub out," Tanner said. "Now!"

"What? Why?" Jefferson said.

"It's coming!"

"What are—?"

"You're wasting time," Tanner said. "If Sharkey dies, it's on you."

Jefferson stared at Tanner for a moment and then pressed the comm button. "Sharkey, bring baby home to momma. Double time."

"We got something, chief," said the coastie monitoring the sonar and radar.

Helicopters roared across the bay, kicking up spray. They were almost upon them. The chop picked up, and the boat listed to port, bobbing back and forth, slowly settling. Wind swirled and pushed the bay in random patterns, and waves broke on the boat from every direction.

"What is it, ensign?" Jefferson said.

"Something big, ma'am, coming up behind the sub." The sonar screen darkened further, a deep blue blob slowly filling the screen.

Two hundred yards off the port bow, the sub's round glass top emerged from the water as its jets drove toward the surface. The Triton 3300 needed deeper water to travel fast, and in the shallow water of the bay, the sub was fighting to pick up speed. Both exterior cameras were white with bubbles, and Sharkey's face looked pale, his eyes dark. Now Tanner really saw the resemblance.

A massive wave rose from the bay, a wall of water twice the size of the one that had chased him off the golf course. Patches of seaweed and tiny water sprouts surged from the bay, their spray falling across the surface with a hiss.

The sound of the copters faded, and Sharkey said, "Oh shit. You seeing this, Houston?"

Bubbles and swirling green water filled the sub's view, and Jefferson ran out on deck with Tanner on her heels. A rotten breeze wafted across the boat and Tanner gagged as he ran to the gunnel. The rank smell got stronger, and Tanner dry heaved and was thankful he'd only had a bagel for breakfast.

A huge water spout surged over the bay and an arced black spike knifed from the water and stabbed at the submersible, just missing it. The black nail jerked back, and struck again as the sub dove and rolled to starboard. The spike missed again. The bay continued to rise and come at them, and Tanner drew his weapon. Randy stood by his side, gun drawn, eyes bulging from his head.

"Yeah," said Jefferson. "Let's go. Lock and load."

Coasties spilled onto the bow, MK18s at the ready. Jefferson fell in behind the mounted machine gun. Water sprayed across the deck as the huge wave crested and the monster dove after the sub.

"Hold your fire!" Jefferson yelled. "We'll hit the sub."

A claw twice the size of a man shot from the bay and fell on top of the sub as it struggled to dig into the water. The giant pincer snapped and bit at air, catching nothing as its weight drove the sub under. The claw pulled back as a dark carapace crested on the mountain of whitewater and landed on the submersible. The sound of crunching metal joined the cacophony of surging water and the hum of the beast.

"Fire!" Jefferson yelled.

Tanner opened up, and the clatter and snap of gunpowder igniting and the whiz of bullets was barely audible amidst the pandemonium. Shots struck the creature's black shell as it fell back into the bay, leaving a frothing jumble of whitewater behind. The sub was nowhere to be seen.

"Sharkey," Jefferson said.

They ran back into the pilothouse just in time to see Sharkey's final moments. The sub's aft camera showed static, but the forward camera revealed a mouth of teeth that rivaled any megalodon. Two fangs pierced what was left of the glass canopy covering Sharkey, and it cracked and popped like a bubble. Sharkey screamed as water poured into the sub, and the jaws opened and a pincer claw reached into the cockpit and yanked him free.

Sharkey's head and shoulders were severed by the pincer and blood filled the water and obscured the forward-view camera. Then the cockpit camera went to static, followed by the aft camera. Through the front window, Tanner saw debris from the sub floating to the surface. Large bubbles popped and whitewater rolled over the monster as mud boiled from the bottom of the bay.

The helicopters were back and the sound of pounding rotors and gunshots echoed across the water. Gunsmoke filled the air, the water flattened, and the natural roll and pitch of the bay returned.

"Tell the copters to leave. I think they're spooking the thing," Tanner said.

"You might be right." Jefferson called off the copters and gave the order to retrieve the remains of the submersible. A smear of blood on the rear bulkhead of the destroyed sub was all they found of Sharkey, and there was no sign of the monster.

8

Randy lived in Stone's Throw, but in a much nicer section than he could afford on his police salary. It was his childhood home, and he had inherited it from his parents. The house sat atop a small rise that sloped down to a canal, with a path that ran south to a community bay beach. Randy's place stood in stark contrast to where Tanner was banished in a trailer park off Montauk Highway, a place most people didn't know existed.

The night was muggy and wet, and with the holiday coming and the beaches closed, Tanner felt a little sweatier than most. He wished he could search twenty-four hours a day, but in the darkness, it wasn't worth the effort and money. Moon glow only helped so much, and often made it worse with its tricky shadows and inconsistent luminescence.

His Jeep rattled as he drove over a pile of sawdust and small sticks. Most of the major impediments had been removed from the roads, but branches, leaves, and tree crumbs still littered the ground, and most likely would for weeks. As he drove, Tanner ran the day's events over and over in his mind, and he was afraid of what the pictures of the beast would show. Jefferson was having the sub video analyzed and enhanced, and Tanner hoped they'd get a good shot of the creature that everyone had dubbed the sea scorpion.

Lucky-shit sat on the bucket seat beside Tanner, mouth hanging open, tongue flapping in the breeze. Fully rested and feed, the animal had shaken off his near-death experience and forgotten his past as only a dog can. LS was ready to be a police dog, and tonight he would be Tanner's babe magnet. He frowned as he thought of his conversation with Jefferson that morning. Was he a pig for loving women as much as he did? Or was he lustful, as one girlfriend had called him?

Tanner pulled in front of Randy's house and killed the Jeep's engine. He sat there a few minutes, finishing his beer and running his hand through his windblown hair. Tanner hated cop parties, and the way they all looked at him because of what had happened. He never felt comfortable. For him, the party was work even though it was at Randy's place, which he spent more time at than his trailer.

LS jumped from the Jeep and Tanner followed. They were both greeted by Randy's wife, Tina, who proved on a daily basis she'd married well below her paygrade when she'd settled for Randy. She whisked LS away to meet the children, and the dog didn't even look back as he disappeared into an adoring crowd.

***

Her name was Tristin, and she was taking quite a ribbing when Tanner rescued her. Do you do everything at a Category 4 level? You seem smaller than I thought you would be. You don't look like a killer bitch to me, were but a small sampling of the comics' work.

"That's enough, dipshits," Tanner said.

All the men turned in his direction, ready to protest. When they saw Tanner, the crowd dispersed, leaving him alone with the woman whose name was now associated with the most devastating hurricane ever to hit her home.

"Thanks," she said. Her face screwed up, and she rolled her eyes and walked away.

"You're welcome." Tanner watched her go, realizing she hadn't needed or wanted to be rescued. He had to stop trying to be the world's white knight. He wasn't strong or smart enough.

Tanner saw the captain across the room; to avoid him, he detoured outside, where he got blocked by two ex-girlfriends. So he grabbed a couple of beers from the cooler and escaped down to the bay. The dock that ran along the back of Randy's property was underwater, but a footpath led across his neighbor's yards to the south, where it turned into a sand path that emptied onto a flooded beach. Signs of the receding water were everywhere: garbage, wood, and pieces of deck furniture were intertwined in large mounds of seaweed that covered the inland beach and wove through the water reeds that lined the shoreline.

Tanner cleared a spot and plopped down onto a pile of seaweed. He opened a beer and took a long pull, staring into the moonlight as it shimmered over the bay's placid sea.

Low tide had sucked out some floodwater, and the smell of rot and shit mixed with salt filled the air. The bay lapped gently against a shore that until two days ago had been covered by floodwaters. Some sections of the coast were lower than others, and would remain flooded for weeks, while higher ground had seen some relief, though the damage left behind was no less significant. With summer ending, people worried that there wasn't enough time to dry out before winter came.

"Hey, cowboy," Jefferson said. She came down the path onto the beach, a glass of wine in her hand.

"Hey, yourself," Tanner said. "The guys with you? They're welcome."

"They hung back, but thanks," she said.

"Didn't expect to see you after…"

"It's OK. Sitting on the cutter crying over it wouldn't do any good. Believe it or not, I've seen some pretty bad stuff."

"I can imagine. What I don't get is why a…" Tanner caught himself. Call me a pig will you. "I just don't get why someone as smart and skilled as you would settle for making no money and sacrifice a more stable life. Adventure?"

"A beautiful girl like me would do this because," she said, letting him know she knew what he'd intended to say. "I was lost. I did good in school, but had no passion, no drive. I thought the military would give me that, and I love the water, so I chose the Coast Guard. It took me a few years to learn that the military couldn't do all that for me. I had to do it for myself."

"You are beautiful," Tanner said.

"So what happened with that woman? Why did she lie?"

Tanner smiled. She'd just cut him some major slack. "I was at the casino over at Davis Park when I met two young women from the city. Ms. Layborn was all over me in minutes, but it was her friend who I wanted to pursue. A beautiful woman named Sherry. All three of us were flirting, and both of them put their hands on me, and I had my arms around them. Ms. Layborn goes to the bathroom, and when she comes back Sherry and I are in a need of a room. We were kissing, embracing, and Ms. Layborn freaked. Starts yelling and getting upset that she thought I was with her. So I, in a very respectful and loving tone, suggested that the three of us adjourn to my friend's house for the rest of the evening where we could have use of a bedroom. Then she slaps me, stalks off trailed by Sherry, and two days later, my captain calls and tells me she accused me of grabbing her ass. Which I might have done, but it would have been when the three of us were hanging all over each other. That is the total truth, exactly how it happened."

"Your statement says she kicked you in the balls," Jefferson said, but she smiled at him.

"A small dramatic embellishment I felt she not only deserved, but sent the message I wasn't above lying if it meant exposing her untruth."

"I'm out of wine. Can we head back to the house and grab more? I have pictures to show you."

"Really? And you're allowed to show them to me? A local?"

She chuckled. "No, I'm not allowed to show them to you." As they headed back to the house, she went on, "The higher-ups had the big heads analyze the sub footage and they think the creature is a *Jaekelopterus*, a prehistoric sea scorpion, mixed with modern Maine lobster or horseshoe crab, most likely both. It has a long, segmented armored carapace that tapers down to a rear attack spike similar to a horseshoe crab's, which we saw today. The *Jaekelopterus'* closest living relative is the horseshoe crab, which as you know is a common crab in the Great South Bay, and that might have something to do with how it ended up here, though the scientists had very little speculation on how the thing could even exist."

"The water is deep out at the canyons," Tanner said. "Who the hell knows what Tristin dug up."

Jefferson nodded. "The Hudson and Block Canyons are about 80 miles off the island, and the water goes from two hundred feet deep to a thousand feet deep in a matter of a mile."

They reached the house, and the party was in full swing. Randy played beer pong, and Tanner and Jefferson made their way through the crowd like sharks, moving and shifting with the crowd as it eddied in its drunken flow. Music blared through the deck speakers, and the night air felt heavy and wet. They plopped down on deck chairs and Jefferson tossed an envelope onto his lap. Tanner opened it and his worst fears were realized.

"The big brains went through the footage frame by frame," Jefferson explained, "but were only able to get the few clear shots you see there. I think the more interesting picture is the satellite image taken yesterday morning."

The top picture was a printout of a satellite photo that showed the shadow of the creature on a sandbar. It was a scorpion-shaped goliath with large front claws and was at least thirty feet long. The other pictures were close-ups that showed a huge mouth of teeth and fangs set in a jaw twice the size of the submersible. There was one clear picture of the creature's underbelly that showed a series of secondary pincer claws, which looked designed to drag prey toward the razor-sharp fangs sticking from immense mandibles.

"Holy shit," Tanner said.

"Fugazi," Jefferson said.

9

The golf course was still flooded, but no longer navigable by dingy. Grass peeked above the water in places, and most of the tee boxes were visible. The road around the golf course was still underwater, so that meant a half-mile walk for Tanner and LS across the wet golf course via a meandering path that led across the semi-dry parts. The smell of rot and decay had subsided, but gnats and flies swarmed them as they walked through shallow puddles and thickening mud. Tanner didn't mind. He'd closed the temporary office and reopened the station, and since it was hard to get to, there'd be no drop-ins by command. If there was a chance their shoes might get dirty, the brass stayed home.

He passed the ninth tee box where only two nights prior he'd had his first experience with the creature. The memory was obscured in a whiskey fog, but the terror he'd felt still sat in his stomach like a bad taco. Tanner pulled free his flask and took a sip of vodka. He was ashamed of being afraid and not completing the hunt, and angry that some prehistoric scorpion had inflicted more damage on his home, which didn't need any more destruction.

The station house was getting back to normal, and the small marina west of the building was back in service; all the functional police boats were moored there. Floating docks were stacked next to the building and several boats damaged by the storm sat in a row before them. The large bay door stood open, revealing the garage filled with supplies of all kinds. The water hadn't reached Tanner's second-floor office, but the moisture made everything damp, destroying files and anything else that absorbed water, so he couldn't use it until it dried out.

Beth waved from the tower as he approached and Tanner waved back. Randy waited under the open bay door. "You sleep well, little boy?" he said. "I saw you and Jefferson hung tight most of the night. Has the great iceberg thawed?"

"No global warming yet, but she's coming around."

"What's the plan today?"

"We're going to meet up with Jefferson and the coasties, and put together another search grid on the inner bay."

Randy made a face Tanner had seen many times. He looked like he was working to push out a turd. "Tanner, I've been think—"

"I know."

"Are you sure you're up for this, boss? You look like you've been run hard and put away wet."

"What are you trying to say?"

"You've been hitting the sauce a bit too much lately and—"

"Who the hell are you? My mom? I didn't realize you were watching me."

"It's hard not to notice. You've—"

"What?"

"I don't know. I just don't like seeing you like this," Randy said.

"Bullshit."

"Bullshit? What's bullshit is you putting me and others in danger because you're off your game."

Tanner stepped forward until he was inches from Randy. "What is this? An intervention?"

"Do you need one?"

Tanner stabbed Randy in the chest with his index finger, but the younger man grabbed Tanner's arm, twisted it behind his back, and shoved him through the open bay door and out of sight. "Have you lost your mind? Are you drunk right now?" Randy said.

"No." Tanner was exhausted all of sudden and he couldn't believe he'd let his rage take over. "I'm sorry."

"Forget it. What're we gonna do if we do find this thing? I mean, we haven't fared very well in our first couple of meetings," Randy said.

"We're gonna kill it," Tanner said. "Come with me."

They entered the heart of the station and made their way to the second-floor storage room and armory locker. Tanner looked around, but didn't see what he was after. "Randy, where are those large harpoons we confiscated from those fishermen trying to spear that mink whale in the inlet last year?"

"They're in evidence," Randy replied.

"At central? Shit."

"No worries, boss, there's a bunch of them stacked with the other fishing gear downstairs. We have four or five of them, and a couple are bigger than the ones you're thinking of."

"Excellent. Get them and load them on your twenty-two. Take LS with you. He has to start following orders from people other than me. Oh, and start thinking about chum."

"Nate, I was hoping for a plan that didn't involve a weapon used five hundred years ago."

"I'm open to suggestions."

"I know a guy in the Army Reserves. I could ask for a high-caliber machine gun to mount on the front of *Big Boy*."

Tanner smiled. "That's why you're in charge. Do it. Fast as possible."

"10-4," Randy said. "Let's go, LS."

The dog looked at Tanner, and he said, "It's OK. You go with him." He pointed at Randy. LS hung his head, but obeyed. Tanner loaded up on ammo and grabbed two extra shotguns, but Randy's words bounced around inside his head like a criticism you don't want to believe, but know is true. Bullets had done little good, but Tanner kept telling himself they'd been surprised, caught off guard. Now they understood what they were up against, and could fight smart, find weak spots. He'd seen *The Hobbit*. He knew how they killed Smaug.

Smaug was the nickname the press had given the sea scorpion. Some child had asked on live TV if the creature in the bay looked like the dragon in that movie, and the reporter had said, "Do you mean Smaug?" The nickname stuck. With the word out, the police were hard-pressed to keep people from monster watching along the shore. The coasties and local fire rescue boats had stopped forty-three civilians from going out overnight. The natives were getting restless, and before long, he'd have fishermen out trying to catch the thing.

The wail of the station alarm rang out and Randy ran to the control tower. "What's up, Beth?"

"We got a sighting over on Carey Beach. Group of kids trying to see the creature. One of the kids got nabbed."

"Oh, shit," Tanner said.

When he arrived at the dock with the guns and ammo, Randy already had the boat's engines going, and the twenty-two-foot SAFE boat was untied and turned toward the canal. LS sat in the command chair behind Randy, unimpressed by the chaos. Tanner jumped aboard, and within three minutes of the alarm sounding, they were skipping across the bay toward Sapphire Point, which was the next town over from Stones Throw.

Randy had the motors pushing at full, and a thirty-foot fishtail jetted from the back of the boat. They barely felt the chop because the boat hardly touched the water. There were no birds in the clear sky, and no fish leapt from the green water. The air smelled fresh and salty, and Tanner sucked it in as though it were the scent of his mother's cooking.

Randy arced the boat toward shore and backed down the engines as he roared across the entrance to Carey Creek. The scene was bedlam as the small cove created by the pier exploded in a mountain of whitewater. The creature was half in the bay and half on the beach. Tanner pulled binoculars to his eyes and gasped.

A human torso was stuck on the black spike as it hovered above the scorpion's back, the beach covered in blood. Tanner gagged when he saw a severed head resting next to a large piece of driftwood. A crowd of kids stood by the beach's concession stand, huddled under an overhang, yelling and screaming at the monster. "Run!" Tanner shouted at them. "What the hell are you waiting for?"

LS barked and flew from his resting place. Tanner slid open the pilothouse door and he and LS ran to the bow. The dog jumped and put his paws on the gunnel and barked at the creature.

Randy cut the engines and the SAFE boat bobbed to a stop. A girl crawled across the beach, leaving a trail of blood behind her. The scorpion's large front claws were snapping at her, trying to pull her into its tooth-filled maw. Tanner pulled his Glock and fired. The bullets bounced off the creature's shell and it didn't even appear to notice.

"Get me closer," Tanner yelled.

Randy engaged the engines and the boat slid forward into the erupting sea. Tanner grabbed one of the long harpoons and braced himself against the gunnel. They were fifty yards off shore when the monster breached, the spike with the body on it flying past in the maelstrom. The monster thrashed, its claws reaching for the girl as she continued her desperate crawl across the beach. She'd made little progress and soon the sea scorpion would have her.

Tanner squeezed the talk button and spoke into the walkie clipped to his life preserver. "Randy, you need to give me a better angle. Bullets won't do shit on its back. I need to get a shot at the belly of this bitch, or front or side at least."

"10-4. Buckle-up." Randy dropped the hammer and the SAFE boat leapt from the water. He pulled around the side of the beast and rammed it. The bay surged and whitewater cascaded over the gunnel.

Tanner lifted the harpoon and held it at the ready. LS barked hard, his little black eyes bulging from their sockets, saliva dripping over his bared teeth. In the distance, the thunder of rotors brought the hope of air support. The leviathan rolled and Tanner loosed the harpoon. It struck home, sticking in the side of the scorpion as it thrashed, but the victory didn't last long.

A pincer claw from the creature's underbelly snapped the harpoon off at the tip like it was a toothpick and the beast flopped over, trying to crush the SAFE boat.

Randy was faster. He threw the engines in reverse and water exploded behind the boat. The vessel eased back from the creature, heading away from shore toward deeper water.

The boat was almost free when the scorpion tossed itself backward, and its right claw clamped down on the SAFE boat's blue inflated pontoon, crushing it. As the section went flat, the claw bit into the hull below. When the pincer released, readying for another power crunch, the boat's backward momentum pulled the vessel free. Randy eased back on the throttle and spun the wheel as fast as he could, then gunned the engines.

The sea flattened for a heartbeat, then a fist of water lifted from the bay behind the boat. Tanner saw the girl on the beach was getting help from her friends. A stream of water flowed into the boat from the gash the scorpion's claw had made, and Tanner didn't think the bilge pumps could keep up for long. A section of the bow was deflated, and bay water poured through the gap.

Lucky-shit barked at the knot of green water that trailed after them.

10

The engines sang as the twin props dug through the bay, but the mound of water behind them was gaining. Tanner stood in six inches of water, and as the SAFE boat swamped it slowed. LS sat in the captain's chair in the pilothouse with Randy, and Tanner crouched behind the aft gunnel with a shotgun, peering into the mist kicked up by their passage. Two harpoons lay on the deck beside him. He needed hand grenades, and that thought gave him an idea.

Tanner ran to the pilothouse. "Randy, do we have any gasoline accessible?"

"Nope. Only what's in the tank and if we were stopped, I might siphon you some, but at thirty knots that ain't happening." Randy looked at him. "I know what you're thinking, and we don't have any bottles or jars. I'm way ahead of you."

"Maybe you should take command," Tanner said, and he meant it.

"Knowing how to blow shit up is no skill," Randy replied. "Get back out there, that thing's right on our ass. Put a few rounds of buckshot into its face."

Tanner sloshed through the rising water and made his way aft, jumped onto the transom, and put the shotgun to his shoulder. Helicopters were attending to the injured, and backup was nowhere in sight. The boat jumped and bounced through the boiling sea and the tip of the gun barrel moved in a tight circle as he strained to aim the weapon. The familiar scent of rot polluted the air, and the creature sang its squeaky hymn.

The beast was almost upon them, and the SAFE boat struggled to stay on plane with more than a foot of water above deck. The boat wouldn't sink, even if all the pontoon compartments were popped, because the hull was filled with foam; unless the boat broke into multiple pieces, it would stay above water. But that didn't mean it would have any speed or maneuverability.

"Full stop!" Tanner yelled. "Cut the engines."

Randy turned and looked back at him through the rear pilothouse window.

"Now. Full stop! Cut them."

Randy pulled the throttle back to neutral, waited a heartbeat, and slammed the engines into reverse for a second and shut them down. The vessel jerked to a stop and the boat's wake broke against the transom.

Tanner fell to the deck, and the shotgun went off and just missed the pilothouse.

The boat lifted on the oncoming wave and then settled as the creature passed under the boat. The SAFE boat was fully swamped, and Tanner worked his way to the bow and sighted the gun. The wave crested, and the creature breached, turning its giant body like a worm and heading back their way.

"Full ahead," Tanner said into his walkie. "Take me right at this bitch."

Randy started the motors and brought them up to speed. He pointed the vessel at the oncoming wave as ordered, but the flooded boat handled like a brick, and it barely made ten knots. LS barked and yipped, but stayed in the pilothouse. Tanner forgot the harpoons aft so he retrieved them. The creature was coming right at them. Two hundred yards and closing. Tanner made his way back to the bow and leaned the harpoons against the gunnel. He checked his Glock 19, then holstered the weapon. He checked his shotgun and jacked a bullet into the chamber.

A black serpent's tail knifed from the water, followed by two huge claws covered in swelling whitewater. A jaw filled with razor-sharp teeth and fangs spanned ten feet, and it opened and moved to bite the boat. Tanner froze; the rank smell of death, the deafening hum, the mouth of teeth between two giant claws, pincers on thin legs jerking and pulling toward the beast's mouth, all made him dizzy. Fear sent a chill through him, and he opened up.

Tanner fired the shotgun until it was empty, then drew his Glock and fired into the open maw of teeth. When the Glock clicked empty, he hefted a harpoon and loosed it.

The ancient weapon struck home and stuck in the sea scorpion's left eye. The deep wail of pain was deafening, and the monster vaulted from the bay like a breaching whale.

Tanner dove to the deck, taking in a deep breath before he hit the water. The sea scorpion landed on the bow, its giant claws flopped back, and the creature's underbelly gyrated as two rows of spidery legs reached for prey.

Still, the twenty-two-foot SAFE boat refused to go down.

The scorpion's smaller claws went after Tanner, who was pressed against the gunnel, his face just beneath the water. The creature blocked the sun, and a cold darkness fell over the water. In that moment, Tanner thought he was done, yet his mother's voice didn't chime in his head. Fear ran through him. He looked up at the scorpion's abdomen as it pitched and heaved, trying to free itself from the boat.

The boat flipped as the scorpion rolled into the sea, and Tanner got tossed against the gunnel. The pilothouse came toward him, and for an instant, Randy and LS stared at him through a window. Then he was sucked away as the scorpion dove and slipped beneath the bay.

The SAFE boat righted itself, and Tanner lay between the gunnel and pilothouse, bracing himself as he sucked in breaths. Black mud oozed over everything as the water drained, and the scent of bay rot filled the air. The creature's hum rose, and the rolling sea once again built and came at them.

A two-foot chop lashed the port side, and the boat filled with water. The advancing groundswell arced toward them and the mouth of teeth tried a second time to take a bite as the spike pulled back, readying to strike.

The bark of Jefferson's M2 was the sweetest sound Tanner ever heard. The coastie boat cut across the creature's line of attack and Jefferson raked the sea scorpion with machine gun fire as she passed. The scorpion stabbed at the coastie boat with its spike, just missing and sending up a fountain of water.

The bullets didn't do much because the beast kept coming, driving through the water with its giant claws as it closed in on the crippled SAFE boat. The spike came up and struck. It pierced the SAFE boat's deck and stuck there as the creature thrashed and bucked, trying to free itself. Tanner peered into the pilothouse, looking for Randy and LS, but he didn't see them. This sent a new spark of worry through him until he realized they were most likely hunkered down out of sight.

A Coast Guard helicopter arrived. Two coasties opened up on the creature from above with their MK18s as Jefferson's boat swung around and laid fire into the creature's flank. The sea scorpion dove, black mud rising to the surface in nasty swirls like diarrhea in green bile.

The shots died off, and a cloud of smoke shrouded the bay's surface like fog. Water lapped against the hull and the whirlybird's rotors thumped, but the hum of the creature died away. Tanner got to his feet and leaned against the submerged gunnel. Jefferson's boat floated toward him, and the coasties were congratulating each other and patting themselves on the back. Tanner searched the bay and saw no sign that they'd hurt the creature. No pieces of shell, no blood slick, no mini-claws. Tanner went cold, and his nerves shook. He couldn't see the creature, but he felt it.

The wind picked up, and the hum returned, except this time it went from low to high in seconds until it was a painful wail that blocked out all other sounds. A giant swirl of water appeared off the starboard bow. The sea scorpion shot from the murky water like a missile, its giant claws outstretched before it. Black dot eyes the size of basketballs tilted Tanner's way, one with the harpoon sticking from it. Tanner dove behind the pilothouse and avoided a crushing blow.

A giant claw clamped down on the bow, cleaving the front of the boat in two. More water rushed into the SAFE boat as it finally gave up the ghost and went down. Tanner swam across the deck as the creature gripped the bow and tossed the crippled boat across the bay like a child's toy in a bathtub.

The pilothouse broke off, and the hull cracked as the claws chewed it apart. Tanner pulled the ripcord on his PFD and it inflated. Water rushed at him from every direction and it was an effort to move, so he gave up and let the surging bay water take him. A deep bellow erupted from the sea and the sky went dark as Tanner was engulfed by the bay.

"Now you've gone and done it," Tanner's mother said.

There she was, the leader of the group in his head that controlled and corrected him when he was wrong. "What'd I do, Momma?" Tanner said.

"You underestimated your opponent, and…"

Blackness took him and his eyes saw no more.

11

Tanner stepped back into the shadows, watching a stunning middle-aged woman in a red dress exit New York Senator Raymond Donald's limousine. The woman was a high-paid prostitute, and the senator wanted to be president. The man was a snake oil salesman of the highest order, and Tanner had a hard time separating his personal feelings from the investigation. He'd been assigned to the DA's special corruption task force, and though Tanner knew the task force existed to embarrass the senator so the DA could run for his seat, Tanner did his job, and Donald was shit. If the DA, as a newly minted senator, felt it appropriate to offer better-qualified people such as himself senior positions, who was he to question a man who held one of the hundred seats that shaped the world?

What pissed him off was he had dinner plans with Audrey. Instead, he was watching an asshole get laid and only getting the G version at that. He'd been tracking the senator for months and cavorting with hookers was the least of his crimes. The deal going down tonight would bring everything together and provide the evidence he needed, and he had to be there. The senator gave bid information to construction contractors run by organized crime. He worked with them all; the Italian mobsters hanging onto glory, the ruthless Japanese yakuza, and the expatriate Russians. The case was so high profile Captain Quinn planned to take the glory bow and do the perp walk old school like Eliot Ness. When Tanner had asked if that was too obvious, his longtime friend and captain in the Suffolk County PD had told him to shut his cake hole.

The limo pulled away and Tanner watched the carefully choreographed falsehood playing out before him. The women entered the apartment building, and in a few minutes, the senator's car would be back, and he'd slip from the long stretch limo like smoke. He'd be in the front door of the apartment building before the limo pulled away. Tanner settled in for a three-hour wait. The captain said the meeting would go down at 11PM, and it was 8:56.

Things went to shit ten minutes later.

The senator's car pulled to the curb across the street—right on schedule. Tanner heard a car door open and then shut. The limo tried to pull away but a black Lincoln Town Car blocked it. A man got out of the Lincoln and sat on the hood of the senator's limo.

The street was deserted. "Let's talk," said the man sitting on Donald's hood. "I won't hurt you. I just want to finish this, and you're the most predictable asshole on Earth. No, man, in the universe."

Tanner strained to see the man and was surprised to see none other than local dickhead and Russian mobster Victor Reznikov. Tanner reached for his gun, then checked himself. Instead, he pulled out his cellphone and started shooting video.

Tanner heard muffled voices and Reznikov got off the hood and disappeared into the limo. Tanner reached for his Glock again and checked himself a second time. What did he have at the moment? Nothing. So he called for backup.

Within minutes, the street was blocked with patrol cars and Tanner slipped from the shadows. Reznikov's men didn't put up a fight, and neither did the senator. Plenty of pictures were taken as the ranking member of the senate judiciary committee got yanked from his limo, marijuana joint in hand, along with the most wanted Russian mobster in New York.

It was 10:41PM when Tanner arrested Donald, and the time had come to go out for beers.

A shadow floated like a giant monster from the depths of the ocean. A black leviathan with claws that could crush the world, and a spike as hard as iron. It was cold, and he was engulfed by the sounds of water and wind.

***

Tanner came awake with a start. That night would haunt his dreams for the rest of his life, and he was thankful he'd woken before its conclusion.

"Easy, buddy, you're all right," Randy said.

LS jumped on the bed and licked his face, walked in a small circle, then sat next to Tanner's pillow.

Tanner's shirt was soaked through, and his throat was so dry it hurt to swallow. "Can you get…?"

Randy handed Tanner a tall glass of water.

"How'd I get here? I thought I was heading to Davy Jones' Locker."

"You don't remember anything?" Randy asked.

"Last thing I recall is the bay sucking me under as that thing broke apart our boat. I see you and LS made out all right. Looks like you guys didn't get a scratch."

"The pilothouse protected us pretty well, though we got tossed around like we were in a clothes dryer. I've got bruises all over my body, but LS made it through OK. He was limping around last night, but he seems fine today."

"What happened?"

"When the sea scorpion chomped the boat in half, I lost sight of you in the whitewater. Jefferson came roaring in with her boat and the coasties opened up on the thing. The monster must have had enough because it dove, and disturbed the mud on the bottom, turning the bay into sewage. We found you unconscious, floating in your life jacket. Jefferson rescued LS and I, then we retrieved you."

"Why wasn't I airlifted to Stony Creek University Hospital?"

"Dude, I knew you wouldn't want that," Randy explained. "I told them you don't do hospitals. If you were admitted, your hunt would be over and I knew you couldn't abide by that. Jefferson didn't buy it, though. She wanted to take you in, but when the boat's medic examined you and your vitals were stable, he said you could go home after an X-ray of your noggin. No surprise, they found nothing up there. How's your head feel?"

"Like your daughter's orchestra is going full tilt in my head," Tanner said. "But it isn't that bad. Feels like most mornings."

Randy said nothing.

"They just let you bring me home?"

"You woke briefly—twice actually—and you told them you were fine and threatened holy hell if they brought you in. You must have a pretty bad concussion if you don't remember any of that."

"It's coming back now. Jefferson called me a baby."

"She did, and she was a bit more concerned than the rest of us. I think she likes you."

Tanner harrumphed. "How long was I out?"

"Twenty-four hours. It's Sunday afternoon."

Tanner sat up, and LS jumped to attention, his tail going back and forth so fast it blurred. Tanner stretched his neck and cracked his back. He got up on shaky legs, and Randy reached out to help him and LS woofed. "I need some air. Let's go outside," he said.

With Randy at his side, Tanner made his way through the trailer's screen porch out onto his small patch of grass and they fell into folding chairs. The trailer park sat in a sheltered cove off Montauk Highway in Stones Throw, and half the people who lived in the town didn't even know the park existed. Tristin had nearly destroyed the Brightlights Residential Park. Several trailers were overturned, and trees and other debris littered the entire area. Tanner was lucky that his metal hovel still stood. He'd tied down his shit-shack, and cut the screens on the porch, and that had helped, but Tanner thought it was the age of the trailer that had saved it. It was an old-school thing from the sixties, made of metal, as opposed to the newer trailers in the park that were only aluminum stretched over wood studs.

"Any sign of the monster?" Tanner asked.

Randy shook his head. "No sign of it since your epic battle."

"Real epic."

"Looked pretty epic from where I was."

"What's happening now?"

"The bay is filled with search boats and in your absence, the command structure is even murkier."

As if his demotion didn't muddy the waters enough. "Sounds dangerous."

"It is. There was a debate about whether the hunt should be suspended and a more experienced team be requested from the Navy. Not surprisingly, it was decided the locals could handle it."

Tanner said nothing. He didn't like the idea of the Navy taking over in his backyard, but if he didn't catch this thing, and soon, he'd have the Navy up his ass for sure. "What do they plan to do if they find it?"

"I armored up a bit since you went down," Randy said. "We got grenades and other weapons from the Army and some citizens have brought some of their personal arsenal to the fight."

"We're gonna have to do better than that. I'll make some calls Tuesday." Tanner passed his hand across his forehead and leaned forward as vertigo took him.

Randy said, "You OK, boss?"

"I'll be all right."

"Get some rest. Why don't you come by the house tomorrow? Have a burger and a beer or four for Memorial Day."

"Nah," Tanner replied. "I'm gonna lie low, rest up, and be ready to get to it Tuesday at sunup." He wasn't up to answering all the questions that would come his way, and Randy's wife would baby him and dote on him as though he were a child. He loved her for it, but it made him nuts.

The wind picked up and stirred the leaves and debris and brought a slight chill. Tanner hugged himself, and his ribs screamed with pain. He got up, went inside, and flopped onto his bed. He was asleep in minutes.

12

If God existed, he'd forgotten about Long Island.

Memorial Day was damp and rainy and miserable. The full moon kicked the tide into high gear, and much of the progress made in the prior week was erased. Floodwaters pressed inland, and though some areas had seen improvement, the low-lying areas on the south shore were still under several feet of water.

Then there was tropical storm Dan ripping across the Atlantic Ocean like a jilted lover, following in Tristin's wake.

Tanner felt much better after another night's sleep. His head only had a dull throb, he could see fine, and he didn't get dizzy when he stood. He skipped his pain meds because he didn't think he needed them. The pills made him feel like shit, and he'd struggled with them in the past because of his bad back. Tanner slapped some peanut butter on bread, ate it with a glass of water, and went back to bed.

He woke to the sound of tapping on his screen door. Tanner pulled on his jeans and a T-shirt and found Jefferson waiting on the porch.

"It's Great South Bay Hopsy Dazy IPA," she said, holding up a six-pack of beer. "Kid at the gas station said it was good stuff. He looked sixteen."

"That Randy's pickup?" Tanner pointed to a red Ford parked in his short weed-infested gravel driveway.

"Yeah, I got a lift to his place and he let me borrow it. He said you wouldn't mind a little company."

"He did, huh? You off-duty?"

"Kind of."

"You want to open two of those beers?"

Jefferson smiled. "Yeah." She leaned forward to snag a couple of beers and her blue uniform shirt fell open a crack, revealing her deep cleavage. Tanner diverted his eyes as fast as he could, but she still caught him and a sly smile crept across her face.

Tanner dragged two lawn chairs into the screen room and they sat. Mosquitoes and flies dive-bombed through the duct-taped screens, and the crickets chirped even though it was mid-afternoon. "So it must be bad. Cough it up."

"What do you mean?" She took a long pull of beer and her face looked like she'd just eaten a bad piece of cheese.

"What did you come here to tell me?" Tanner asked. It hadn't occurred to him until that instant that she'd come to hang out with him.

Her eyes widened and her lips tensed into a thin line. Tanner's eyes shifted to the cracked concrete slab that served as his porch. "I wanted to bring you up to date on the sea scorpion. Figure out what's next," she said.

"I'm glad you came."

They were silent for a few minutes, but to Tanner it felt like an eternity.

"So how does a marine cop who makes six figures end up living in a thirty-year-old trailer?"

"Didn't get the subtlety merit badge, did we?"

"Never tried for it."

"My wife left me. I wanted the kids to have a normal life, so they stayed in the house and I came here. It's not bad, really, and…let's just say you're not seeing it at its best."

"I could say that of your entire island."

Tanner laughed. "You could at that."

"So why'd she leave you?"

This was dangerous territory for Tanner, and his experience had taught him to say as little as possible. Not because he had something to hide, but because the probability of him saying something inappropriate or stupid was high. "It's complicated."

A light rain still fell. "We got time," she said.

"OK, so maybe it's not that complicated," Tanner said. He'd just meet this woman, but he felt like he'd known her a long time and owed her the truth. The crisis they'd shared and their battle with the beast had melded them together quickly like lava hardened by the sea. "I wasn't there, and I didn't prioritize her in my life."

"Don't give me that counselor psychobabble. That the real reason you didn't want to go to the hospital? Afraid of the psych evaluation to get back on duty?"

"No, really. I would have agreed with you a few years ago, but the counselor had a point. I was distant, and it was a problem."

"Why is that?" Jefferson asked.

"Why you grilling me?"

"Curious to know what I'm dealing with," she said. Then she laughed and took a long pull on her beer and Tanner's heart raced as a sheen of perspiration broke out on his forehead. Jefferson's light brown skin was flawless, her deep brown eyes wide with life, and they sucked him in and stirred feelings he hadn't experienced in a long time.

A bird sang as the rain stopped. She was looking at him with eyes that deserved an answer, so he gave the best one he could. "Two years ago, we were supposed to go out to dinner one Saturday night. I had a real bad day and had to cancel because of a stakeout. When I got home that evening, she had some of my stuff packed and asked me to leave. She said it was a long time coming, and that she was sorry, and that this was the best thing for both of us even if I didn't understand that yet. So I left. My kids are in high school and couldn't give two shits about me anyway, so I split."

Jefferson looked at the cement floor and said nothing.

"Hurt more than I wanted to admit, but like our marriage counselor, Audrey had a point. She deserves better," Tanner said, and he meant it.

"Sounds like a real battle."

"Not really. With me out of the picture, they seem to be doing fine, which is confusing since I was hardly ever there to begin with. I guess knowing I'd come home at some point affected their lives. The life of an unwilling asshole."

"Sorry I asked," she said.

"No, it's OK." Tanner shrugged. "It's one of those things. I'm not even mad anymore. Hurt that my kids never come around, but they're teenagers. I figure that might change someday."

Jefferson glanced at the row of empty booze bottles on the windowsill, then down at the cracked concrete, but said nothing.

Breaking the silence, Tanner said, "On to more important stuff. Any news on our underwater friend?"

"No. Those pictures we got are OK, but unless you saw the thing with your own eyes, it's hard to believe."

"I get that. How can such a thing exist?"

"The Atlantic Ocean covers forty-one million square miles and has an average depth of twelve thousand feet. The Hudson Canyon isn't that far from here, and it's deep in spots. The coastie big heads think that might be where this thing came from, as you thought from the beginning. Seas cover seventy percent of the Earth, and it's believed there are countless species in the depths we haven't discovered. The sea scorpion is most likely one of a kind, or part of a tiny family. A long-lost hybrid of a creature that hasn't lived for hundreds of years that's also part lobster. The spike most likely developed over time for protection, like its relative the horseshoe crab."

"And nobody's ever seen this freak of nature before?"

"Like I said, it's a big ocean and it may be the only one, or one of a small family," Jefferson said.

"The question is, where the hell is the thing?"

"If you were a huge bottom dweller, where would you go?"

"Out of the bay for sure, but maybe it can't find the breach? Like a crab stuck in a crab trap?"

"Maybe it doesn't want to leave. Maybe it likes it here," Jefferson said.

"I can see how it might. Food, mud, and plenty of places to hide."

"So, if not out on the bay, then inland?"

"Exactly," Tanner said. "We need to hit the flood areas."

"The thing is smart, not your normal brainless creeper. It could be hiding in a flooded building."

"I'll go through the charts tonight and mark the low areas. You do the same with your fancy equipment onboard the *Vigilant* and we'll compare notes in the morning. You'll be surprised to see that some areas have drained considerably while others remain badly flooded due to differences in elevation, heights of bulkheads, and natural and manmade low areas. Several channels have been formed. I plan to bring *Big Boy*, but we may need to switch to smaller crafts to go deep into the flood zones."

"What's our objective? Search and destroy? That hasn't worked out very well so far."

"We've upgraded our armaments, and we can always run and lead the thing out into the bay where we'll have support." Tanner took a long pull of beer. "Listen, the captain will take me off the hunt in the morning, bring in other people, so I need to get out early."

"Why?"

"With the visibility and seriousness of the situation escalating, this loosey-goosey command structure we've been working under will no longer work for him as he shifts into ass-covering mode."

They sat in silence for a long time, and the rain picked up again. Dusk shrouded the world in a gray haze. Jefferson finished her second beer and put the empty back into the cardboard six-pack holder. She got up and stretched her back. "I'll meet you out there tomorrow? Sunup?"

He wondered if she saw the disappointment on his face when he said, "Leaving?"

"Yeah. I got to get back to the cutter. Just wanted to touch base. Have a good night, Tanner." She turned and pushed through the screen door. Tanner watched her as she got into Randy's truck, started it up, and pulled away.

His stomach tightened. Why did he care so much what this woman did? He hardly knew her, but a chill ran through him and he was sweating. He wiped his brow with the back of his hand and pulled his flask free. He took a hit, grabbed the beers, and headed inside.

13

The trip to Carey Creek only took five minutes. Tanner drove through the predawn dusk, yawning, and wondering who would voluntarily get up before dawn every day. It explained why so many people were already pissed off by lunch most days when he was just getting into the groove. Randy was picking him up at Carey Creek instead of the station because the captain was known as an early bird and he might throw a wrench in the works and show up extra early.

Many people took the day after Labor Day off from work, and traffic was light. Most of the signal lights were working thanks to backup generators and smart electrical engineers, and other than a layer of tree crumbs along the shoulder of every road, Long Island's highways and byways were in good shape. Everything was passable in both directions though it would take months for the public works guys to backtrack and pick up all the lumber. Tanner didn't think there'd be much left by the time they got around to it. With gas and oil prices through the roof, he had a hunch tree companies and civilians fond of playing with their chainsaws and looking to save a buck would take care of many of the fallen trees.

Carey Creek cut through a flooded residential area so Tanner was to meet Randy at the canal head on Monroe Avenue. He made a left off Montauk Highway and drove past his old elementary school and made a left on Monroe. Carey Creek was over flooded and the surrounding streets were under two feet of water. Many of the houses stood like islands and Tanner hadn't gone far before he had to stop.

The captain's white Tahoe was parked across the road in front of a yellow barricade. Quinn and Randy leaned against the truck, watching Tanner as he stopped before them and jumped from the Jeep. Just past the captain's truck, the Great South Bay lapped over the blacktop, half-a-mile inland from its normal demarcation point. A police SAFE boat waited fifty yards off and Tanner was thankful he'd remembered his hip waders. He'd need them to get to the boat, and he had a feeling he would be waist deep in shit all day.

Tanner gave Randy the hardest look he could muster, which wasn't much. Randy returned the stare, and Tanner understood his partner had been threatened. The two men spoke to each other telepathically; at least that's what it felt like.

"Before you get pissed at him, I gave him a direct order," Captain Quinn said. "He had no choice."

"You always have a choice, but I understand," Tanner said. He shot Randy another glance and his partner headed for the boat.

"Hang out, Randy. This concerns you as well," Quinn said.

Randy returned like a scolded child.

"Where's your new partner, Tanner?"

"Today's gonna be a long one, and I'm not coming back until this thing is dead, or it kills me, so I figured the responsible thing to do was give Lucky-shit the day off." The dog had barked up a storm when he tried to leave the trailer, and he was still carrying on as Tanner pulled from his driveway.

"Easy, Ahab. While that's the most responsible thing you've done in months, you're not going out there today," Quinn said.

"You shitting me?" Randy said.

"Ears only, Randy," the captain said.

"You shitting me?" Tanner said.

Randy snickered and Quinn turned to him. "No, I'm not shitting you. When I get to my office, I'm calling the Chief of Police and I'm going to let this crap flow upward. By the end of the day, the Navy will be on the way."

"Fine. That gives me a day. Let me get going."

"No can do," Quinn said. "This thing is getting big and it won't be long before the nation's cameras are turned this way again. It would be best if those cameras don't focus on you. For your own good."

"For *your* own good, you mean. If the press shows up, I'll make myself scarce, they won't even know I'm here. Like I said, I ain't coming back without a pelt, and by then, it won't matter. I'll be dead or the beast will be."

"If it was up to me, I'd let you go, but the death of cops, then a coastie, to say nothing of the civilians, makes that impossible. We're not equipped to handle this, and it's snowballing out of control."

"What's the real reason you're impeding my investigation? Don't want to take a risk because you might fail and look bad? What the fuck happened to you?" The contempt Tanner felt had him trembling, and his stomach burned.

"Stand down, Tanner. Don't take our friendship for granted and put me in a bad position."

"Friendship? Is that what this is?" Tanner said, and he immediately regretted it. The captain had saved his ass so many times he'd lost count. He'd probably be pumping gas without him in his corner. Quinn's shoulders sagged, his head tilted, and he frowned. Tanner said, "I'm sorry, OK? You know I'd give my life to save yours. This goddamned monster has killed, Terry, right before my eyes, and I guarantee you it will kill again. Jefferson and I think it's coming inland into the flooded areas. We have no time to lose."

"I know, but this is business," Quinn said. "Randy, take the boat and go meet the coasties. Tanner is staying with me."

Randy didn't move.

"Did you hear me, Randy?"

Tanner shifted his gaze from the captain to Randy, and his best friend lowered his head, turned, and slowly waded into the water heading toward the boat.

"I'm calling *Newsday* today, my friend," Tanner said. "Giving them the whole thing. Good luck then." Dredging up what happened that night was the last thing he wanted to do, but his recent struggles pulled his past into the present like the tide.

"You know damn well what happened wasn't my fault," Quinn said. "It wasn't yours either. It was dark. The kid had a toy gun. A toy with all the orange reflective markings colored over in black marker to make it look real. You couldn't have known."

"We shouldn't have been there at all. You get that? The senator hadn't been enough. You pushed me into that situation, and now I live my life knowing I killed a thirteen-year-old boy who thought he was protecting his sister." Pain raced up Tanner's back, and he shook with rage, clenching his fists and biting his tongue.

"The boy was wearing a navy blue sweatshirt, Tanner. Holding a toy gun in a drug house."

"We should have waited 'til daylight. Rested up and gone in with backup, but you had to have the twofer, and I had the hat-trick."

Quinn sighed. "Audrey's my fault now, too? You didn't mean to kill that boy. It wasn't our fault." Quinn was pleading, and to Tanner it seemed like he was trying to convince himself more than him.

"Doesn't matter," Tanner said. "He's dead because of your glory, and my stupidity, and I took the blame for it so you could stay clean. Marine division. Why didn't you put me in prison? I would have retained at least some of my respect there."

"You'd kill our careers to get back on the bay? Destroy my reputation? Because the record says I wasn't there, and if you say I was, what happened doesn't even matter."

"It does to me, and I don't care. I'll go to Florida and be a charter boat captain, and you can go fuck off."

"All right," Quinn said. He sighed and breathed deep. "We can't have this loose command structure anymore. The coasties have been informed of your removal."

"Randy's in charge," Tanner said. "I'll advise him."

"What about Jefferson?"

"Don't worry about Jefferson. We're going to war and she's got no beef with me."

Randy had reached the boat and was taking his time looking for the mooring rope, which was underwater.

"I'll tell the brass I missed you, but expect to be called in," Quinn said. "I don't have the final say."

"Expect me to disobey that order," Tanner replied.

The captain smiled and held out his hand. "Good luck and try to come back alive. Don't give your life away for nothing."

Tanner took Quinn's hand and said, "I won't."

The SAFE boat's engines rumbled to life and Tanner waved at Randy, who shut down the motors and rushed out onto the deck like an expectant bride.

The captain left as Tanner pulled on his waders.

"You need help with anything?" Randy shouted.

"Nay, be there in a second." Tanner hid the Jeep's keys under the seat and trudged out into the floodwater. The houses to his left stood just above the encroaching bay, and the water went from two inches deep to two feet deep by the time he'd reached the SAFE boat.

Tanner climbed aboard and clapped Randy on the back. "Thanks for waiting."

"You kidding? What would the Sundance Kid do without Butch? The crew is waiting with *Big Boy* at the mouth of the creek."

Tanner sparked the Hondas and backed the SAFE boat into deeper water. Trees, street signs, and houses stuck from the green bay water, and the buzz of hydraulics echoed through the pilothouse as Tanner lifted the motors a little. Debris floated just beneath the surface and he didn't want to damage the engines.

The sun rose in the east, pushing away the dusk and illuminating the shattered world. Tanner turned the boat south and headed for the open bay.

14

The bay was flat and covered in thick fog. It would burn off by noon, but until then, visibility was minimal. There were no whitecaps, and the wind was a light three miles per hour out of the north. Tanner inched the SAFE boat through the canal mouth into the bay and *Big Boy*'s red navigation light and aft emergency light cut through the fog like mismatched eyes. The deep bellow of *Big Boy*'s horn echoed across the water and Tanner headed toward it. The air was thick and humid, and his blue uniform shirt was already wet in all the tight places.

"Orders, boss?" Randy asked.

Tanner chuckled. "I advise you to…"

"Lt. Tanner, I order you to act as captain of the SCPD vessel *Herman*, AKA *Big Boy*, until further notice. Is that clear, sailor?"

"Sailor?" The two men laughed and Tanner clapped Randy on the back. "We both have to lead today, brother. But thanks."

Randy hailed the coasties, and they agreed to meet at the breach where they'd set the day's search pattern and exchange updates. They reached *Big Boy* and Tanner prepared to disembark.

"I want you on this twenty-two. Piloting a craft you're comfortable with. I'll send you Toby, and I want you to be my wingman. You got me?"

Randy nodded.

"You remember that stupid movie, right? Never leave your wingman. I was able to forgive you the night you met Tina, but they'll be no acceptable excuses tonight except one."

"Which is?"

"You have kids, and they're like my kids, and—"

Randy revved the engines, but they were so quiet he had to turn up the radio.

"Randy, I'm not screwing around," Tanner said.

"I know. I won't do anything stupid. If I have to retreat and leave you, I will."

"You don't have to be so flippant about it. I mean, pause for a little contemplation for shit's sake." Tanner left the wheelhouse as Randy brought the boat close to *Big Boy*.

"Kim, you there?" Tanner said. *Big Boy* was shrouded in fog.

A woman with short-cropped blonde hair and black-rimmed glasses walked to the bow. "Yeah, I'm here. Tanner? What are you doing here? Our orders—"

Randy's voice boomed from the exterior public address system. "Tanner is in command of *Big Boy* at my order. Toby is with me."

The SAFE boat crept alongside the gray patrol boat. Tanner stepped up onto the SAFE boat's blue pontoon gunnel, and then down onto *Big Boy*'s dive platform. Officer Toby Overbier, better known as Otto, said hello to Tanner and jumped onto the SAFE boat and joined Randy in the cabin. Both boats came about and headed across the bay toward the breach.

Big Boy's wheel trembled beneath Tanner's hand. The *Herman*, AKA *Big Boy*, was a forty-two-foot powerhouse made of thirty-six tons of aluminum that'd been beaten and hardened over twenty years of use. It had a flying bridge, thick tubular guardrails, and two old-school diesel engines pushing 4,000 RPMs each. The vessel sounded like a ferry to Tanner, but when he jumped on it, the old mother could go forty knots. Its command console was replaced two years prior, and its modern lines and current equipment made it look out of place in the old pilothouse. The boat could house four men for a cruise of ten days and was similar in style to the war boats that had gone up the Mekong River in the Vietnam War. The harder you pounded *Big Boy*'s aluminum hull, the stronger it became. Behind the pilothouse, a short-range tactical Zodiac waited in its cradle. A heavy-duty boom arm sat folded beside it and when deployed, it could launch the boat in minutes. Tanner ordered the smaller craft stocked with ammo in case they needed to get into it fast.

Tanner was pleased with the modifications to *Big Boy*, the largest of which was the addition of an old M1919 Browning heavy-duty machine gun Randy had borrowed from the local Army reserve base. It came with a thousand rounds. In addition, two midsized M60 machine guns were mounted atop tripods on the upper deck, and a case of grenades sat open on the forward deck. Next to the grenades was an M9 bazooka with two three-and-a-half-inch shells stacked beside it. Everything was secured under a cargo net. All the improvements were military issue, and thus technically weren't allowed to be used by civilian police departments, but given the situation, the reservists had made an exception with the proviso that Randy never reveal where he'd gotten the stuff, no matter what happened.

The fog was already dissipating and lifting when they crossed the center of the bay. *Big Boy* pushed through the green water at twenty-eight knots, with Randy running alongside him. Tanner was on the bow, surveying the water and sky for any signs of animal life. Normally, flocks of piping plovers, geese, ducks, and seagulls filled the sky, and little shiners jumped from the water, but there were no signs of them. The scent of rot and decay permeated the air. Dead fish lay in thick patches of seaweed, and the bay was quiet and still. Several PD and fire rescue boats searched, but many waited on full readiness standby, waiting to be called in.

Two SAFE boats with orange pontoon gunnels raced through the breach toward *Big Boy*. The tide was going out, and bay water ran through the breach like a river, the current pulling anything in its path out into the Atlantic Ocean. Sandbars created by the strong currents loomed on both sides of the Coast Guard vessels, and the SAFE boats were forced to pass single file through the breach.

Tanner went to the bridge. "Full stop," he said, and the hum of *Big Boy*'s engines lessened. They floated toward the breach channel, the tide and wind moving them along at a steady three knots.

Broken shells covered the sandbar to port, and Tanner sighed when he saw no clam or oyster shells among the mollusk wreckage. The Great South Bay had once been the Mecca of oysters and sea scallops, and Blue Point oysters were still served all over the globe despite the fact that no oysters had been commercially harvested from the bay in over fifty years. Overfishing had killed off the oysters and scallops, and clams were on the way out. When Tanner was a boy, hundreds of boats would venture out onto the bay each day in search of bounty, and that had shrunken to little more than a dozen in recent years.

"Captain, the coasties are asking to board," the helmsman announced over the PA.

Tanner went back to the bridge. "Get Randy over here as well. We'll meet in the wardroom."

Ten minutes later, Jefferson entered the wardroom with her security escort and strode up to Tanner, who regarded her from where he sat at a table with a chart of the bay laid out before him. "Lt. Vernon?" she said to Tanner.

Tanner sighed. He thought she was going to arrest him for an instant. "Aye, ma'am," he said.

Jefferson's mate stared at the floor and Randy snickered.

"You have taken over for Lt. Tanner? I was informed by the brass he is no longer on duty."

"That's correct," Tanner said, playing along with the ruse.

Jefferson's security guy had never meet Tanner, and if questioned later, Jefferson could tell her superiors she'd made a mistake, and the locals hadn't set her straight. It wouldn't work, but it was better than outright disobedience and it might save her tail if things went to hell.

"Coffee?" Randy asked.

"Please."

Randy fetched coffee and sat next to Tanner.

Jefferson took a long sip and closed her eyes, savoring it. "Thank you. You guys do coffee way better than we do."

"We aim to please," Tanner said.

"Quiet out there this morning."

"It's as if every living thing knows a new alpha is in town except us."

"Isn't that always the way with the alphas?" Jefferson said.

"Guess so."

"Can we get to it?" Randy said.

Tanner shot him a dirty look. "I think we should head out to Bellport. The coastline there is still flooded, and the sea scorpion could penetrate way inland there."

"What about Carmen's River?" Randy asked.

"Possible, and if we don't have any luck this morning, I think that'll be out next stop."

"I've got two boats and so do you," Jefferson said. "Should we split up?"

"I think we should," Randy told her. "It's not like we're talking long distances here. If we need a full force, it would only take a few minutes to make that happen."

"So let's stay together until we get to the mainland," Jefferson said.

"Should we get underway while we talk?" Tanner said.

"Makes sense."

Jefferson's security man, seaman First Class Tito Leppords, left the wardroom to go give the orders from *Big Boy*'s bridge.

"Do we wanna chum the water?" Randy asked. "I brought two barrels of the nastiest shit I could get. The crap would wake the dead."

"Maybe we should leave a slick through the breach out into the ocean. The thing might follow it out," Jefferson said.

"Really?" Tanner said. "It killed one of your men, and two of mine. You'd just let it walk…crawl off?"

"No," Jefferson answered. "But let's hold off on chumming the water until we get inland and see what we're dealing with."

"Agreed."

Big Boy shuttered as the engines engaged, and the boat listed for a second as it got underway. The hum of the motors, the sound of rushing water, and the bump and rattle of the stores in the wardroom's cabinets made talking hard, but there wasn't much left to say.

Tanner's stomach ached, and it wasn't from anything he'd eaten. The stern expression on Jefferson's face told him she was having similar thoughts, but neither of them said anything as *Big Boy* churned across the bay.

15

The call from command came as *Big Boy* pushed across Bellport Bay. A white haze hung in the sky as the last of the clouds burnt off and the sun shone through. It was seventy-five degrees, the humidity was at eighty-six percent, and it was only 9AM. A steady breeze kicked up chop, and the sea spray left a sheen of water on every horizontal surface. A line of clouds marched across the sky to the west and by 2PM it would be raining. The air was crisp and fresh, the scent of rot and shit only an undercurrent. Tanner, Randy, and Jefferson had moved up to the command bridge, and the PD boat and the two coastie boats flanked them.

"This is the *Herman*. We copy you, command," Randy said.

"Randy, this is Monteeth. Is Lt. Tanner with you?" the chief said through light static.

The question hung there and Jefferson and Randy both stared at Tanner, so he pressed the comm and said, "No, sir." His Randy voice was pretty good.

"Is he on the vessel?"

"No, sir."

"Do you know of his whereabouts?" The chief's voice cracked as he strained not to yell.

"No, sir."

"Bullshit, Vernon. You two are as thick as shit and maggots. I'll bust you both down to crossing guards or worse. Especially your partner. You there, Tanner? I know you are, you fuckin' turd!" The chief had lost the battle with himself and was screaming full tilt. "You better get this bitch, Tanner! The Navy is on the way, and when they get here, whatever the hell is going on out there is going to end. You can hide now, and I'm not coming for you, but you better catch this thing or you and Randy and every asshole on your team are done in marine."

"Copy, sir," Tanner said. "Randy out."

"Screw you, Tanner. Command out."

"Sounds like a good guy," Jefferson said.

"He is," Tanner said. "But you know how bosses are, always have to be putting you in your place so they can feel superior. Sad really."

"Try being a female officer in the military."

Tanner grunted.

"You think the creature will hunker down for the day?" Randy asked.

Tanner said nothing.

"I'd better get back to my ship," Jefferson said.

Tanner nodded.

"See you on the other side," she said, and slipped from the bridge.

Tanner watched her climb aboard her boat: the fine lines of her ass, the gracefulness of her walk. Old senses stirred in him and he drove them down again. When this was over for good or ill she'd be gone, and whatever they might have been would be lost.

"Time for me to go as well," Randy said.

Tanner stared out at the bay, unable to find words. When he turned to wish his friend luck, Randy had left.

"Bring me down a few notches, helm," Tanner said. He relinquished the controls so he could move around the boat. As *Big Boy* came off plane, the three SAFE boats did the same, like they'd all come out of hyperspace at the same moment.

The light tower at the end of Beaver Dam Creek stood four feet out of the bay, and that was the only thing marking the submerged jetty. Rooftops and the second stories of houses stood above the floodwaters, and small rolling waves broke through smashed windows.

"Take us in," Tanner instructed.

They had the sonar on, but it looked clear of thirty-foot sea monsters. They hadn't seen any of the creature's waste, or any other signs, for that matter. The water was four feet above the bulkhead, and all the homes along the canal were flooded and mostly abandoned. A few houses had dinghies tied to front porch railings, but most of the houses sat quiet. Tops of cars, street signs, trees, and other vegetation stuck from the water, and debris bobbed on the miniature tsunami caused by their passage.

"We're in six feet of water, sir," the helmsman said.

"Full stop," Tanner said. "Keep us here and get *Little Boy* ready to deploy."

"Sir?"

The kid's face was priceless. It said, "Sir, are you out of your mind going out in the floodwaters in a sixteen-foot boat with the sea scorpion around?"

"Prepare to deploy *Little Boy*. Now!"

Tanner put six grenades and the bazooka and its shells in the Zodiac. He checked the Glock 19 on his hip and fetched an MK18 on loan from the coasties from the gun cabinet. Once everything was in the boat, he hailed Randy. "Randy, you copy?"

"Go ahead, boss."

"I'm going on point. Stay right behind me. I'm leaving *Big Boy* here to hold the mouth. Have the coasties flank you. Be ready to move up when I signal."

"Come get me, over," Jefferson's voice came over the radio.

"That's a negative," Tanner said.

"Not a request, sailor."

Tanner sighed so long he thought he might pass out. "10-4," he said.

Tanner got in *Little Boy* and braced himself as the boom arm lifted the short-range tactical Zodiac powered by a thirty-horse Honda outboard and dropped it in the water. Tanner put the motor down and started it. It roared to life, and he slipped it in gear and headed for Jefferson's boat. She waited on the bow and stepped easily into the smaller boat.

"Why are you doing this?" Tanner asked.

Jefferson said nothing. Instead, she sat on the gunnel, her MK18 between her legs, and stared into the wreckage of the drowned world.

The desolation was complete in this area. Lives floated in the flotsam and jetsam; pictures, clothes, shards of wood that had once been part of a world people took for granted. With all the people gone and the rot of water filling every crack and empty space, there was no tomorrow for this neighborhood. When it dried out, it would be bulldozed and the battles would begin anew between those who wanted to rebuild and those who felt it was throwing good money after bad as the increase in global water temperatures created more hazardous and more frequent hurricanes.

The outboard gurgled as they slid across the placid surface, down a side street that was still four feet underwater. A woman waved from an upper window, and cats lived on rooftops. They came to a boatyard, and two giant metal warehouses blocked their way, their large doors open. Tanner turned and made a fist, and the three SAFE boats held their positions. Tanner killed the motor and glided into one of the warehouses.

Tops of boats protruded from the water, and cushions and other garbage gathered in one corner. Nothing on sonar, and sea bottom was hard-packed. Tanner started the motor and backed out.

They repeated this process several times, covering the entire neighborhood and seeing no sign of the creature. They headed north back out to the main canal and deeper inland. The flood waters were getting lower, but the wind had done a particularly wicked job here. Roofs were missing, entire walls caved in or gone altogether. Trees toppled on cars and houses, and everywhere piles of garbage, both natural and manmade.

Tanner said, "Reminds of me of a time the Navy dumped us off in Africa to support some militia that had agreed to bring vaccines to the people in the area suffering from an Ebola outbreak. That's dangerous shit, and it's important to stamp that crap out no matter where it is because it could get here easy. So we head up the Congo River to meet up with the locals, but someone dropped the dime on us and we were attacked on the river. Lost all my guys. The devastation was amazing."

"You were the only one to survive?" Jefferson said.

Tanner looked at her, but said nothing. He piloted the boat through backyards, over submerged fences, and across streets and parking lots. Nothing moved except the gentle push and pull of the water as it continued its assault on what was left of man's creations. A helicopter cruised by overhead and Tanner got on the radio to Randy. "Why are there whirlybirds in the air? I thought we'd grounded them because they spook the creature?"

"That's a 10-4, Tann..." Silence over the comm channel. "That's a 10-4. I'll get on it."

Tanner smiled. Randy thought their communications were being monitored, and he was probably right. The chief said he wasn't coming after him, but that didn't mean he wasn't keeping an eye on him.

Randy said, "Some good news. Apparently, civilians are searching for the thing using their toy drones. The footage isn't bad. The captain put out the word that people should email their footage links to us. As they come in, they'll be examined."

"10-4. Keep us appraised."

They continued searching though Jefferson was getting visibly frustrated. After an hour she said, "I don't think it's in here."

"Why?"

"No signs. Wouldn't we see waste? Broken buildings and other stuff the monster rampaged through?"

Tanner didn't want to give up, but she had a point and there were plenty of other places to search. It was noon when Tanner called it.

Clouds filled the sky and a light rain fell as Tanner dropped Jefferson off at her boat and headed back to *Big Boy*. The boom arm eased overhead, and Tanner attached the lanyard of the lift cables to the boat at four points and gave the go-ahead to the bridge. As the boat lifted, it poured huge drops that filled the Zodiac and drenched Tanner through. The tiny fleet motored through the rain, and Tanner hoped their luck changed soon. They were running out of time.

16

The Great South Bay was a blown-out mess. Whitecaps dotted the boiling sea, and rain fell sideways in the twenty-mile-per-hour wind. Somewhere above the clouds, the sun had passed noon, and the storm showed no signs of easing. Three-foot waves crashed inland, battering houses that had already seen significant damage. The navigation tower stood out through the thick rain as they exited Beaver Dam Creek. Visibility was only half a mile, and *Big Boy* rolled side to side as the motion of the sea embraced her and they entered the bay. Huge windshield wipers worked double time clearing the rain, and the sound of them smacking back and forth soothed Tanner's nerves.

He said, "Bring her up to one quarter, helm."

The diesel engines rumbled and *Big Boy* lurched forward through the turbulent sea. The bow lifted and fell as they cut through the chop, and Tanner gripped the arms of his chair. Sea spray hammered the front bridge window, and the helmsman used the computer more than her eyes to navigate. Directly across the bay, hidden by the storm, was the breach, which was the main reason the section of the south shore they'd just searched had been hit harder than anywhere else, and why it was still severely flooded more than a week after Tristin had bid Long Island adieu.

The good news was the longer the storm lasted the longer it would take the Navy to arrive. The destroyer USS *Gridley* was on the way, but the Atlantic pounded Fire Island with a six-foot swell and that would slow things down. The USCGC *Vigilant* was anchored nose into the waves, and Jefferson had described a night of non-sleep that would have had an old seaman like him puking. Tanner didn't do the sleeping on boats thing very well. Cost him endless ribbing in the Navy and always reminded him that fear of the water as a boy had led him to trying to overcome it, which led to the Navy and ultimately to being a cop. Maybe being a marine cop hadn't been his dream, but it was better than most jobs.

Officer Kimberly Jansen was at the helm, and she held the wheel steady as she examined the display screens mounted atop the dashboard: GPS, front and rear extra cameras, engine status, and the track of the storm all neatly organized before her. Tanner knew she didn't like him because she let him know it every chance she got. She thought he was a chauvinist pig, and there were times he'd have to agree with her. The world had changed, and at forty-two, he was a dinosaur.

"What's this weather looking like, helm?" Tanner said.

"It should blow through in the next couple of hours," Jansen answered. "Clouds will hang around, but visibility should improve."

"What about Hurricane Dan?"

"One moment," she said. "It's on track to hit the east end, but the final path is still unknown. We could see severe wind."

"Check in on Ally and Sal," Tanner said.

Jansen called down to the engine room and got an all clear and then did the same with Sal, who was below in the wardroom preparing sandwiches. Tanner checked in with Randy and Jefferson via SAT phone.

"Everything's OK here, boss," Randy reported.

"Stay on the line while I patch in Jefferson," Tanner said.

"10-4."

"Jefferson? You there?"

Static boomed from the phone in short bursts, and then Jefferson's voice came through clear. "I'm here. What's the plan?"

"I'm open to input."

"This is your sandbox."

Static filled the line again and Randy said, "We tried the basic stick together route with no bait, and we've wasted a good chunk of the day. We need to do better than that."

"I said monitor, Randy. Ears only," Tanner said.

"He's got a point," Jefferson said.

Tanner sighed and leaned back in his command chair. "Yes, he always has a point."

Static filled the silence and Tanner worked the problem. If they split up, they could cover more area, but if the thing showed, it might take too long to bring the other boats into the attack. The sea scorpion moved fast, and Tanner wanted to kill the thing the next time he saw it. No games. No more chases. He wanted it hanging from a hook on the pier with him standing next to it on the cover of *Newsday*. If they stayed together, they might search all day and night and never find the thing, and by tomorrow he'd be off the case. Hell, he might even be locked up.

"Let's split up," he decided. "I'll head over to Fireplace Neck and head inland as far as I can with *Big Boy* then penetrate further with the Zodiac. Randy, you head west, Jefferson east. The second Coast Guard boat should hold position and serve as emergency backup."

"Works for me," Jefferson said.

"Keep in touch," Tanner said.

"10-4," Randy and Jefferson said at the same time.

"Time to chum and get a slick going?" Randy said.

"Do we want to fight this thing inland?" Jefferson said.

"Ideally, we'd flush it into the bay so we can hit it with everything at once," Tanner said. "In tight quarters, that might be a challenge."

"We'll wait for a sign then," Randy said. "What about hanging a chunk of rotten fish off the back of the boats? That'll create a small slick and might draw the thing out it."

"Makes sense," Tanner said.

He went out on deck and opened one of the large plastic barrels Randy had brought onboard. The scent of rotten fish almost knocked him over, and when the maggots crawled on his hand, he dry heaved and almost coughed up a lung. *Big Boy* slowed to a crawl and Jefferson and Randy came in close. He tossed them each a chunk of rotten fish. Jefferson saluted him and Randy flipped him the bird. Jansen brought *Big Boy* about as Tanner tied heavy-gauge fishing line around a chunk of fish and tossed it off the back of the boat and tied the line off on a cleat.

Fireplace Neck was a maze of canals with a large marina at its center. It was a relatively new development, and most of the houses still stood thanks to hurricane strapping and building code enforcement. Unfortunately, there was no code that could protect you from Mother Nature's most powerful tool: water.

Tanner headed back to the bridge and looked over Jansen's shoulder at the GPS navigation chart. The maze of canals was created so each house in the development could have a boat slip, and the center marina had a manmade island at its center with a restaurant, gas pump, and a small general store that stocked mostly marine supplies.

"Head up main canal. You'll hold position in the marina and I'll head in on the Zodiac. Can you handle things here?"

Jansen turned her head and tried to crack her neck. "Aye, sir," she said.

Tanner smiled. If she thought he was a chauvinist pig, then he might as well give her what she wanted.

The rain let up a little, but the wind didn't. The canal mouth wasn't visible so sonar led the way. Debris filled the water, and all manner of garbage bounced off *Big Boy*'s hull as they pushed inland. The houses along main canal were flooded, and there were no boats or other signs of life. When they reached Fireplace Neck's central marina, *Big Boy* came to a stop and Tanner deployed the Zodiac. With Sal by his side, the two men set off into the narrow waterways that ran behind the houses, the rattle of the outboard echoing through the destroyed community.

They spent two hours in the rain, powering up and down canals, floating into backyards and hollowed-out structures. Tanner and Sal ate their sandwiches, checked their weapons, but it wasn't until the end of Tippit Canal that they noticed the strange scale-like shells floating on the surface. The panels were black as night and looked intact, as though they'd been shed, not broken.

Tanner plucked one out of the flotsam and examined it. It was oval, three feet long tip to tip, and smooth to the touch. It was also thin and somewhat pliable. One side had a coating of mucus or some other excretion, and it smelled of rotting flesh.

"What do you make of this?" Tanner said as he handed the specimen to Sal.

"Looks like the thing rubbed up against something, or got snagged on something."

"Yeah."

It was 3PM, and the rain started again. Thunder rumbled, and off to the west lightning streaked across the sky. There were eight scales floating in the jetsam, and the longer he studied them, the more they reminded him of the tip of a lobster tail, what were called the uropods. Tanner stacked all eight in the boat and continued on.

"Should we head back?" Sal said.

Tanner stared up into the rain. "Not yet."

17

"What's that?" Sal said. He was pointing toward a notch where two six-foot stockade fences came together above the water. At first, Tanner saw nothing special, but when his eye caught the broken harpoon, he froze, unable to process what he was seeing. He sat there for several moments, doing nothing, the fight with the beast rushing back in the form of a waking nightmare. He'd pierced the sea scorpion's left eye, and if this was that harpoon, it meant they were close.

Tanner jerked the engine's control arm and headed toward the harpoon. It was his all right, he could tell from ten feet away. He recognized the grip, the tip was broken off, and it had the same rope lanyard tie-off at the end of the handle. Tanner put the motor in neutral and eased himself to the bow of the boat. He leaned on the rubber gunnel and was about to dip his hand into the water when he remembered the many horror movies he'd seen where the unwitting protagonist puts his hand down a dirt hole, or into wall, or the most common use of this trope, sticking his hand in water known to contain danger.

Tanner cracked his neck and grabbed the broken harpoon. It had once been nine feet long, two-thirds handle and one-third steel tip, with the last foot being barbed. Half the steel tip was gone, cut clean off as if done with a laser cutter. There were no twists in the remaining metal, no signs of stress.

"Looks clipped clean off," Sal said. "Just like the first one you hit it with."

"You're very observant."

Sal looked at him and squinted, confusion filling his face as he tried to figure out if he was being insulted.

The rain had stopped and thick mist hung around every corner. Somewhere a screen door banged ceaselessly against its frame as an easterly wind tore through the flooded neighborhood. Tanner continued on and heard a chainsaw screaming to the north. The water was three feet above normal this far in and the outline of the bulkhead on both sides of the boat could be seen below the surface.

Tanner pulled his radio free and looked to Sal, who gave him nothing. Sal was two years out from retirement and wouldn't take any unnecessary risks. Tanner pushed him. "What do you think? Call in the cavalry?"

"I think the scales and harpoon might have been here five minutes or days. No way of knowing. We haven't seen any of its shit, or anything else we could claim was a recent sign. I'd hold off."

It was good advice. The problem was Sal didn't have Tanner's gut, which was telling him the thing was close. They came to the canal's end and cut up a driveway to the east and through a backyard to the next canal. They floated across a lawn covered in three feet of water, and children's toys and garbage eased back and forth on the grass below with the roll of the tide.

To their left, an oversized house missing two walls and its roof had a fountain of bubbles leaking out the front door. Tanner got a grenade and readied his MK18. He killed the engine and, using the boat's momentum, he guided the Zodiac around the side of the house to get a glimpse of whatever was causing the bubbles.

The boat slid toward the opening on the side of the house and a mass of bubbles and whitewater roiled from what had been somebody's living room. As they eased closer, the bubbles dissipated, and the water went flat. An eerie silence settled over the destroyed house. No birds squawked, no shiners jumped from the water. There was no sign of life.

"You think it heard us?" Sal said.

"At first, I thought it was some type of leak, maybe a broken natural gas pipe, but it stopped when we approached." Tanner was concerned. They were floating within the house and if the creature surfaced, it would do so directly beneath them.

Tanner detached the oars held in place on the side of the Zodiac by two short bungee cords. He flipped up the oarlocks and fit in the oars. He rowed gently, lifting the oars from the water delicately, trying not to disturb the water or make noise, and the Zodiac inched backward.

Tanner breathed a sigh of relief when they were outside, under the blanket of dark clouds. Tanner moved the boat away from the house and stopped next to the house's lamppost, the top of which stuck from the water like a forlorn tree in a decimated forest. He tied the Zodiac off on the post and leaned back, sighing and running his hand through his hair as he sucked in air. Sal watched him intently, waiting for Tanner to declare their next move. It was obvious to Tanner by the look on Sal's face that he would rather have been anywhere else in the world at that moment.

Several minutes passed and Tanner said nothing. Sal couldn't contain himself any longer. It was fun watching his fellow officer's stages of frustration and anger play across his face. "We just gonna sit here and wait until the thing gets hungry?"

"No. Not you, anyway. I think I've got a plan," Tanner said.

"Ruh oh," Sal said, doing his best Scooby-Doo impersonation. "You think the thing's in there? How could it fit?"

"In the basement, though I don't know how it got in there. A caved-in foundation wall, maybe."

"What do you mean not me?" The excitement was clear in Sal's voice.

"See that broken window there?" Tanner pointed to a house across the street that had a double-sized doghouse jutting from its roof, its blown-out double window facing the street.

"Yup."

"I'm thinking you drop me off over there, and I sit up in that window and wait with the bazooka. You start the motor and make a big show of leaving, and as you do that, you can leave a chum slick right here where we're sitting. Draw the thing out and I'll nail it." It sounded even crazier now that he'd said it out loud.

Sal's face brightened again. "That might work, but what happens if the thing attacks the house? You'll have nowhere to run."

Tanner hadn't thought of that. "Once you get clear, call Jefferson and Randy. Pull them into the marina and be ready to engage when I call you."

Sal nodded vigorously as if he was still trying to convince himself that this madness was a good idea.

Tanner untied the boat and rowed across the street and inched the Zodiac up to the house's front porch. He tied off the boat, gathered his weapons, grabbed a sandwich and a bottle of water, and stepped onto the flooded porch.

"You almost forgot this." Sal handed Tanner a radio.

"That would have sucked," Tanner said.

"Good luck. See you in a bit." Sal untied the boat and let it drift back toward the street. Tanner watched as Sal opened a small container filled with the rankest rotten flesh he'd ever smelled, and the officer ladled the decomposed maggot-infested chum into the water. The slick floated toward the target house. Sal saw his slick growing and where it was going and quickly sealed up the container and started the outboard. He wasted no time bringing the motor up to full power, and within a minute he was gone, leaving only his wake and the faint sound of the engine whining.

The house's front door was locked, but it didn't take much to spring it open. Water lapped across the plush carpet of someone's living room. Household debris floated in the floodwater, an LCD TV hung on one wall, and everything else had the beginnings of green mold covering its surface. The stairs were straight ahead and Tanner mounted them, pushing the urge to cry from his mind. It was difficult witnessing the destruction, the lives destroyed, and the families broken and displaced. Again he wondered what the people who'd live here would do, and where would they go?

Once upstairs, he moved a chair in front of the window and planted himself in it. It was the perfect spot to view the house across the street. No sooner had the sound of the Zodiac's motor faded than bubbles poured from the front door of the house across the street.

Tanner laid out the bazooka and the two shells he'd brought next to the chair and placed a grenade on the windowsill before him. Then he checked his Glock and his MK18. He sighted the rifle, making sure he could get a good bead on both sides of the house, and waited.

The crinkle of paper being unfolded as Tanner unwrapped his sandwich filled the room and he paused, staring across the street with trepidation. There was no sign the sound had stirred anything, so he finished and ate. Twenty minutes later, his sandwich was gone, he'd drunk his water, and he was bored. How did hunters sit in a tree all day waiting for a deer to come by?

The clock ticked on. Tanner took a pull off his flask and waited.

18

Tanner dozed, and it was after 4PM when the bubbles increased in strength and snapped him to attention. Sal's slick had spread across the area, and the odor was so strong it made Tanner gag. He lifted the MK18 and placed his forearms on the windowsill. The weather had cleaned up, but it was still overcast and damp, the humidity so thick it was like breathing Jell-O. Sweat dripped down his face and into his eyes and Tanner wiped them away with his shirtsleeve.

Whitewater poured from the house across the street, bubbling over what was left of the walls and out through the missing roof like a soda that's been shaken and then opened. Seaweed and all manner of flotsam surged forth, and a section of the house's front wall collapsed. Two large pieces shot across the flooded road.

The leviathan emerged from the mound of bubbles, its black scimitar-like tail appearing first, ready to strike. Huge claws floated to the surface, followed by the creature's black segmented carapace. Floodwater heaved around the beast's underbelly as its spiderlike appendages beat and pushed at the water to keep the monstrosity afloat. Tanner sighted the MK18 where he thought the scorpion's head would surface and flicked off the safety.

The MK18 was a close quarter's combat weapon developed by the US Navy. It was a short-barreled variant of the AR15, and its gas-powered rotating bolt churned out thirty shots in seconds. The shorter barrel makes the gun compact and easier to use in tight spaces like ships or submarines. Tanner had fired similar weapons in the past, but he'd never fired this particular weapon, and that worried him.

The sea scorpion's head inched from the water and Tanner jerked back in astonishment as he got a good look at the immense creature for the first time. He'd studied pictures of fossils showing the prehistoric *Jaekelopterus*, and other than the front claws being much larger and the giant antennas, that was exactly what the beast looked like. The antennas were a foot around where they met the hard black shell of the creature's head, and they ran twenty feet in length. Its mouth hung open, revealing rows of teeth accented with two long fangs. Above its mouth, two black eyes the size of basketballs rotated and scanned the area. The left eye had blue blood around it and Tanner saw the steel tip of his harpoon sticking from it. The beast's good eye swiveled in his direction and Tanner felt it searching for him as if it could sense his presence.

Tanner's dad used to say even the most docile of creatures would become violent if cornered. Instinct took over and the animal's learned responses were put on hold as its primordial brain asked itself the question of flight or fight. Though Tanner sat in wait for the creature, his caveman mind considered the same question. He could sit tight, hide, and the thing would leave or submerge. Or he could attack it and send it back to hell.

Tanner dropped to the floor and held his breath. Suddenly, he didn't feel so tough. The steady sound of bubbles eased, and he lifted his head above the windowsill and took a peek. The beast was floating about, sucking in the slick, searching for its source. With all the wildlife fleeing, the sea scorpion would have no source of food. His father's words came back to him again: the only thing more dangerous than a cornered animal is a hungry animal.

Tanner loaded the bazooka and leaned it against the wall. He wanted to hit this thing in the face, so he'd have to get it to come right at him. Then when the leviathan was bearing down on him, he'd put the two-and-a-half-inch incendiary rocket right down the bastard's throat. Tanner smiled and braced himself on the window again as he sighted the MK18.

The sea scorpion didn't have much room to move between the houses, and the water wasn't deep enough for it to swim, so the beast scuttled across the flooded neighborhood looking for food, its antennas always searching. When it came parallel to Tanner's position, he fired.

The quick burst of bullets struck the creature's armored carapace, and the monster bucked, kicking up sea spray as it tried to dive. It hit the blacktop road below with a loud thud and sprang up. Tanner loosed another burst and it struck the armored shell around the creature's face. The scorpion spun toward Tanner. He opened up, spraying the creature with bullets and emptying the MK18.

Tanner dropped the weapon and lifted the bazooka, setting it on his shoulder as he flipped up the eyesight. It was an older weapon that still worked because of its basic design. The M9 rocket launcher was thirty-one inches long and weighted sixteen pounds. It could penetrate armor plating up to four inches and its solid propellant shells traveled at two hundred sixty-five feet per second and packed quite the punch. Tanner had never fired such a weapon, but he'd been told it was recoilless so he didn't think it would be hard.

Blue blood streaked across the creature's face as it turned and came right at Tanner. Water swelled as the beast clawed through the flood, ripping up blacktop and turf. Tanner held the bazooka steady, but his hands shook and sweat dripped into his eyes. The sea scorpion was forty yards away and closing, and the deep hum of its voice rose above the crashing water as Tanner prepared to fire. The creature roared, its mouth opening as it lunged toward the house.

Tanner pulled the trigger. The solid propellant in the rocket ignited and a flash of fire spit out the back of the launch tube. Tanner flinched, and the nose of the bazooka flicked upward an inch as the shell streaked from the tube and flew toward the monster.

The one-inch barrel lift grew exponentially as the rocket closed the forty yards between Tanner and the creature's open mouth, and when it reached its target, the rocket's trajectory had changed enough to allow the shell to pass inches above the scorpion's head. It struck the house behind the monster and exploded in a dazzling display of black smoke and fire. The remains of the house burned above the floodwater and smoke filled the area.

Tanner heard the beast coming on but couldn't see it. He fumbled for the second rocket but as he did so, the creature crashed into the house and he was thrown to the floor. Boards creaked and snapped and the floor beneath him collapsed, the corner to his right sinking precipitously at an angle. The house shook and walls cracked and pieces of the ceiling fell. His heart raced in his chest, and he heard his mother's voice in the back of his head yelling at him to be careful.

Through the swirling smoke, Tanner saw the sea scorpion's spike rearing and preparing to strike. It stabbed downward and came through the roof ten feet from where Tanner lay. The cicada-like buzz grew until it blocked out all other sound, and Tanner's ears rang. Floodwater lashed against the house as the creature thrashed about, blue blood smattering the water and the remains of the house.

Tanner fitted the rocket into the launcher and got to his feet. He felt for his Glock and found it in its holster on his hip. He checked for his flask and radio and gasped. The radio was no longer clipped to his belt. He searched about him and saw it sliding toward the corner that was caving in. He went for it, snatching it up and carefully backing away as the floor buckled beneath his feet.

The black spike pierced the roof feet in front of Tanner, and he jumped back and drew his Glock. He fired four times, each bullet hitting home and taking small chunks from the spike as it retracted and disappeared from view. The creature bellowed, and the spike came down again, this time right next to Tanner. He ran for the door in the back of the room, but the front of the house was falling away and the floor was going with it. A bed and large dresser skidded past him as he fought to keep from slipping into the wreckage.

The window darkened as the beast breached from the water and attacked the house, claws grabbing wood and the great spike smashing through the roof. The floor gave out, and the roof collapsed. Tanner fell, clutching the bazooka as though it was the last thing he'd ever see. Wood rained down as he fell, and the roaring and confusion engulfed him as he plummeted into the floodwater below.

19

Tanner had once paddled class four whitewater on the Green River, and he'd been thrown from his kayak and sucked into a hole where he endured the most difficult four minutes of his life. A powerful torrent of water had pressed him beneath the surface, and after great effort, he'd emerged into fresh air for an instant only to get sucked under again, as though he were in a clothes washer and endlessly spinning on the rinse cycle. As the house collapsed around him and water filled his mouth, he remembered how good it felt when he'd freed himself of the river.

He hit the floodwater hard, but it broke his fall. He landed on his right side and crashed into the floor with a splat and waves of displaced water washed over him. A chunk of the floor fell on him, and Tanner rolled toward a wall hoping for protection. Everything went dark as wood and debris pushed him into the turbulent water. He took a deep breath and dove, pain crippling his right leg.

He thought of Audrey. When they met. The biggest mistake in his life was letting her go. He thought of Jefferson. Now he wouldn't even get the chance to mess that relationship up. Tanner sucked in water and coughed. Wood and soggy sheetrock rained down on him, but some light had returned. Forty-two years old. Disgraced.

A boy swam before him in the debris. The boy he'd shot and killed. His dark eyes watched Tanner as he was buried beneath the falling house. The boy's hair floated above his head, and he wore the same dark shirt, a bullet hole drenched in blood on its front. A small crab came out of the boy's ear, scuttled across his face, and moved down his neck into the bullet hole.

"Why?" the boy asked. Bubbles leaked from his lips and he smiled, sharp teeth slipping over gums.

"I didn't mean it," Tanner yelled. He kept yelling it until he couldn't hear himself anymore.

"So that's it, huh?"

It was Mom.

Tanner fought to get his head above water, swimming beneath a large section of floor wedged against the remains of a wall. He surfaced under this protective pocket, gasping for air as the raging water tried to suck him under again. Small waves pushed him as debris sloshed around in the maelstrom.

The water settled as Tanner floated on his back beneath the fallen floor. Wood creaked and the hum of the monster faded. Tanner's breathing and the pounding of his heart echoed in his ears. He lay there motionless for several minutes, staring up at the chunk of wood two feet from his face. He inched over and worked his way into the rubble like a worm and slowly climbed out of the wreckage.

He emerged onto a section of collapsed roof where he sat to collect himself. His entire right side was badly bruised, but nothing appeared broken and everything functioned. His right leg hurt, but with the adrenaline running through his veins, Tanner was ready to move. He got up and sat right back down. He felt dizzy and sweat streaked down his forehead. He stiffened, and reached for his flask. He sighed when he found it, pulling it free and taking a long pull. The alcohol felt good as it burned his throat and warmed his stomach. His nerves settled. Tanner slipped the flask into his pocket and took inventory.

The rocket launcher was gone, as was the MK18. The Glock was still on his hip, and he pulled it from its holster and snapped out the clip. Glocks would fire after being submerged in water, and the version issued to the military and law enforcement functioned normally even while fully submerged. Despite this, Tanner shook the weapon out and blew down the barrel, then snapped the clip back into place and returned it to its holster. He pulled the radio free, twisted the ON knob to maximum, and pressed the comm button.

"Anybody there? Mayday! This is Lt. Nate Tanner. I'm down and in need of assistance! Over."

No response. No static. No nothing.

Tanner turned the radio off and clipped it on his shirt collar. If he had the opportunity, he'd open it up and see if he could dry it out a little and maybe it would work. The way his luck had been going, the odds of that were somewhere between zero and negative one.

Large pieces of the destroyed house floated burning in the floodwater, and Tanner saw nothing stable or big enough to hold him. He'd have to walk through the water until he found a better way. His hip waders were back on *Big Boy*, and he cursed himself for not having them on, but he wasn't worried. The water was calm and most of the wildlife hid or had fled and he'd know if the scorpion was coming his way.

Tanner stared at the desolation around him and considered which way to go. He could head south toward the bay, which would mean a mile trek through flooded neighborhoods, or north into the woods and eventually he'd hit dry land. West made no sense; *Big Boy* was to the east. After the explosion, his guys would be out looking for him and they'd be coming from that direction, so he headed for *Big Boy*.

Tanner edged off the broken section of roof into the floodwater, carrying his Glock above his head. He knew all about how it worked wet, but he also knew bullets and water didn't like each other and the last thing he needed was a misfire in a critical situation. The turf beneath his feet was soggy and his boots sunk into the saturated earth.

The sun started its descent to the horizon, but there was still plenty of light, though Tanner couldn't see what was beneath the water before him. His hands shook and his neck ached. Somewhere in these waters was a pissed-off thirty-foot sea scorpion, and he was traipsing about like a bird rinsing itself in a puddle. He sent waves rolling across the desolation, and garbage bobbed and shifted with each movement.

Tanner reached the road, and the water reached his belly button. The slick still covered the surface of the water and the rank stench hadn't faded. The oily sheen formed a ring around his waist, and flies and water bugs danced on the slick, taking in whatever nourishment it provided. Tanner crossed the road and cut between two houses that didn't appear to have fences blocking off their backyards, but when he reached the nearest house, he saw a three-foot chain-link fence marking the properties boundaries just below the surface.

Tanner mounted the fence and slipped over, his feet landing on the muddy bottom. Green grass and brown dirt floated to the surface, clouding the water further. The area had been flooded for eleven days and most things below the waterline were deteriorating. The last rays of the setting sun cut across the desolation, and for the first time, Tanner was struck with a sense of uselessness. What did it matter if he killed the creature? The home he'd known was gone, and the new Long Island that would emerge wouldn't be the place he knew and loved.

The faint sound of an outboard cutting through the stillness brought hope, but the sound faded as it headed away from him. A jet inched across the sky, and its thunderous roar made Tanner smile. The airport was running a full schedule, and people were coming home to find what was left of their lives, and start the process of rebuilding. Many had fled before Tristin, and FEMA had given the OK to return only three days ago. Most water services had been restored, though the Water Authority was providing free testing kits so people would have confidence in what came from the tap.

Tanner smelled the creature's shit before he saw it. He came to a backyard boxed in by a six-foot wooden fence that stood three feet above the water. Several sections were gone on the southern and northern sides where the force of the tide had pulled them down, and through these openings Tanner saw a pileup of debris in a corner. Two large piles of brown waste that resembled chocolate mousse rested atop seaweed, along with pieces of wood and plastic, and an aluminum lawn chair that was somehow still floating.

Tanner put his back to the fence and worked his way to the next street, where he cut across the flooded road and swam to the roof of a shed and scrambled onto it. There he rested and surveyed his progress. He'd gone three blocks. He was already exhausted and his entire right side screamed with pain. His wet socks had chafed his feet, and his underwear rode up his ass. He had to take a piss, but held it in for fear of leaving a scent the monster could follow.

A low hum began to build, and Tanner lay on his stomach, trying to hide atop the shed. He couldn't determine if the hum was coming his way, or if it was just in the general vicinity. He pulled the radio from his belt and tried it again. No luck. He drew the Glock and held it out before him and chuckled at his futility. So far, the 9mm rounds hadn't done much more than annoy the scorpion, but he had nothing else.

Tanner slid off the roof and followed the humming sound. If he found the creature, what would he do? He went on anyway, the realization of his obsession clear in his mind, though still not fully in control. Tanner would hunt this animal until he killed it or it killed him, but for now he'd stalk it, track it, and wait for his opportunity to…do what? He didn't know, but he sloshed through the floodwaters anyway.

"Don't call me Ismael," he said to himself. "Call me Ahab."

20

Tanner hadn't gone far when he heard the tone of the creature's hum change and become more of a sharp click-buzzing sound. Large ripples in the floodwater rushed over debris, cars, and around houses as the beast came his way. The house to his right had no front door and Tanner waded into it. Directly in front of him was a set of stairs that lead to a second story and he mounted them and headed up. Water dripped on damp carpet as he made his way down a narrow hall to a bedroom at the corner of the house. There he looked out a window.

The sea scorpion worked its way up the street from the south, its black shell and tail gliding above the surface. The water wasn't deep enough for the huge creature to swim and the blacktop street below provided no mud to nestle into. The scorpion's spike glistened, its black carapace blending into the fading light. It occurred to Tanner that this moment might be the perfect time and place to attack the beast where it couldn't dive and hide beneath the surface.

Tanner checked the Glock and rested it on a nearby table. Then, he undid his pants. He had to take a leak and couldn't hold it any longer. He sighed as a steady stream of urine drenched the green wall-to-wall carpet before him. When he was finished, a smoking stain was all that remained as the hot pee met the cool damp carpet. The room instantly smelled of urine, and Tanner thought again about the creature's ability to sense his scent.

They knew little about the sea scorpion other than what they'd witnessed, so Tanner had no idea what the beast could do. Did a horseshoe crab smell stuff? Did it even have a nose? He'd seen so many of the odd creatures over the years and he'd never given them a second thought. Who knew they were direct descendants of dinosaurs and had been prowling the bays of Earth for four hundred and fifty million years? If the sea scorpion had a sense of smell, it didn't detect him because the creature swam past his position and disappeared around a bend in the road. The beast's shrill cry faded and then stopped. Tanner grabbed the Glock and headed downstairs, back into the water.

Despite having had a sandwich only two hours ago, he was starving and thirsty. He had no water or food, so he turned around and went back into the house. The kitchen was half underwater, but he searched and found nothing of use in the fridge. A cabinet had a package of stale crackers, some condiments, and a loaf of bread with green mold around the edges. He peeled off as much of the mold as he could and ate the bread quickly, not looking at it. He'd had worse when he was in the military. Some field rations are inferior to what they feed the canines on base.

Once back in the floodwater, Tanner pushed through the wreckage. He swung out onto the main canal; in the distance, *Big Boy* sat right where he'd left her. The water was a little deeper in this spot because the road dipped into a hollow, so he headed north a few blocks to where the water was a more manageable depth. The tide was coming in, and soon the sun would be down and he'd lose all light. He had no flashlight or illumination of any kind and he didn't relish walking through water in the dark with the scorpion swimming around.

The sound of an outboard motor and the hum of the beast echoed above the sloshing water. Both sounded subdued, but were coming his way. A hundred yards off, a large oak tree stuck from the water in front of a half-submerged brick ranch house. Pushing through the water as fast as he was able, Tanner made his way to the tree and wasted no time climbing into it. From his perch, hidden in within a cluster of leaves, he had an unobstructed view in every direction.

The sea scorpion came around a corner and surprised him. Its spike tail passed beneath him as the beast roamed the area. Had it sensed him somehow? Or was it wandering about looking for food? Either way, he was a sitting duck. If the creature saw him, it was game over. Tanner exhaled as the creature disappeared around a bend and stillness settled over the devastation.

A bird landed on a branch next to him and Tanner flinched and almost fell. The small thrush preened itself, paying no attention to him. Tanner smiled, watching the bird like an infant who'd never seen one before. He'd been out on the water all day, and this was the first bird he'd seen. In fact, he couldn't remember the last time he'd seen a bird. Suddenly, the thrush froze, its head jerking to the east. Then it leapt into the air and flew away. Tanner heard the beast coming his way again a few seconds later.

Floodwater lapped against the tree trunk and the beast's scent added another rank layer to the odor of the slick. The creature slowly passed beneath Tanner again and he held his breath. It took a six count for the entirety of the beast to pass by, and the stink it left in its wake was unbearable. Tanner's meal of green bread fought to come up.

The sea scorpion stopped and floodwater washed over its back as its antenna flailed about, searching. The big heads figured the antennas provided the same function to the scorpion that they did for a lobster, and served as sensors that helped the beast navigate. The creature turned around, moved side to side, but appeared to give up and continue on. Then it abruptly breached from the water and headed for Tanner's tree.

The sound of the whining outboard was music to Tanner's ears. Coming up the road was Randy in *Little Boy*. He had it full open, and the Zodiac sliced across the still water, a ten-foot rooster tail shooting out behind it. With the boat in motion, Randy stood, sighted his rifle and fired twice. Then he sat and jerked the motor control arm toward him. The Zodiac made a tight turn and disappeared behind a house.

The sea scorpion took up chase.

When the beast was out of sight, Tanner climbed down and headed for a small cluster of willow trees three houses down. The willow's leaf-covered branches hung to the surface of the water and he hid within. The sound of the outboard and the buzz of the creature were fading, but then Randy backtracked his way. Tanner heard the outboard getting louder and waves rolled in the floodwater.

When Randy rounded a corner up the street, Tanner leapt from his cover beneath the trees, yelled his friend's name and waved, jumping up and down in the water like a drowning cat. Randy saw him and brought the Zodiac to a partial stop in front of him.

"Fancy meeting you here," Randy said.

"How did you know where I was?" Tanner grabbed the boat and hoisted himself onto the gunnel.

"I saw you hiding in the tree and when the thing came for you, I figured it was time for a diversion. Hurry up, it's on my tail."

Behind the Zodiac, the creature's tooth-filled mouth cut through the water and came at them. Tanner fell over the gunnel into the boat. Randy flicked the throttle switch to maximum and the inflatable jumped from the water. Tanner pressed his back into the bow, Glock held out before him and trained on the beast. It was chirping and wailing as it came, pushing the debris and vegetation in its path aside.

Randy spun the boat around and headed for *Big Boy*.

For no other reason than the anger growing in him like a fungus, Tanner fired at the scorpion, first aiming at the mouth, and then the eyes. Twelve shots rang out in the fading light, and none of them even slowed the beast. If anything, it seemed to come on faster, and only five hundred yards separated the creature from *Little Boy*. When his Glock was empty, Tanner holstered the weapon and wedged himself into the bow of the Zodiac again, trying to limit wind resistance. *Big Boy* waited in the distance. They were closing fast and would reach the patrol boat in seconds.

The sea scorpion roared, as if it understood what Randy and Tanner were trying to do, and it would have none of it. Water surged around the creature as its sixteen legs pushed and pulled at the floodwater, pushing the scorpion forward with amazing speed.

"It's gaining," Tanner said. "You got any more in that motor?"

Randy laughed and shook his head. "Told you to buy the fifty horse. What was it you said? Why would we ever need that much power, you said. Why should we spend the extra two thousand clams, you said. The boat's not for our pleasure, you said."

"Next time make sure I listen to you, will you?"

"I'll do my best, but you're not always the most receptive person," Randy said.

They had twenty yards to go and Randy backed-down the throttle. Tanner took up position in the bow and prepared to jump off. Kim Jansen stood on the deck above, watching the scene unfold with horror etched on her face.

Tanner yelled up to her. "Get things ready to go. Fast!"

Jansen disappeared from deck as the Zodiac made its final sprint to *Big Boy*. Randy cut the motor, and the boat smacked against *Big Boy*'s dive platform as both men jumped out. Randy tied the boat off and headed for the bridge and Tanner headed for the bow and the newly installed machine gun. In the distance, the monster was on a line to attack them; its tail raised to strike, mouth open wide, and all its claws, big and small, chomping and biting at air in anticipation of grinding aluminum.

Tanner got in behind the Browning M1919 and pulled back the slide, loading a .50 caliber round into the chamber. *Big Boy*'s engines rumbled to life and Randy eased the boat forward, bringing it quickly up to speed.

The game of chicken was on, and the winner would live and the loser would die.

21

The machine gun shook Tanner's body violently as it fired. Empty shells fell to the deck and rang like tiny bells and Tanner released a primal scream of fury. He concentrated fire on the creature's forward flank and the beast dove beneath the water of Fireplace Neck's inner marina. He kept firing; the shots hit the water and threw up small columns of seawater.

Big Boy listed to port as the sea scorpion rammed the boat. Water surged over the gunnel and the deck flooded for a few seconds before draining. Tanner spun the machine gun to port, but the weapon wouldn't allow an angle that sharp and Tanner was forced to abandon the Browning. He ran along the gunnel, pulled his Glock, and fired, but only got the dull click of an empty chamber. He hadn't had time to load the weapon.

The beast passed them, but couldn't find the outgoing canal. It pivoted when it reached the end of the marina and had nowhere else to go except back or up on land. Two antennas searched for a way out, but were unable to locate one. A mountain of water emerged in the center of the marina, off *Big Boy*'s starboard side, but the beast didn't appear to be coming their way.

Tanner ran to the bridge and found Randy and Jansen waiting for him. The SAFE boat Randy had come in on was docked to the north. Tanner briefly considered fetching the vessel so he could draw the animal away from *Big Boy*, but then thought better of it. Jefferson was positioned at the creek mouth awaiting instructions. The water settled and the creature's hum lessened as it swam wide circles around *Big Boy*.

"What the hell happened out there?" Randy asked. His eyes never left the mound of water that circled them like a shark waiting to strike.

"Thing almost got me," Tanner said. "Saw me, or sensed me somehow."

"Saw you?"

"Remember this thing is like a horseshoe crab. They have two sets of eyes, and several in their shells, and they can sense light in a spectrum beyond human abilities, so who the hell knows how the thing sensed Tanner, but it did," Jansen said.

"Looks like its confused now," Randy said.

"Yeah. Randy, call everyone in and we'll finish this."

Randy never got the chance.

As if it had heard their conversation, the sea scorpion changed course and headed straight for *Big Boy*, rising from the water like a nightmare, teeth chomping on water, claws and pincers snapping together with such force the sound carried over the surging water.

"Ram the thing," Tanner told Jansen.

"What?" She looked scared and no longer wore her superior smirk.

"I said ram it. Now!"

Jansen eased the throttle down and *Big Boy*'s engines moaned and coughed as the forty-two-foot aluminum boat drove through the water. They were playing chicken again, but this time Tanner was prepared, and if the beast changed course, he would match it. Pain cramped his neck, his side hurt worse than any injury he'd ever had, his heart pounded, and soon he'd fall down from exhaustion and lack of food. Tanner's day had started fourteen hours ago, and he was losing steam faster than he could produce it.

The beast was twenty yards out and closing, and Tanner leaned past Jansen and pressed *Big Boy*'s throttle all the way down. The boat plowed forward at full speed.

The impact was bone rattling, but little happened. A sharp scraping sound filled the cabin as the sea scorpion's shell rubbed against the metal hull, but there was no tearing or crunching sounds of destruction. *Big Boy* had taken the hit with no major damage, and the creature passed on the port side and stabbed at the boat with its spike, but missed because of the angle. The spike kept pulling back and striking, over and over, but hitting nothing because it wasn't lined up correctly. The beast's forward claws were also useless because of its position as it swam alongside the boat.

Tanner jumped from the bridge onto the deck. He'd remembered the grenades. They sat on deck in a wooden crate and he fetched two and ran to the stern. The creature was just past them. Tanner pulled the pin from one of the grenades and tossed it after the beast. It hit the water directly behind the sea scorpion and the explosion sent a geyser of water shooting into the air behind the beast. Tanner pulled another pin and threw the grenade, but the leviathan dove and the grenade blew on the surface.

"Shiiiiiiiiiiiit," Tanner yelled.

The creature circled them again, but this time further off.

"Damn thing's smart for a living fossil," Tanner said.

"Wha?" Randy said.

"Horseshoe crabs have been around so long they're classified as living fossils," Jansen said.

"Aren't we an encyclopedia today," Randy said.

"Don't know about it being smart, but it's definitely an apex predator," Tanner said. "I'm gonna kill that fucking thing if it's the last thing I do. Randy, did you call Jefferson and the others during the confusion?"

"On the way." Randy looked at the deck. Silence fell as the fist of water circled *Big Boy*. Randy looked sheepish, then said, "Hey, listen, since you're already pissed, I might as well heap some more bad news on those narrow shoulders."

Tanner watched the beast as it circled *Big Boy*. "What now, you gonna tell me you're gay and you've been in love with me all these years?"

"Audrey has a boyfriend," Randy said.

Tanner jerked back like he'd been punched. "What? Who? When?" He'd known this would happen, just not so fast. Audrey was a beautiful woman, and she could have any man she wanted. They were done, and he had no hold over her any longer.

"Names Fred Jasper. He's a fireman in Rescue One in the city," Randy said.

"You've met him?" Tanner said. "Nice timing, dipshit." He couldn't believe they were having this conversation with a man-eating prehistoric animal tracking them and circling their boat.

"Tina and Audrey are friends, you know that. We went out to dinner a couple of times. He's not a bad guy."

"Dinner a couple of times? When the hell were you going to tell me?"

"When you were really pissed-off already about something else, like now. I know this isn't a great time, but you're already—"

"Screw you," Tanner said. He left the wheelhouse and slammed the bulkhead door behind him.

"Come on, man—"

The door cut Randy off and Tanner felt guilty. His friend was trying to tell him what no one else could, and he'd just torn him down. Frustration got the better of him and he'd lashed out at someone close to him. It had been an issue with Audrey as well, and it was the main reason she'd suggested he seek professional help to work through his issues. This just made him angrier, which she said proved her point, and around and around they went.

He breathed deep, sucking in the foul sea air. A boyfriend. Goddamn. What did he have to say about it? Since they'd broken up, he'd dated several women, so why he thought that was OK and Audrey dating wasn't was crazy. He knew he was wrong, but that didn't stop the deep burn in his stomach that told him he still cared for her, deeply, and maybe the time had come to tell her so. That is, if he made it through the night.

Tanner rolled his shoulders and cracked his back. He felt clammy, his wet clothes sticking to his skin, the salt water drying on his face making his skin tight at the edges, like it might rip if he moved too fast. He had fresh clothes in his locker below, and he had just decided to go change when he realized he no longer saw the sea scorpion circling *Big Boy*. It had changed course, and was moving around the edges of the marina as if searching for an outlet.

Tanner bolted back into the pilothouse. "How far out are reinforcements?"

"Sixty seconds," Jansen said.

"Cut the thing off and don't let it out of the marina."

"But how—?"

Tanner stepped to the controls and motioned for Jansen to step aside. He took the controls and spun *Big Boy*'s wheel as fast as he could. The boat turned in a tight arc, putting it on an intercept course with the sea scorpion. The beast didn't appear to notice and continued its search around the edges of the marina. It made no sound, and its claws were hidden by the water and its spike was bent vertically in swim position.

"I think it's trying to escape," Tanner said.

The screaming of outboard motors running at full tilt filled the air. Two coastie boats and two PD SAFE boats raced up the main canal toward them. All Tanner had to do was block the creature until they arrived. Like a defensive back closing in on a receiver, he adjusted his angle to intercept the sea scorpion.

The creature disappeared beneath the water, and all that remained was a swirling vortex of water. Tanner eased back on the throttle and *Big Boy* slowed to a crawl. He picked up binoculars and searched the horizon. There was no sign of the sea scorpion. The wind eased, and the rank stench of the beast cut through the sea air.

"There," Randy said.

Aft, past their wake, the creature swam in the opposite direction.

"It played possum," Tanner said. "Full stop."

"You don't want to chase it?" Jansen asked.

Tanner said nothing. He watched the sea scorpion cross the marina and when it hit the opposite side, it turned left and traced the edges of the quay again. A bruised sky stretched to the horizon as the sun disappeared below the rim of the world. Twilight hid the desolation, and Tanner could barely see the creature in the dying light.

It was 8:19PM.

22

Tanner ordered all *Big Boy*'s exterior floodlights turned on, but the glare of the lights made it harder to see in the growing darkness, not easier, so he had them shut down. The sea scorpion waited across the marina, bubbles streaming to the surface marking its location. Stars shone overhead, and the temperature had already gone down a little, but the humidity was still brutal.

Jefferson's SAFE boat had joined *Big Boy* at the entrance to Fireplace Neck's marina, followed by two PD boats and the second Coast Guard boat. Jefferson's orange gunnels and the white Coast Guard logo stood out in the dark. Outboard motors wound down and Jefferson's boat bumped *Big Boy*'s aft dive platform. She stepped off her boat and Tanner watched her make her way up to the bridge.

"Sorry we took so long," she said as she entered. When she saw Tanner's clothes and his mud-streaked face, she added, "What the hell happened to you? You OK?"

"Fine," he said. Randy snorted and Jansen made no sound.

"You don't look fine. What happened?"

She wasn't her normal beautiful self. The long hours without sleep and the lack of food had taken its toll. Black bags hung beneath her eyes and her face was haggard. She'd been worrying. About him? He doubted it, yet he had that familiar warm feeling in his stomach as he looked at her and there was heat between them. But hadn't he just decided he needed to make things right with Audrey?

"The beast and I had a…a tussle," he said.

"The thing came after him and kicked his ass," Randy said. "Almost killed him. I found him hiding in a tree."

Tanner shot him a glare but said nothing.

"Where is the thing? Did you get it?" Jefferson was excited. She had the wrong impression.

Tanner said nothing, but instead pointed out the port window.

Jefferson followed his finger and peered through the darkness.

"It's sitting on the opposite side of the marina. What's it waiting for is the real question. I think we spooked it."

"I can't see it," Jefferson said. She stood inches from the bridge window, squinting, and Tanner watched the frustration grow on her face.

"Its shell is black. Good camouflage at night," Randy said.

"So, what? You're just waiting for it to come and invite you to tea?" Jefferson said.

"Not exactly," Tanner told her. "Are your guys up to attacking this thing? I think we've got it cornered in here, and the water isn't deep, only twelve feet at the center."

"Yeah, we're up for it, but you better make it fast. The USS *Gridley* has arrived, and it's anchored out by the *Vigilant*, so it won't be long before we're not calling the shots."

Tanner grunted.

"It's not so bad. They can help us."

"We'll see," Randy said.

Jansen, an ex-Navy helmsmen, said, "They're more qualified to handle this than we are. Why aren't we pulling out? Letting them take care of this?"

"We can handle it ourselves," Tanner said. His voice was laced with anger, and he ground his teeth in frustration.

"Evidence to the contrary proves otherwise," Jansen said.

"You want off the boat?" Randy asked her. "I can have one of the SAFE boats take you out, Sal also if that's what he wants, and anyone else that feels the way you do."

Jansen said nothing, but returned to monitoring her command console.

"Speaking of Sal, where the hell has he been?" Tanner asked.

"He's down in the hold," Randy said. "We sustained minor damage in the attack and he's attending to it."

"So are we're going to stand around and argue about nothing? Or do you have a plan?" Jefferson's frustration showed via red blotches forming on her perfect brown skin.

"I propose we leave two PD boats at the mouth of the marina, backed up by a coastie boat. Then Randy in a twenty-two, and you in your rig, and me in *Big Boy*, ride down this thing's throat and blow it to hell."

"You still have the rocket launcher?" Jefferson asked.

"Nope. Fired one at the thing and missed. I lost it when...when I ran into trouble." The house collapse story would have to wait for another time.

"So we've got two heavy machine guns, a box of grenades, and small arms. That going to be enough?"

"Hasn't been so far," Jansen said.

"Should we bring in air support?" Randy said.

"Coast Guard and PD units are standing by," Jefferson told him.

"I don't want to spook the thing before we get a shot at it. We'll bring in air support as needed. As to will it be enough, you've forgotten our most powerful weapons; the boats, specifically Big Boy. When I tried to ram the thing, it fled."

"Sounds a little too Captain Nemo for me," Jefferson said. "I think you're a bit obsessed."

"The thing has killed our friends, Kim. You want out?"

She said nothing.

"Let's get to it then," Tanner said.

Jefferson paused a moment, looking at Randy as if she expected a counter-proposal, or other suggestions, but Randy focused on the deck and added nothing.

Jefferson headed back to her boat and within moments, all the vessels were shifting positions and preparing to fight. The machine guns were checked, and Sal came above deck carrying an armload of guns and ammo. Sal piloted *Little Boy* and took Randy to his twenty-two and transferred him and his weapons to the PD boat.

When Jefferson flanked *Big Boy* on the port side, and Randy had the starboard side, Tanner gave the order to move ahead slow. The small vanguard slipped across the surface of the water, the sound of motors rumbling in the stillness. When they were a hundred yards from the creature, Tanner ordered a halt. A cluster of bubbles fought to the surface, but the sea scorpion was submerged and only the rounded shell of its back and its spike tail could be seen.

Tanner opened a comm channel. "All units keep this channel open for the duration and limit chatter to necessary communication. Copy?"

"Aye," came Randy's voice first, followed by Jefferson and the others.

"OK. Let's do this," Tanner said. He took a deep breath. "All exterior lights on."

The night was drenched in white light, creating a pocket of luminescence in the blackness. The bubbles ceased at once, and the beast's humming sound started.

"Hold," Tanner said. Then he turned to Jansen. "I'll man the main gun." He walked to one of the bridge side windows and slid it open a crack. "Keep an ear out for me. I may need you to move."

"Aye," she said. The young marine cop's face was drawn, her brow furrowed and her usually full lips drawn into a thin line.

Tanner exited the pilothouse and made his way to the bow, where the Browning rested on its tripod. He moved in behind it and aimed the heavy-duty machine gun at the swirling water where the bubbles had been.

There was nothing else to do, so he ordered Sal to toss a grenade and wake the thing up. Sal, moving as slowly as Tanner had ever seen him move, inched across the deck and retrieved two hand grenades. "I can't reach from here. I'm not Aaron Rodgers for shit's sake."

"Bring us in closer," Tanner yelled.

Big Boy's engines cycled up and the boat slid forward. When they were thirty yards out, Jansen stopped the vessel. "Kim, be ready to back away as soon as Sal tosses his surprise."

"10-4," she said.

Sal wedged himself into the bow and pulled both grenade pins at once and tossed the explosive devices into the swirling water.

"Now!" Tanner yelled.

Big Boy jumped backward, and the water before them geysered as the grenades detonated and displaced hundreds of gallons of water. A great cry rose above the tumult and the sea scorpion surfaced, flailing wildly, its spike stabbing empty air as its claws snapped closed in search of prey.

"Fire!" Tanner yelled.

The rattle of machine gun fire and the boom of shotgun blasts growled like thunder. Smoke filled the air and Tanner coughed, but he didn't pause. The Browning rattled as it cycled through its bullets, Tanner's eyeballs shaking in his head.

The creature vaulted from the water directly at the forward coastie boat. The beast's spike came down, piercing the Coast Guard vessel and sending its crew running for cover. The spike lifted and came down, again and again, and some of the coasties, including Jefferson, were forced to jump into the water.

Sal ran to the gunnel with two more grenades, but stopped when he heard Tanner yelling.

"Cease fire! Cease fire! You'll hit them!"

To starboard, Jefferson's SAFE boat was broken in two and going down. Indecision gripped Tanner and fear crippled him. The coasties yelled for help as the scorpion pounded the sinking ship. Sal acted without orders. He ran aft and jumped in *Little Boy*, started the engine, and tore off toward the coasties in the drink.

"No. Sal, I order you to return to the ship," yelled Tanner, but it was too late.

Little Boy raced across the water toward the chaos, but didn't make it. One of the monster's claws speared from the water, and before Sal could react, he was caught in the giant claw. It cleaved him in two and his broken body fell into the water, his legs disappearing beneath the sea. His torso floated on the surface, his blue inflatable PFD deployed.

"You fucker!" Tanner opened up with the machine gun again, firing indiscriminately into the mass of water that hid the creature. A coastie floated in the water face down, but it wasn't Jefferson. The sea scorpion rolled toward *Big Boy*, and Tanner screamed, "Full ahead!"

The floodlights cast the scene in black and white, and time slowed. Water gushed over *Big Boy*'s gunnel as the beast used its shell to crush the PD patrol boat and everyone on it. *Big Boy*'s forward momentum pushed the aluminum bow into the creature's underside and drove it back. Tanner fired, the machine gun popping like synchronized fireworks, a smile creeping across his mud-streaked face.

23

The sea scorpion rolled, and the ensuing splash knocked Tanner across the deck. The machine gun went silent, and the wail of the beast sounded over the water. The railing around the bow was splattered with blue blood, as was the deck and gunnel. It looked greasy and slippery, and reminded Tanner of a chum slick.

He got to his feet and drew down. The Glock barked, and blue blood gushed from the creature's face cavity as it lunged forward and bit the boat. Then *Big Boy* was past the creature and Tanner jogged aft, emptying the Glock as he ran. He dropped the empty clip, snapped home a new one, and sighted the creature as it disappeared outside their sphere of light.

"Bring her about and get on the bastard's tail!" he shouted.

Jansen turned the ship's wheel and *Big Boy* spun in place as the starboard maneuvering props churned the water. Randy had picked up Jefferson, and they flanked *Big Boy* in a twenty-two. Pieces of Jefferson's boat bobbed on the boat churned water, and Tanner didn't see the guardsman's body floating amongst the wreckage.

"We're taking on water, sir," Jansen reported.

"Oh, shit," Tanner said. "All pumps at full."

"They're already at maximum capacity. Go check how bad it is."

Tanner almost told her he gave the orders, and then realized how stupid that would be, so he said nothing. He was barely her superior officer at the moment, anyway. He ran out onto deck and jumped down the ladder leading to the main deck. He stopped at a sealed bulkhead hatch, spun the dog handle, and pushed it open. The passageway beyond serviced all sections of the ship, and it was dry. He walked down the passageway ten paces and climbed down a ladder through an open deck hatch.

He landed in water.

"And I repeat, oh shit."

Bay water shot through a hole the size of a baseball in *Big Boy*'s hull. To Tanner, it looked like a tooth hole. If he could get that flow stopped, it would buy them some time. The scent of oil and seawater filled the compartment, and steam floated above submerged hot pipes. The engine rose from the deck at the rear of the section and soon it would be underwater and unable to function.

Tanner sighed, pulled free his flask and took a long pull, and then slipped it away. The vodka sharpened his senses and woke him up.

A metal folding chair sat before a row of engine gauges. It was steel, with a flat metal seat. Tanner folded the chair and sloshed through the water to a bulkhead where a fire extinguisher, a portable defibrillator, and a bottle of spray sealant were mounted to the bulkhead. The sealant was made of cutting-edge expanding polymer technology and was designed to make emergency repairs on all types of metal: boats, dames, and pools; plus, it hardened while immersed in water.

Tanner sprayed the sealant on the underside of the folding chair and pressed it against the inflowing water. He threw all his weight against the chair, driving it as hard as he could into the bulkhead. The water lessened considerably, but didn't stop.

Big Boy shuddered and listed hard to port, and for a heartbeat, Tanner thought they might be going three-sixty. He slammed against the bulkhead and fell beneath the water. He emerged moments later, coughing and spitting. The chair patch held, and he tried to get up as the boat rocked back and forth, slowly settling.

Jansen's voice burst from the comm speaker mounted on the bulkhead. "It's attacking us. Need you up here. Randy and Jefferson are in trouble."

Tanner examined his patch, and saw a trickle of water running down the bulkhead beneath it, but he'd stopped most of the flow.

The water was still rising fast.

Tanner searched the compartment for more leaks, but saw nothing and realized there must be additional damage below the flood line. He dove beneath the water as it sloshed around like a pool that's been disturbed by playing children. His eyes stung as he opened them beneath the water; the salt and accumulated grease and dirt and dust all clouded the water and hurt his eyes. Despite this, he detected the problem easily.

When the sea scorpion bit them, it left a series of small puncture holes beneath the larger one where the beast's smaller teeth couldn't fully pierce the thick aluminum, leaving only small holes instead.

He surfaced and grabbed the can of sealant, which was almost empty. He dove again and felt along the bulkhead for inflows of water, and as he did so, he sprayed the sealant wherever he felt a hole. After two minutes, the tank of sealant ran out, and he surfaced, tossed the can, and headed for the door. As he left, he saw the flooding had slowed significantly, but not enough for the pumps to keep up.

Slowly, inexorably, *Big Boy* was going down.

***

"How bad is it?" Jansen asked as Tanner entered the bridge.

"Not good. I'd estimate we've got about ten minutes before *Big Boy* is sitting on the bottom and we'll have no maneuverability." The sonar said they were in twelve feet of water, and *Big Boy*'s lower levels would be flooded, but the bridge would stay above water.

"Great."

To starboard, the creature thrashed about, its claws snapping, mouth open, its spike stabbing at the water, causing spires of water to shoot into the air.

"Before we're dead in the water, ram it again." Tanner's voice was harsh. He was lost in the frenzy of battle and thought of nothing else but killing the creature. If he went down with it, so be it.

Jansen increased speed and headed straight for the beast. Randy, realizing Tanner's last gambit, backed away from the animal as the remaining coastie boat fired at the scorpion.

The creature turned north and fled.

Tanner opened the comm channel. "Follow me, we'll drive it to the marina's edge and finish this."

"That's 10-4, *Big Boy*."

The sea scorpion was fifty yards ahead, but they were closing. Randy and Jefferson were on the starboard side, the remaining Coast Guard boat to port.

"You sure you want to do this?" Jansen said.

She had a point. Sal had been cut in half, another coastie was dead, *Big Boy* was sinking, one of the coastie boats had been crushed, and the monster still powered on as if made of metal or some unknown indestructible material. They'd damaged the creature, that was proven by the blue blood covering the surface of the water and *Big Boy*'s deck, and yet it appeared unaffected.

"You see that, Tanner?" Randy's voice came through the comm speaker. "The claw?"

Tanner strained to see the creature in the darkness, the floodlights only penetrating a hundred feet into the blackness, which was now complete. A giant claw floated in the water before them, and *Big Boy* almost ran it over, but Jansen made a last-second adjustment and avoided it.

"What the hell happened?" she said.

"Must have broken off when it attacked us and or maybe it fell off when the beast ran."

"Gonna need an Olympic-size pool of butter for that thing," Jansen said.

Tanner's stomach growled. He hadn't eaten since the moldy bread in the abandoned house, and even though that was only a few hours ago, his stomach ached with hunger, and his throat was dry as ash.

"Is it slowing?" Jansen asked.

They were almost at the northern edge of the marina and once they reached the submerged bulkhead, the creature would have nowhere to go.

One of the many things Tanner had learned about prehistoric sea scorpions was that they were one of the first species of marine life to leave the sea. The scorpion's distant relatives had crawled from the primordial ooze millions of years ago, only to be driven back into the ocean by larger predators. So Tanner wasn't that surprised at what happened next.

The leviathan rose from the water: first its spiked tail, then its black carapace.

"All hands prepare for impact!" Tanner saw nothing but the red-hot anger of war.

"Are you seeing this?" Randy's voice came through the comm.

In the harsh light of *Big Boy*'s exterior floodlights, Tanner watched as the beast climbed from the canal and lumbered through the floodwater, which once out of the marina was only two feet deep.

"Full stop!" Tanner said.

Jansen, mesmerized by seeing the creature's full size for the first time, hesitated for an instant, then jammed the throttle into neutral, then reverse, but it wasn't enough to stop *Big Boy* from slamming into the submerged bulkhead. The jolt threw Tanner to the deck, and Jansen barely stayed on her feet as she clung to the ship's wheel. The boat creaked and groaned as it settled, and a few seconds later, seawater leaked beneath the wheelhouse door.

"End of the line," Tanner said. Then he yelled into the comm, "Randy! I need you."

"We know." It was Jefferson. "Port side."

Tanner looked out the port side window and saw Randy pulling his twenty-two alongside *Big Boy*. The water was up to Tanner's ankles, yet Jansen griped the wheel, the creature only twenty yards in front of them. Tanner put a hand on Jansen's arm. "That's enough. Let's go."

She looked at him with dazed eyes and nodded.

They made their way out onto the deck and down the ladder to main deck where Randy waited. *Big Boy* hit bottom, and a shudder ran through the old boat. A twinge of sorrow passed through Tanner. He and *Big Boy* had been through a lot together; now, the vessel was scrap. Another score he needed to settle with the sea scorpion.

Randy eased his SAFE boat to the dive platform, and Tanner stepped aboard. Jansen waited for the next PD boat, which would take her to safety.

"How ya doin'?" Jefferson said as Tanner hopped aboard.

He leaned against the transom, his legs rubber and his stomach howling with pain. "Alive," he said.

Jefferson threw her arms around him and said, "You're one crazy son-of-a-bitch."

Ahead in the darkness, the creature splashed through the shallow water and disappeared between two houses. Without orders, Randy nudged the SAFE boat's throttle down, and continued the pursuit.

24

The hamlet of Fireplace Neck had been around since the whaling days and had changed little in the last hundred years. Mainly composed of residential neighborhoods, the town itself was nothing more than Main Street stacked with old buildings and two cross streets. There was one traffic light, and Beaver Dam Road ran north to Montauk Highway two miles to the east.

Tanner and crew had run out of water and abandoned their boat. They followed the sea scorpion's tracks on foot, trudging through the mud and darkness. Randy, Jefferson, and a coastie named Ravac followed him, weapons drawn. Tanner didn't want to think about what would happen if the beast attacked them. Without the Browning and *Big Boy*, they didn't stand a chance, and neither did Fireplace Neck.

"Randy, does your radio work?" Tanner asked.

"I think so." Randy unclipped the handset from his belt and gave it to Tanner.

He accepted it, twisted the ON knob to full, and pressed the comm button. "Calling the Suffolk County PD. Anyone out there?" Nothing but static for a few seconds, and he tried again. Nothing.

He was ready to give up when a raspy voice echoed through the static. "Please refrain from using this emergency channel. It is reserved for—"

"This is Lt. Tanner of the Suffolk County PD marine division. I need to speak with command immediately." A pause. "We don't have time for bullshit. Fireplace Neck is in grave danger."

"Repeat, please. Over."

"Send everything you've got to Fireplace Neck. Now. Copy?"

"Copy. What is the source of the emergency?"

"Do you want me to teach, or are you going to act? Delay and the blood will be on your hands. I repeat, send all available units to Fireplace Neck. ASAP." Tanner turned off the radio and tossed it to Randy. "Not much more we can do."

"You could have told them what was happening," Jefferson said. She frowned as she considered her words. "I see your point. Even if they believed you, how long would it take to convince them?"

"Should you call in your people, Jefferson?" Randy said.

"They're already standing down to the Navy, and they'll be on the creature soon enough. Do you think I'd get through to them?"

Randy shrugged.

The creature lurched through the tree break a half mile in front of them, branches snapping as it went. It left a clear path of destruction and blue blood in its wake. No crickets chirped, no frogs bleated, nothing moved as the apex predator cut through the center of Fireplace Neck, heading straight for town.

"What are we doing?" Jefferson said.

"Good question," Randy said. "What do you mean to do? What if it backtracks, or senses us? We've barely got any weapons."

Tanner said nothing.

"No idea, huh?" Jefferson said.

Tanner stopped and turned on his companions. "Look, I don't have the answers, OK? Never said I did. What would you suggest? We do nothing? Let the thing escape and hide somewhere? We're here and I don't see anyone else."

To that, no one had any response, and they continued forward. The floodwaters hadn't reached this far inland and civilization appeared all around them. House windows glowed with candlelight, generators rumbled in the night, and headlight beams cut the darkness ahead. The creature traveled along the road, not slowing or pausing, as if it had a destination in mind and it wasn't stopping until it got there. Tanner heard its legs and pincers digging into the blacktop. It sounded like the scuttling of a million cockroaches.

Headlight beams lit the darkness, and a loud roar and the sound of crunching metal brought Tanner to a stop. A scream pierced the night, and Tanner broke into a run.

The scorpion attacked a car, crushing it with its only claw and stabbing it with its spike. A woman ran toward Tanner, panic spilling across her face, a smear of blood on her cheek. "Help. Please help. It has my husband."

Jefferson took the woman by the arm and led her to a patch of grass and made her sit down. As she consoled the woman, Randy grabbed Tanner. "This is getting real, brother. I think it's time to pull back."

"Stay here with them. I'm going on," Tanner said.

Randy sighed. "Give me a minute." He went to Jefferson and when he returned, she was with him, along with Ravac. "We're coming with you."

"No way you're getting all the glory after all this," Jefferson said.

In the distance, the sound of breaking stone and twisting metal marked the beast's location.

"It's reached the neck," Tanner said.

Normally, the town would be visible from a mile away in the blackness, but with the power out, the only light was the traffic light, and a few emergency lights spinning blue and red.

"They listened," Randy said. "For once, they listened."

"Don't get too excited," Tanner told him. "It could be a deputy sheriff and a fire truck." It was 9:47PM and he'd been going full speed ahead for over seventeen hours. His back ached, and his feet were so waterlogged and wrinkled that each step was painful.

The party, led by Tanner, came up a side street, and what they saw when they arrived on Main Street reminded Tanner of a Godzilla movie.

Two police cars blocked the creature's way as it crashed through town. Fire trucks backed up the PD cars, but the monster didn't pay them much attention. Its spike stabbed at the cops as they fired at the sea scorpion to little effect. Its remaining claw crunched a nearby building, and the old stone tumbled onto the police cruisers, extinguishing their lights. The creature's hum echoed off the buildings and its underside pincers clawed at the road, tearing up sections of blacktop and concrete as it pulled itself forward.

The scorpion climbed the pile of rubble, and to Tanner it looked as though the tooth-filled mouth opened in a grin. Smoke and fire consumed both police cruisers, and the monster bellowed and scuttled off the pile onto the road.

Tanner froze, unsure what to do. Randy waited on his right, Jefferson his left. The creature turned and plowed into a tall wooden structure that housed a restaurant and card store, and the building came down with a horrible crash that sent a smoke cloud billowing across town, obscuring the sea scorpion from view. Every few moments, the beast's spike tail would drive away the smoke as it searched for prey.

The gunshots stopped, and someone wailed in pain. The scorpion rumbled across the remains of the building it had brought down and a minor explosion lit the night. "Take that you son of a bitch," Tanner heard someone yell. Then the ground shook as a second explosion sent a fireball into the air and filled the area with more black smoke that smelled like gasoline.

"Somebody threw a Molotov cocktail at the thing," Randy said.

"Yup," Tanner said.

From their hiding position behind a van, Tanner watched as the town of Fireplace Neck burned. The irony wasn't lost on him, and as the beast disappeared around a building, the sound of helicopters approaching filled the night.

"Let's hang back now and let the big dogs handle this," Jefferson said, but Tanner wasn't listening.

He walked forward in a daze, his eyes transfixed on the destruction the sea scorpion had caused.

"Wake up, buddy." It was Randy.

Half of Main Street was on fire, and the creature's humming faded as it moved east behind the buildings lining the main avenue. Two copters dropped in; one was the Coast Guard, and the other was gray and bore the logo of the US Navy. The Navy copter was equipped with two stinger missiles mounted beneath the fuselage.

Tanner ran up an alley to a back street so he could see what was happening. He arrived at the rear of Ted's General Store just in time to see the stinger shoot from its tube and streak toward the beast, which had taken up position inside the shell of a brick building.

The missile hit what remained of the building, bringing the rest of the structure down onto the scorpion. There was a deep wail, then the creature vaulted upward, and bricks shot outward like bullets. Mortar dust filled the air, and bricks fell all around Tanner. There was a squeal of metal, and the Coast Guard copter's rotor threw sparks as bricks and debris pelted it. The sound of tearing metal dominated the chaos, and then the helicopter was falling from the sky like a bird with a broken wing. It landed atop the bank and exploded, spraying metal shrapnel and fire over Main Street.

Tanner dove for cover. As he lay prone on the road, he watched the Navy bird disengage, and the sea scorpion's hum lessened as it moved east.

To the east was Carmans River, a large waterway that ran from Bellport Bay all the way north to Middle Country Road. It ran through woodlands, under roads, and behind neighborhoods. If the sea scorpion found its way into Carmans, they would have a hard time finding it. The river gets shallow as it goes north, and most of the boats and their related weaponry would be useless.

The creature moved away and Tanner followed it. He looked back; his three companions were behind him, and they didn't look happy. When they reached the end of town, the creature turned right and rambled through low brush into the forest.

"Shit," Tanner said.

Police cars came screaming up the road, followed by fire trucks and ambulances. It was time to become scarce. If the police saw him, they'd want to question him, and once that began, he'd never be allowed to rejoin the chase.

"Where are you going?" Randy said. "You gonna fight this thing with your bare hands? Tanner the scorpion fighter? Come on, it's over."

"Bullshit. It's not over until that thing is on a hook or I'm in a box," Tanner said.

"Yeah, I know."

Tanner stopped and looked at his mates. He didn't have the answers, and they knew it. They were out of ammo, had no boat, and no way of tracking the beast into the wetlands that surrounded the river. He said, "You guys hang back. I can't. I'm going to track this thing. Give me your radio."

Randy sighed but handed over his radio.

"Go back, get a twenty-two, answer their questions, then call me and come find me. I'll be on our hush-hush channel."

"But what—?" Jefferson said.

"No buts, and you go too. I'll be fine. I'll hang back and track the thing and I won't do anything until backup arrives. Promise." Tanner looked at where the creature had disappeared up the street. "We can't let it get away and hide."

Tanner turned his back on them and ran into the darkness, following the trail of blue blood.

25

"Hey, wait up!" Jefferson ran beside him and Tanner stopped.

"What are you doing?" he asked.

"I'm coming with you, and before you start with all your macho bullshit, let me remind you I'm a Coast Guard officer, not some delicate flower." She still wore her light blue uniform shirt, but it was stained and ripped in several spots. Somewhere along the line, she'd lost her ribbons and her cover, and her patent leather shoes no longer shined. In the moonlight, he saw mud on her face, and her eyes stood out against her brown skin, which was slick with sweat. Despite all this, she still looked amazing.

"I just thought you'd be more help with the others, that's all. Don't give me the equal rights garbage. I was thinking of your safety."

"And I was thinking of yours," she said.

Tanner said nothing and resumed trudging through the woods. Thin oaks, scrub pine, and underbrush of pricker bushes and weeds filled the forest, but it didn't appear to be slowing the sea scorpion, which trundled along, breaking trees and pushing them aside like a snowplow. The blue blood trail was getting thicker and wider.

They walked in silence for several minutes, the sound of cracking trees filling the stillness. The longest day of Tanner's life was showing no signs of ending, and it had become an effort just to put one foot in front of the other. Jefferson looked a little better off, but not much. She was dragging, and her breathing had become labored.

"Do you have a girlfriend?" she asked. "I never came right out an asked you when we had our beer the other day."

The question threw him, and he looked at his feet, considering what he should say. He didn't have a girlfriend, but did he want her to know? He'd always heard women were more interested in men able to commit and will overlook the "stealing your boyfriend" thing if they felt the man worthy of a long-term commitment. This was ridiculous to Tanner. What made people think a cheater would stop cheating?

"OK, that's a no," Jefferson said.

"Why do you ask?"

"No reason." She flashed him a half-smile.

Ahead, the sound of breaking trees had stopped, and Tanner listened hard, the way they'd taught him at the shooting range in boot camp. He filtered out the wind, the pounding of his heart, and the sigh and rustle of leaves.

To Tanner, it sounded like the massive beast was taking labored breaths, wheezing and gurgling in between intakes of air. "It's hurt," he said.

"Maybe it will die and save us a lot of trouble."

"You don't know me well. If you did, you'd understand there's no way that's happening."

"Why is that?"

"'Cause I'm the unluckiest bastard alive," he said.

"Really? Huh, 'cause I think all the dead people are a bit more unlucky than you. You've been attacked by this thing how many times? And you're still here."

Tanner said nothing.

The heavy breathing continued, and they inched forward until the beast's outline became visible in the darkness. It had stopped at the edge of a field of water reeds, their brown broom-like tops swaying in the breeze. The scorpion appeared to be surveying the area, its head rotating back and forth, antennas darting about.

Without warning, the scorpion jerked forward, throwing itself into the reeds, wriggling side to side, burying itself in the black mud that made up the river bottom. The rank smell of rot and shit assailed Tanner, and when the creature stopped working itself into the mud, it couldn't be seen.

"Now we wait," Tanner said. He sat and leaned against a tree and was asleep in minutes.

***

The annoying radio call sounded like Tanner's alarm clock, and it brought him upright. Darkness pressed in around him, and the silence made him uncomfortable. Normally, the crickets, frogs, and other creatures of the night created a symphony so loud it made talking in a normal tone difficult.

The creature hadn't moved. The mound of mud still sat amidst the flattened water reeds before him. He lowered the volume on the radio and stayed still. The ground trembled for an instant, and the pile of mud lifted a few inches, and then fell still.

"White Whale, you copy?" Randy said.

"Copy."

"Heading into the mouth of the Anduin. Location? Over."

"I'm south of the fishing dock just inside the mouth," Tanner said.

"That's a 10-4, White Whale. Out."

Tanner looked at Jefferson and smiled.

"You two play war when you were kids?" Jefferson asked.

"That obvious?"

"I'm a trained professional," she said. "How long?"

"The Anduin is code for Carmans so not long at all."

"So you're Middle Earth boys?"

"There are things he and I instinctively know the other will also know with a hundred percent certainty. We would kill on a game show like that one where they separated couples and asked them questions and then compared the answers."

"The Newlywed Game," Jefferson said.

"How old are you?"

"Thirty-seven."

"You've seen The Newlywed Game?"

"TV Land, dinosaur," Jefferson said. She put up a hand. "Listen."

The sound of outboards gurgling in the stillness brought a smile to Tanner's face. He pulled free his radio and turned it on. "White Whale calling Solo. Copy," Tanner whispered into the radio, trying not to disturb the creature.

"Copy, White Whale. How we doing this?" Randy's voice crackled through light static.

"End dock on the south end. Come in slow and dark. There's some tall poles sticking above the dock which is still underwater. You'll see us, but the scorpion is right here, so run silent. Copy?"

"Be there in two. Out."

"Let's go. We need to work our way to the end of this small marina. I'll find the dock and we'll walk out."

Jefferson looked south toward the bay, then back to Tanner, but said nothing.

"What is it?" he asked.

"They let Randy come alone?"

To the west, the skyline was lit by helicopter searchlights as they focused on responding to the emergency at Fireplace Neck, but soon some intrepid officer would trace the path of destruction and find their position. The beast had traveled part of the way on the road, but it wouldn't take Sherlock Holmes to discover where it entered the woods and dug its foxhole.

The sound of outboard motors came closer and they reached the end of the marina. A hundred yards off, Randy's SAFE boat was outlined in the darkness.

"I need to risk some light," Tanner said. "Grab my belt, and stay right on me while I lead us down the dock. Keep an eye on our little friend." He did his best Al Pacino impersonation on the last part.

"Scarface. Great flick."

Randy turned on the radio's emergency flashlight, and a thin beam pierced the night. Two feet below the surface, the dock waited like a slippery unmoving eel. He stepped forward, checking his footing before taking another step. So it was that it took five minutes to go twenty feet, but they avoided falling into the drink and arousing the sea scorpion.

"Damn good to see you, brother," Tanner said. "You also, Ravac."

"You two are alone? How'd you pull that off?" Jefferson said.

"We didn't officially check in," Randy said. He looked at Tanner, a smile splitting his face, his eyes looking for praise.

"You done good, Randy," Tanner said. He had. "How long we got?"

"An hour. Maybe two."

Tanner sighed, but said nothing.

Ravac spoke, addressing Jefferson, his superior officer, as if making a status report. "Ma'am, they're blocking the channel beneath Smith Point Bridge, and they've closed William Floyd Parkway. CNN is running cellphone footage of the scorpion destroying Fireplace Neck. It's like a kaiju movie teaser. The Army and Marines have deployed teams, and they'll be here within the hour. The Navy is moving in as we speak."

Nobody spoke. That was it. Game over.

Tanner said, "What do we have weapon wise?"

"Not much," Randy said. "9mm shells for the guns. Shotgun loads. Two MK18s. One harpoon, and two grenades."

Tanner said nothing. They all stared at him. He didn't think they'd given up, but they definitely didn't exude confidence.

"You got any food? Water?" Jefferson asked.

"Yeah," Randy said. He went to a white cooler mounted behind the pilothouse and brought back bottles of water and peanut butter and jelly sandwiches wrapped in deli wax paper.

"Where'd you get these so fast?" Tanner needed a few minutes to think, and he didn't want to be asked questions, so he asked some.

"We slipped through the emergency operations tent. It was chaos, so getting supplies wasn't hard. There were local civilians in there locking and loading."

"Great," Tanner said. "The forests around Carmans will be an open season shooting gallery." It was starting to look like a lost cause. With the big guns coming in, he had to consider the possibility of friendly fire.

He and his crew weren't authorized to be on the river, and military commanders didn't screw around. For all he knew, they might plan a major offensive using any number of tactical weapons that would leave him and his team fried. He couldn't let that happen to Randy, or Jefferson. Shoot, even he and Ravac the stoic deserved better than that.

"Perhaps we should quit," Tanner said. It was gut-wrenching to say the words, but sometimes that's what leaders had to do. Flee and live to fight another day.

As if a god above had heard his admission of doubt and decided it would not stand, a spotlight shone down from above and the *whomp whomp* announcing an approaching helicopter broke the stillness.

"Shit, Randy, they must have followed you," Jefferson said.

"That might not be a bad thing," Tanner said.

26

Tanner's entire gambit depended on who was in charge of the approaching team, whether he got a cowboy or a player. A cowboy wanted to get the job done no matter the cost, and a player wanted to be in control no matter the cost, even if it meant losing. If he got the latter, that meant game over for him. If he got a cowboy, someone who would ignore orders to send him back because they needed his local knowledge of the area, then he had a chance.

The helicopter was loud, and the monster stirred, first throwing up its spike and then its claw.

Tanner set his radio to the emergency channel. "Whoever is coming in on the copter, back off. You're scaring the thing away! Back off!" he yelled into the radio. If they heard, they ignored him, because the spotlight got bigger as the copter descended toward the surface of the river.

The sea scorpion was a hundred yards away and shaking off mud. The beast didn't seem to notice them, and as it eased into the water, Tanner let out a sigh of relief. Within seconds, the creature had disappeared into Carmans River, and only the outline of its dark black spike was visible in the moonlight.

"Shit, it's taking off," Randy said. "Pursue?"

Tanner looked upriver at the scorpion as it swam toward Montauk Highway, then out toward the bay, then up at the whirlybird dropping from the sky. "No. Let's wait for these guys. It won't go far. As soon as this copter leaves, it'll bury itself in the mud again up river."

"What's that?" Randy said.

The copter's spotlight beam was intermittently blocked by something dangling beneath the fuselage. A black rectangle hung in the white light above, and it swung in a wide arc when the copter pulled up and settled, treading air and holding steady. The gale caused by the SH-60 Seahawk flattened water reeds, tore leaves from trees, and stirred the water.

"It's an NSW," Jefferson said.

"What?" Randy yelled. The pounding of the rotors and churning winds made talking difficult.

"Naval special warfare insertion," Ravac said. Tanner and Jefferson inched in close. "The copter is an SH-60 Seahawk. Very good craft. A heavy lifter. Has a top speed of a hundred and sixty-eight miles per hour with a load capacity of five thousand pounds. That's a Zodiac special ops boat hanging from cables beneath it. Something like *Little Boy* but better. Much better, I'd guess. These guys are probably SEALS. They'll have all the newest shit."

The boat continued its drop from the sky toward the middle of the river.

"Randy, light it up for them," Tanner said. "Shows we're here and that we want to help."

"Wow," Randy and Jefferson said at the same time.

Randy switched on the SAFE boat's exterior floodlights and the area was illuminated in a ball of harsh white light. When the incoming boat was ten feet from the surface of the water, a soldier stood up and pulled a quick release and the Zodiac dropped the last ten feet. It landed with a loud smack and started toward them straightaway.

"They rowing?" Tanner said. No outboard rumbled.

The whirlybird's exterior light went out, and the copter's engine cycled up as it lifted away. The copter rolled, and before their new friends were within fifty yards, the Sikorsky was nothing but running lights and background noise.

The black Zodiac cut into the beam of their bow light and came straight on. They were under power but Tanner couldn't tell what was powering the vessel. Dark figures sat along each gunnel, and a man in fatigues and rain slicker stood on the bow, staring into Tanner's spotlight like he was pissed Tanner hadn't turned off his high beams when he came around a bend in the road.

As the newcomers got closer, Tanner smiled. Two guns, barrels down, were mounted on the boat's bow, though he couldn't tell what type they were. Soldiers in full body armor and helmets with tinted face shields sat at attention on each gunnel, their dark silhouettes casting long shadows across the swaying water reeds.

A faint buzzing sound rolled across the river and as the black Zodiac slowed, the sound lessened. Randy's SAFE boat rocked as the inflatable bumped into the twenty-two and the man in the green fatigues stepped aboard. He strode across the bow, slide open the pilothouse door, and said, "Who's in command here?"

Randy looked at Tanner who looked at Jefferson who stared back at Tanner.

The man chuckled and said, "Guess it's you." He gestured toward Tanner.

"Lt. Tanner, sir. This is Petty Officer First Class Belinda Jefferson of the Coast Guard and her mate Ravac... Don't know his last name or rank. Officer in charge is Lt. Randy Vernon there. Who are those Stormtroopers?"

"They're my support team," the man said. "Five of the most skilled special ops soldiers on the planet. They're face shields allow for night vision." Silence fell as the man sized them up. "You know where it is?"

Tanner looked at Jefferson, and said, "Yeah. I do."

"I take it you're familiar with this area as well?" the man said.

"Who am I talking to?" Tanner asked. "I mean, I called you sir because anyone that can drop out of the sky like that is of higher rank than me, but forgive me if I'm suspicious. It's been one of those days."

"I heard," the man said. "Harry Silva. I work for the federal government and specialize in anomalies, and I think your creature qualifies."

"You Navy?"

"I'm everything," Agent Silva said.

"Aren't we confident," Jefferson said.

The agent's gaze flicked to her and when Jefferson stared back defiantly, Silva got in her face. "Are you aware this man Tanner is wanted by his people? That he's not supposed to be on this case? That he's been busted down in rank and essentially AWOL?"

"Aye, sir, I'm aware," Jefferson said. Her chin was out, her eyes stern. "I'm also aware that I'm in command of my people, and I'll decide the best course of action for them."

Tanner had more respect for her in that moment than he'd ever had. He felt something for her, he couldn't deny that, and it was more than just a sense of responsibility and commitment born of their shared experiences. She made him warm in places that had been cold for a long time.

"So I take it we need him?" Agent Silva said.

"That's about the size of it," Jefferson said. "And he knows it and handles himself as you might expect a local to."

Silva chuckled and Tanner grit his teeth and cracked his neck. "Glad you two agree. You do realize you scared the creature off with your diva entrance. I don't give a shit who you are or where you came from, this is my backyard."

"Do you realize I could lock you both up for insubordination without saying a word?" Silva said. "All it would take is a nod of my head. No questions would be asked. You care about your home? Fine. I want to leave it. But first, I need to clean up your mess. So save the tough guy stuff for the Nassau County PD."

Tanner chuckled. He couldn't help it.

"You said you knew where the creature is? You bullshitting?" Silva said.

"I don't know exactly where it is, but I'm confident I can take you to it."

"OK, let's roll then," Silva said. "We can fit you and one other."

"Whoooh. The thing can sense the slightest movement and sounds," Tanner said. "It'll hear us coming."

"We have a state-of-the-art electric motor. Did you hear us come in?"

"A buzzing sound," Tanner said. "It was pretty quiet, though."

"So what?" said Randy. "How are you going to kill the thing? Its shell sheds bullets like tempered steel and it's lost a claw and a lot of blood and hasn't slowed down. In fact, it's running around on land and if it's anything like its ancient ancestors, it doesn't like that too much."

Agent Silva shifted his weight and looked up as if asking for divine patience. "You see those five guys? They've got missiles," he said. He held out his hand and one of the soldiers stood and displayed a sleek shoulder-fired rocket launcher. "They've got grenade launchers, and armor-piercing bullets. See those two guns on the bow of the Interceptor? One fires twenty shells per second, and the other is a laser. Anymore concerns about weaponry?"

"Laser? Like Star Trek?" Randy said.

"Just like that. A light ray passes through a lens made of some magical mixture that focuses the beam."

"All due respect, this thing has taken some hard hits and keeps on ticking," Tanner said.

"That why there's a blood blue slick on the river?"

"A scrape can look like a deep gash."

"Look, you got a better option? I'm done playing games. You want to help? Get in the boat. Otherwise, you can wade your ass ashore and wait to be arrested. Your choice, Tanner." Tanner opened his mouth to speak, and the agent shot him down. "Don't give me your tale of sorrow. Right now, I don't care. All I care about is removing the danger from the path of American citizens. Help me and you can tell me your life story over dinner and we'll figure out at the rest of the shit later. Agreed? You know this area like it's your backyard. I've never been here. Help me get this thing. Do right by me, and I'll help you out with the bigwigs."

Tanner believed the guy. He didn't know why, because usually he had to know someone a long time before he trusted them. Shadows danced beneath the trees and in the water reeds and the faint rumble of chaos from Fireplace Neck could be heard above the wind. The air smelled rank with rot and decay. Dawn was still several hours off. Every muscle in Tanner's body pulled and jerked in pain, and he didn't know how much longer he could go on.

27

"Now that doesn't work for me at all," Ravac said.

"Me, either," Randy said.

"You two can back us up in the PD boat," Silva said. "I'll even give you one of my stormtroopers to make room in my boat." He gave a sidelong glance at Tanner.

"I won't—" Ravac started.

"You will. That's an order," Jefferson said.

"You too, Randy," Tanner said.

His partner's face twisted. "Can I have a fast word?" Randy said.

Tanner sighed and he and Randy stepped out of earshot.

"What? Not a great time," Tanner said.

"You up for this? You don't look good, boss."

Tanner didn't feel good. His flask was empty, he hadn't eaten or slept, and now Randy was pissing him off. "What are you trying to say?"

"Maybe you should stay back with me."

Tanner rolled his soldiers and cracked his neck. "I appreciate the concern, but mind your own business. Follow me on the twenty-two and sit tight with Ravac and await orders. Got it?"

Randy said nothing and wouldn't look at him.

Tanner left Randy alone and he and Jefferson and boarded Silva's boat. "So what's the plan?" Tanner asked.

"Locate and destroy," Silva said.

"It's not that simple. We don't want to excite this thing and send it on another rampage. Did you see Fireplace Neck?"

Agent Silva nodded.

"We go in full stealth. I'll be able to find it. Then we surround it and hit it with everything we've got before it can move on us."

"You put a couple of those SPIKE-MR missiles down its gullet and that will be all she wrote," Jefferson said.

"You were paying attention before and know your weapons," Silva said. "The SPIKE-MR is a shoulder-launch, man-portable, fire-and-forget missile with a 200m to 2500m range and it will turn the scorpion into chum."

Nobody laughed and Tanner grunted.

Tanner and Jefferson squeezed into seats along the gunnel between the soldiers, who sat stoic and silent, their expressions hidden behind their face shields. The motor whirred to life and Silva took up position in the bow as the Zodiac slid through the still water, heading up river.

The rumble of Randy's outboard broke the stillness. Silva's head whipped around and he ran aft. "Kill that. Kill it," he shouted to Randy, who cut the motor. "We're going in slow and silent. Throw me a line and we'll tow you in."

"Gets shallow as you go north, so we'd end up doing this eventually anyway," Randy said to Ravac. He tossed Silva a bow line, and he tied it off on an aft cleat and returned to his spot in the bow. They were underway again in seconds, the electric motor dragging the extra weight without a problem. A soldier handed Tanner and Jefferson MK18s. Tanner wrapped the shoulder strap around his arm for stabilization and pointed the weapon into the oncoming gloom.

Darkness pressed in around them and pale daggers of moonlight cut across the shadow-filled landscape. Still no insects buzzed as the animal kingdom hid from the living storm that just wouldn't pass them by. Tanner missed the ear-splitting night sounds. The forest was somber, with only rustling leaves filling the silence. Carmans River narrowed and lost depth as one went north, and forest and protected bird sanctuaries flanked the river on both sides, though it passed under several roads, including the Long Island Expressway, and Sunrise and Montauk highways.

A slick of blue blood snaked down the center of the river.

"There are two bridges coming up that we might have to portage around," Tanner said.

"Might? I thought you knew this place?" Silva said, but he was smiling.

"So you're a nutcracker, huh? Ever hear of the tides? Do you get pissed when people bust your stones back?" Tanner didn't mind a little banter; in fact, he enjoyed it, but if it became bullshit it became a problem, and he wasn't looking for any more of those.

"I can take a joke, but that's easy to say when you're in charge," Silva said. This time, he wasn't smiling.

"What is it exactly that you do for Uncle Sam again?" Jefferson asked.

"Track, catalogue, investigate, and deal with anomalies of all types."

"What branch does that fall under?" Tanner asked.

"Federal Bureau of Investigation," Silva said. "You might have heard of us."

"Maybe," Tanner said. "So you're like James Bond?"

Silva laughed. "Not really. Most of the time I'm tracking random mutations that amount to nothing. Biological oddities are on the rise, and I often see living things that shouldn't be possible based on science as we know it, yet there they are. Right in front of my face, clear as day, undeniable."

"Is that what you think this thing is?" Tanner asked. "Some kind of biological freak?"

"We'll know more once the scientists get hold of the corpse and run some tests, but based on what we have so far, we believe this thing is old. Really old. Possibly on the order of two hundred years old, and the big heads think mutations and species combinations over millennia led to this creature. But they're just making educated guesses. They think it's one of a kind, but there could be similar creatures in the depths. Most of the really deep spots of our oceans haven't been fully explored."

Jefferson spoke softly and everyone on board turned toward her. "The sea is everything. It covers seven-tenths of the terrestrial globe. Its breath is pure and life-giving. It is an immense desert place where man is never lonely, for he senses the weaving of creation on every hand. It is the physical embodiment of a supernatural existence. For the sea is itself nothing but love and emotion. It is the Living Infinite..." Jefferson noticed everyone staring and said, "Captain Nemo."

Tanner said, "How is it nobody has even seen this thing before?"

"We're not sure no one has," Silva said. "The hurricane that ripped through the Atlantic and laid waste to your island tore through the canyons and stirred things up. As I'm sure you're aware, there's a steep drop-off about a hundred miles offshore and the big heads think the storm dredged up things that haven't been this shallow since the dinosaurs roamed the earth. The strange storm currents have had all kinds of odd effects on the Atlantic."

"I've heard all that, but it's hard to buy," Tanner said.

"It comes down to what your primitive mind can accept as real. Like your sea scorpion. If I told you of its existence and you hadn't seen it with your own eyes, would you have believed me?"

"I'd probably think you embellished."

"Fair enough, but that's the same thing. You would have doubted the account. Who wouldn't, but all that changes when you see it for yourself."

"So you have a lot of power? Can move armies and such?"

"I have major threat authority," Silva explained, "which means if I determine the security of the United States is in jeopardy, I can call on any resources available to the U.S. government without approval or discourse."

"Damn," Tanner said. "The weight of the crown and all that."

"I've never needed to bring down the house, but others have."

"I suggest you put troops in the woods on both sides of the river from the shoreline to Middle Country Road," Tanner told him. "Put vehicles on Sunrise and Montauk and light up the tunnels that pass below."

"Already done," Silva said. "I could handle that much by looking at Google Maps. I've also got two Apache copters waiting to pounce if the creature heads into the woods. They can be here within two minutes of a call from a foot patrol."

Tanner looked back and saw the outlines of Randy, Ravac, and the soldier in the moonlight. They sat on the blue inflated gunnel of the twenty-two, staring forward, the soldier in the black armor and helmet sitting off on one side alone. Carmans was wide this far south, and both boats floated in deep water down the center of the river. Water reeds hemmed them in on both sides, and gnarled stands of pine stood beyond them. They wove back and forth around the river's sharp bends, making their way north.

"Any word on Dan?" Tanner asked.

"Upgraded to a hurricane, and it looks like its outer edge is going to hit Long Island," Silva said. "We should be wrapped before it gets here."

"Yeah, but we're still struggling from the last one," Tanner said.

Jefferson changed the subject and said, "Strange coincidence this creature is a close relative of the horseshoe crab, when Long Island is a primary habitat of the species."

Silva looked at her. "Horseshoe crabs live all over the globe, they're far from unique to this region, but yeah, it's strange."

"Sure is big for the brother of a crab," Tanner said.

Silva and Jefferson laughed.

"It's called abyssal gigantism," Silva said. "Like I said, this thing most likely came from way down deep in the canyons out by the drop-off."

"Yeah, my people said something about that," Jefferson said. "Abyssal gigantism is supposedly caused by the creatures adapting to scarcer food sources, and greater pressure or colder temperatures in the deep water."

"There are many examples of this," Silva said. "Giant isopods, the giant amphipod, the Japanese spider crab, the giant oarfish, the deep-water stingray, the seven-arm octopus, and several squid species have all shown signs of growing much larger than normal when living at great depths."

"There are specimens of the colossal squid over fifty feet, and giant squid over forty," Jefferson said.

"And let's not forget the most iconic of these oversized beasts, the Greenland shark and the Pacific sleeper shark, though they are of a much different variety because they visit the surface and are not larger than comparable species that spend more time in shallower water, such as the great white," Silva said.

"But they're big," Jefferson said. "I've seen a sleeper shark up close. Not as scary as a great white, but not something I'd want to meet while out taking a swim."

"So I'm fairly certain the creature is a product of the deep sea," Silva said.

"Makes me wonder what the hell else is out there waiting to be woken," Tanner said.

One of the soldiers coughed, and Tanner looked his way, but the man's expression hid behind his face shield.

The group fell silent.

Dark water lapped against the boat as it churned through the darkness. Clouds moved in, but there was still plenty of moonlight and starlight. Tanner felt the butt of his Glock, and fingered the trigger guard on his MK18. He wanted to end this. He felt like he'd been chasing this animal longer than Ahab had chased the famous whale, and it was difficult to believe it had been less than two weeks since Tristin laid waste to his world.

The river looked like oil in the darkness, the black surface rolling and undulating as the Zodiac and SAFE boat drove deeper inland. They'd seen no sign of the sea scorpion other than its blood, but it was here, Tanner was certain of that. Where could it have gone without them knowing? They had it penned in, and it was only a matter of time before they found it.

As if on cue, the water reeds to their right were flattened and broke, and the blue blood slick got thicker. In the distance, bubbles popped like grease in a frying pan.

"Slow up," Tanner said.

Silva cut the electric motor, and the Zodiac glided forward, disappearing under an outcrop of trees.

28

The boat came to a stop beneath a black gum tree that hung over the river and blocked the moonlight. Tanner couldn't see his hand in front of his face, and when he turned to Jefferson, she was nothing but a silhouette in the darkness. The bubbles moved upriver, away from their position, leaving a nasty blue blood trail in their wake.

"Dang, can't be any quieter than that," Jefferson said.

"It senses the slightest vibrations in the water," Tanner said.

"Vibrations," Silva said. Tanner couldn't see his face, but the tone of Silva's voice hinted at something sinister, as though the FBI man had just gotten an idea that might prove fatal to them all.

"What is it?" Tanner asked.

"You just gave me a horrible idea," Silva said. "You ever hear of a sonic weapon?"

"A what?"

"I have," Jefferson replied. "I've even dealt with them. The effects of them, anyway."

"Really?" Silva sounded incredulous. "That's top secret stuff. How do you know about it?" Suddenly realizing the monster had moved off and they'd fallen behind, he added, "Ahead slow. Oars only." The soldiers dipped short paddles into the dark oily water and the black Zodiac slid silently across the placid surface. Randy and crew paddled hard behind them but were already falling behind as they eased out from beneath the tree cover.

"I was on active duty in the Caribbean a few years ago," Jefferson said to Silva. "Standard tour, no real mission other than training and patrol. I was in a little seaside bar on St. Croix, when my second-in-command calls me in a panic. Says we need to make for Cuba, double time. President Obama had just lifted the sanctions. I assumed it was citizens in distress and we were being called in as a rescue force."

"I take it you were wrong?"

"Big time. Our orders were to evacuate more than half of the diplomatic staff, all of whom complained of headaches, nose bleeds, and dizziness. Several staffers had fallen, just lost their balance for no apparent reason. The CIA thought Cuban dissidents were using a sonic weapon of some kind. A device that focused powerful sonic waves at the US embassy."

"I remember that," Silva said. "Some of our people worked on the initial investigation."

"Does the U.S. have such a weapon?" Tanner asked.

Silva said nothing, but the white of his toothy smile shone in the blackness.

"You bet your ass we do," Jefferson said. "I've talked to Marines who claim to have used sonic guns that emit a strong focused pulse that can incapacitate an average-sized man."

"You ever see one?" Tanner asked.

"No," Jefferson said. "But I believe the guy."

"What's that there?" Silva said, pointing at a pile of seaweed and debris piled atop bent and crushed water reeds. A concrete train trestle rose in the darkness before them. The debris floated before the entrance to the tunnel that ran beneath train tracks. Graffiti decorated the stone bridge, but most of it looked old. Tanner recognized some of the band names painted in bright colors: RATT, Motley Crue, and Def Leppard.

Upstream, a sharp bray split the night, something in great pain calling for help, but Tanner's first thought was one of confusion. He'd seen no animals during the endless day. He listened hard, but whatever had made the sound had been silenced.

"Full stop," Silva said. He slammed his fist on the gunnel. The tide was coming in and the tunnel beneath the old trestle was unpassable.

Tanner leaned over the side and examined the debris tangled in the seaweed patch. Mixed with the seaweed and shrimp shit was a brass belt buckle, part of a black boot, and some splintered wood, paper, and a scrap of dark blue fabric that looked to be of the same material as Jefferson's pants. Tanner fished the blue material from the tangle and held it up.

"I think that's a shred of Sharkey's uniform pants," Jefferson said, and sniffed.

Tanner's stomach burned. He untangled the brass belt buckle and examined it. There were no engravings or logos other than a stamp that proclaimed the item made in the USA. He held it out in the palm of his hand for Jefferson to inspect.

"Probably Sharkey's also," she said. "It looks standard issue."

"No logo or anything?" Tanner said.

Jefferson pointed at her buckle, which was exactly the same as the one he held—plain shiny brass. She let her head fall in her hands.

"You OK?" Tanner asked. He slipped the belt buckle into his pocket.

Her head bucked up and if looks could kill he'd be dead, but after a moment, her face softened and the tense muscles in her neck eased. "Yeah. Sorry. I'm fine. It's just…"

"I know. I've lost three men, all friends, and we haven't had a second to mourn them and lay them to rest. Doesn't feel right."

"It isn't, but what choice do we have? I know Sharkey and Dave wouldn't want me to stop the pursuit until their killer is dead, but that doesn't make me feel any better, and it certainly doesn't make it any easier."

"No, it doesn't."

Silva came over to them. "So, what now? There's another one of these ahead?"

"Yup, and that's before we get to the tunnels," Tanner said.

"All right," Silva said. "I don't like it, but we need to portage the boat. We're going through that gap in the woods."

To the left of the bridge, a patch of weeds filled the embankment that led up to the train tracks. It was steep, and there was no way Randy's twenty-two was getting portaged over. The soldiers got out of the Zodiac and dragged it up and over the embankment, Silva on point.

"Tanner? You leaving me behind?" Randy said.

"No way he's kicking anyone else out of our boat. Stay here and keep an eye out," Tanner said.

Randy opened his mouth to say something, then decided not to. Randy's face said all it needed to. He wasn't happy, and it bothered Tanner that his friend didn't trust him.

A look passed between Ravac and Jefferson and he lowered his head.

"We'll be right back," Tanner said. He turned his back on Randy and started climbing, and he felt his partner's stare boring into his back long after he'd passed over the trestle and was back on the river.

The blue blood slick was twice as large and thick as before.

"Looks like it had a problem getting under that bridge," Silva said. "How far up is the next portage?"

"Right before Montauk Highway, then we'll hit the tunnel under Sunrise," Tanner said.

"You figure that's where we'll get it?"

"Yeah. It's smarter than you think and it knows it's being chased. I'm sure of that. It's looking for a place to lie low, and the tunnel would be perfect. It's big, deep, and with the road closed, they'll be no noise. We'll get it under there and bring everything down on it."

"Destroy the road?"

"Fuck the road," Tanner said

The sound of paddles dipping into the river and the drip of water as they retracted was barely audible beneath the wind, which had picked up. The pitch pines swayed in the breeze, their evergreen needles making a faint tapping sound as they collided. They came around a wide bend and the river narrowed. Water reeds loomed like walls on both sides.

"Oh, boy," Silva said. "Right side dig 'em in. Left side rest."

The Zodiac spun to port, and Tanner saw what Silva was going after. Something floated in the water at the stream's edge tangled in the water reeds. The boat inched closer, and the water changed color from a greasy blue to a deep red. The blood slick was fresh, and pieces of fat and gristle floated within. A deer leg cut off at the hip lay half in and half out of the river, fresh blood still leaking from the severed limb.

The Zodiac eased to a stop when it hit the reeds, and Tanner pulled a small mag light from his pocket and risked some light. The limb had been cleanly cut as if by a sharp knife, the muscle, tendons, and gristle neatly shorn.

"Guess that guy didn't get the memo," Jefferson said.

"Deer around here can be very trusting," Tanner told her. "They're protected in here, and people feed them. They'll take seed corn right from your hand."

"Yeah, but it must have been a dumb one," Silva said. "Everything else feels the danger of this thing a mile away."

Without a word, the soldiers began paddling again, and Tanner looked back down river. He could still make out the outline of Randy's twenty-two. He'd be fuming by now, but this was for the best. There was no way he'd be able to tell Tina and the kids Randy had died. He couldn't live with that, and he'd known from the moment Silva suggested Randy follow in the twenty-two that he'd have to leave his old friend behind, and in this case, that's exactly what he wanted.

The second portage was easier than the first because everyone knew what to do and there was less underbrush surrounding the metal bridge. The structure was unpassable no matter the tide, and when they got over it, the river opened up. A light wind sent waves skidding across the surface. Moonlight lit the water, and as they paddled, the blue blood slick filled the entire river.

"Looks like it won't be long," Tanner said. "Maybe it's going off to die?"

"Not as crazy as it sounds," Jefferson said. "Animals go off alone to die all the time."

Ahead, moonlight marked the dark maw of the tunnel leading under Sunrise Highway.

29

"The Mines of Moria," Tanner said.

Jefferson chuckled. "Say friend and enter."

"Mellon," Tanner said, spreading his hands as Gandalf had done before the entrance to the fictional mines.

"You two geeking out over there?" Silva said.

"Private joke," Tanner said.

"Not very private. I've seen *The Lord of the Rings*."

"Seen? Not read?" Jefferson asked.

"I'm a child of the movies, what can I say?"

Tanner harrumphed and Jefferson chortled. Apparently, they made too much noise because Silva placed a finger to his lips. Jefferson flipped him the bird.

"Full stop," Silva said. His men reverse paddled, and the boat came to a stop beneath the tunnel opening. Lights from emergency vehicles flashed on the road above as they blocked off Sunrise Highway. The sound of crashing water came from the northern end of the tunnel where Southhaven Lake split through its dam into Carmans River. The top of the arced tunnel stood fifteen feet above the water and was equally deep and stretched into blackness. This far north, the tidal patterns no longer applied and the constant flow of water from Upper Carmans through Southhaven Lake ruled this section of the river, pushing everything south.

"Get on the laser," Silva said to the soldier next to him. "Back us out of this opening a little. I don't want to be under here when this thing comes down."

The waterfall at the opposite end of the tunnel was loud and disturbed the water, so Tanner couldn't tell if air bubbles popped on the surface of the river. He saw no sign of the scorpion other than some blue blood, and he remembered how it had backtracked and tricked him, not once, but twice.

As if reading his mind, Silva said, "You think it's in there?"

"Has to be," Jefferson said. "No way it could have gone over and around without the guys on the road above seeing it."

"Agreed," said Tanner. "The blood trail leads right in there. Kind of a roadmap, and there's no way it snuck under us."

"I'm going to risk a brief burst of light before I waste my time chumming the wrong area," Silva said. He made his way to the bow and retrieved a spotlight clipped to the gunnel. He directed it into the tunnel and flicked the light on for a second, then flicked it off. He didn't need to do it a second time.

"Everybody see it?" he asked.

"Yup," Tanner said. He'd seen the creature's spike tail pressed flat against the tunnel roof, the upper portion of its carapace sticking above the water, and its antennas bent backward across its shell.

"OK. Looks like it's all the way at the other end. Can it get out down there?" Silva said.

"Probably, though it would be difficult," Tanner said. "The tunnel ends about thirty feet from the dam, which is only ten-foot high. There's a chain-link fence at the top of the dam, but the sea scorpion could go right through that."

"We need to draw it toward us," Silva said. "Get it under the road." He headed aft and got a plastic jar that looked like a container used for commercial food storage. He grabbed some line and went back to the bow. A smile crept over his face as he screwed the lid off the jar.

The smell hit Tanner like a hammer. He'd found dead animals in various stages of decomposition. He'd even found a body once, half rotted and stinking, but he'd never experienced anything like this. It was far worse than Randy's chum. Tanner dry heaved and covered his mouth. Jefferson had her head over the side, puking.

A couple of the soldiers coughed. Silva laughed and said, "It's a tuna out of a shark's stomach. It's half-digested and months old. Some Navy friends of mine had it on ice for just this type of special occasion." He tied the line around the decayed fish and tossed it in the water, playing the line out through his fingers as the tuna floated into the tunnel, and then started back his way.

He reached into the dark water and grabbed the rotten fish, and this time, he threw it thirty feet into the tunnel. "Come on. Come and get it, you piss-crab."

The rotten fish floated in the tunnel, its rank odor filling the underpass. The slick created by the chum was moving down river, away from the sea scorpion, but the scent of free food would be impossible for the beast to ignore. Silva fastened the line tethered to the chum fish onto a bow cleat. Then he fell in behind the mounted machine gun and sighted it into the darkness of the tunnel.

The air reeked of rot, shit, and decaying fish. A low hum echoed through the tunnel as the beast surfaced and a giant claw shot from the water. The river boiled and pitched, and the creature's antennae pressed against the underside of the tunnel next to its tail. Despite being in a confined space, the sea scorpion's primeval instincts took control, and it knew only one thing: get food.

Jefferson was beside Tanner, her MK18 held out before her. Silva was surrounded by his men on the bow where he manned the heavy-duty machine gun. Two of the forward soldiers had grenade launchers, and two others had shoulder-fired missiles.

"Hold incendiaries until my order," Silva said. "Ready with the grenades. Target the creature and then bring the roof down on her."

The claw heaved forward as a giant black hole ringed with teeth surged from the river and took the tuna, crashing back into the water and sending waves over the gunnel. Silva opened up with the machine gun and its muzzle flash lit his face. He was somewhere else, probably reliving an old war story, and he grinned as the gun barked faster and harder than anything Tanner had ever heard.

The monster splashed back into the river and rolled against the rounded tunnel wall. Gunfire erupted as the line with the chum at its end went taught, and the Zodiac was dragged into the tunnel's maw.

"Give me reverse thrust full. Fast!" Silva yelled. A soldier turned on the motor and it whined as the prop tore at the water, dragging the boat backwards, creating a mountain of whitewater.

The chum line was as tight as piano wire, and it tinkled and creaked as it was stretched to its limit. It broke with a loud twang, and the Zodiac rocketed back out of the tunnel. Tanner was thrown across the deck and he bounced off the inflated gunnel as the Zodiac almost flipped. A wave of water threatened to capsize them, but the self-bailing Zodiac again proved its worth.

"Fire grenades and get down," Silva said. "All hands brace for collision."

Two pops reverberated in the tunnel, and a second later, two massive concussions sent a wall of heat and flames shooting down the tunnel toward them. Dust and debris bounced off the walls, and the shockwave river tsunami lifted the Zodiac and pressed it backward. Tanner saw that the entire middle section of the tunnel was gone, and stars blinked down through the hole. Red and blue lights back-lit the smoke and dust, and the sound of crashing water was like thunder. The debris pile of bricks and dirt undulated and moved, then went still. Dust filled the darkness, and spotlights rained down from above. There was cheering and screams of joy. Horns beeped, and guns were fired.

Tanner and Jefferson hugged, but when Tanner tried to hug Silva, he brushed him off. The agent walked to the bow and peered into the darkness. Bricks still fell and rolled, splashing into the river which was already flowing past the wreckage.

"Bring me in closer," Silva instructed. "Get a light on it. I want a corpse."

"I'm good," Jefferson said.

"Me too," Tanner said. "I'll settle for a picture."

Silva ignored them, and the Zodiac eased forward into the tunnel mouth. Two handheld spotlights added to the illumination from above, but it was still difficult to see through the smoke and concrete dust. A steady breeze blew down the river, and the hole in the tunnel roof was acting like a chimney. Tanner looked at Jefferson, whose eyes were the size of quarters.

Every muscle in Tanner's body ached and moaned, and his bruises and scrapes and cuts all stung. He needed a drink, but for the first time wondered if he'd get the opportunity. He'd been going nonstop for almost twenty-four hours straight, and sometime soon the ghost would give it up, and he'd go down like a drunk after the last shot that breaks the bartender's back.

They'd only gone in twenty feet when Silva said, "Full stop." The beam of his mag light revealed loose stones above. Mortar was missing between many bricks and several looked like they might fall. A little further in, large gaps in the rounded tunnel roof opened to the sky.

A large section of bricks fell into the water with a loud splash, and everyone's head snapped around. Tanner peered through the swirling smoke, but he was tired and didn't trust what he was looking at. The rubble pile was shifting and moving, and bricks tumbled into the water. The river heaved and pushed the Zodiac back several yards as Tanner tried to brace himself, his heart racing and his mouth dry.

The sea scorpion crawled from the wreckage, its head cracked and crushed, dark blue blood covering its shell. One antenna was gone, and its remaining large claw had been torn off, leg and all. The dark spike tail still curved above its back, poised to strike, though it didn't have much room to maneuver in the tunnel. The creature lurched forward, away from the wreckage and toward the Zodiac.

A surge of displaced water swamped the boat and Tanner crouched behind the gunnel. The creature half-swam, half-crawled around the Zodiac, and for an instant, the beast was feet from Tanner. Its one remaining black eye swiveled his way. Blue blood dripped over the boat and the sea scorpion's tail impaled a soldier as it passed, dragging the screaming man beneath the boiling river.

"Did that just happen?" Tanner said. He pressed against the inflated pontoon. The flooded Zodiac was already bailing itself out thanks to a gap between the deck and gunnel, and even as he caught his breath, the surrounding water drained away. Silva and his remaining men coughed and cursed while one fished for the radio. It took Tanner a moment to realize why the radio was so important, and he froze, his stomach going cold with dread.

Randy.

30

Tanner joined the search for the radio, but before it could be found, Silva had the electric motor fired up and the Zodiac jumped into the creature's blood wake. Tanner worried for Randy, but surely his friend had heard the commotion and had figured out what was happening.

Daybreak came on, and the darkness faded. The creature pushed down the river ahead of them, its tail poised above its back. The animal's blood slick appeared thicker than it had been, and that meant it was only a matter of time, but how much time? Tanner felt like the thing had been bleeding for days and he suddenly felt sorry for the beast. What did it know? The scorpion hadn't come here on its own. The storm dragged it from its home, forcing the animal to deal with one of the most vicious and lethal predators on earth: man.

They were gaining on the beast and needed to catch the thing before it went under the steel trestle. If it got through there, the chase was over because they wouldn't be able to portage the boat fast enough. Randy would be forced to confront the creature with the help of one soldier, Ravac, and a heavy-duty machine gun. That wouldn't be enough. It was also possible the wounded creature would try and hide along the shoreline like it had earlier.

A cloud passed before the moon and it got darker, the world becoming a gray nothingness beyond a hundred yards. The roiling water atop the scorpion went flat, and then came at them, a giant wave rising like a fist from the river. The scorpion had turned back and was on collision course with the Zodiac. Tanner cursed. What had he done to make everything go so terribly wrong on this never-ending day? He sucked in a breath and waited. There was nothing else he could do.

The wave before the sea scorpion washed across the river, and the boat rocked and listed. The leviathan surfaced, and Tanner braced himself and fired his MK18 at the beast's giant mouth as it hovered above him, huge fangs dripping blue blood. The beast's one black eye focused on him, and in it Tanner saw death. Not the creature's, but his own. He pulled the trigger until the gun clicked empty, but the bullets had no effect on the beast and it continued to come on like a bull. Tanner let the empty clip drop to the deck and slammed home a full magazine of thirty 45mm armor-piercing shells.

"Ready incendiaries," Silva said. One of the soldiers lifted a missile launcher onto his shoulder. "On my command! It's too close."

Jefferson rushed to the bow, her movements considered and steady as she settled in behind the laser. The bark of the machine gun vibrated the entire boat, and the empty shells fell into the murky water. In the east, the purple-orange glow of sunrise was a dark bruise spreading across the horizon.

The river was suddenly full of blood. Tanner realized one of Silva's men had been caught in the monster's jaws, and it was ripping and tearing at the man as he disappeared down the sea scorpion's gullet. The man's black helmet and dark faceplate were visible within the closing mouth and Tanner raised his MK and fired, putting the man out of his misery.

The massive jaws closed, and a loud crunch shot a nasty pain down Tanner's back. Jefferson screamed and lit up the predawn dusk with the flash of the laser. It shot upward, off target, and cut across the sky like a stray beam from a light show. She swiveled the cannon as best she could, but the weight of the thing jerked her around, making it hard to get a steady shot.

Tanner's mind spun and rage grew in him as the creature flailed above him. A hand gripped his shoulder, and Silva screamed for him to move. Tanner rolled to the side, wishing he'd listened to Randy and Jefferson. They needed more men, more firepower. The distant sound of helicopters approaching filled Tanner with dread, and his stomach burned with angst. If they arrived, the beast would panic, and that would make things worse, but they were still miles off, and wouldn't make it in time to do more than clean up the mess.

The scorpion's mouth opened again, and the cavern behind the teeth and fangs was bottomless. The monster exploded into the Zodiac, and the boat lifted from the water as it was tossed like a toy toward the water reeds that lined the river's edge. The creature's hum became a load clicking sound, and the world spun as the raft and everyone in it flew through the air.

As the elixir of adrenaline flooded his body, Tanner heard the chorus from the theme song of one his favorite childhood TV shows. "High on the rapids, it struck their tiny raft, and plunged them down a thousand feet below. To the laaaaaand of the lost. To the laaaaaaand of the lost."

The Zodiac landed with a jarring crash atop water reeds that cushioned the fall. Jefferson tried to sight the laser, but she couldn't get a bead on the thrashing creature. For the laser to be effective, it had to remain focused for several seconds, and with the sea scorpion fighting for its life, it just wouldn't cooperate. The animal bucked and heaved, kicking up mud and leaves as its tail stabbed at the river.

The spotlight blinked out, and everything fell behind a curtain of gray dusk. Tanner jumped into the dark water, scrambling to bring up his MK18 as he fired. If he could draw the creature away, it might give Silva enough space to fire the missiles. His feet sunk into the soft river bottom as he headed into the water reeds, the MK18 held above his head. All around him chaos ruled as the turbulent water engulfed the Zodiac and silenced the machine gun.

"Fire missile!" Silva yelled as he was engulfed in the torrid river.

The whoosh of the SPIKE-MR leaving its tube jerked Tanner's head around, and he watched the missile streak across the river and strike the sea scorpion on its hard carapace. The explosion was ear-piercing, and it sprayed flames across the river. Water reeds caught fire, going up like tinder, and in the firelight, Tanner saw the beast struggling to stay upright. Its tail stabbed wildly as it was engulfed in flames, and columns of river water shot twenty feet in the air as the spike missed its mark. A giant ball of black smoke rolled toward him, its heat so intense Tanner closed his eyes and got low in the water.

The Zodiac surfaced amidst a mound of boiling water. Silva fired the heavy machine gun again, focusing the shots on the fiery hole left by the missile. The scorpion wailed and cried as fire tore through it. The reek of burnt fish filled the air, and black smoke made seeing anything more than a few feet away difficult. The beast screamed again and flopped into the river with a crash that sent a wall of water at Tanner.

He dove underwater as fire covered the surface of the river. The water heated, and he was boiling to death beneath flames that threatened to cook him. The river vibrated, as if the Earth had been shaken. Above, an orange-white glow filled the sky and the water got hotter. Tanner's lungs burned, and when he couldn't hold his breath any longer, he came up and entered hell.

The sea scorpion tossed and jerked in its death throes, tossing itself around and trying to extinguish the fire. Its giant jaws chomped on nothing, and its tail stabbed randomly, hitting nothing but water. Massive cracks in the monster's carapace leaked blood, and white meat pushed out through the shell. Tanner had a twisted vision of a giant lobster tail cut open, covered in paprika and baked with breadcrumbs, a pool of butter next to it. The scorpion breached into the air and came down with a bone-rattling wail and fell still. It laid upside-down in the river, its legs twitching, its pincers chomping at air.

The Zodiac floated a few feet away. Jefferson stood and released a primal scream and emptied her MK18 into the corpse. The creature spasmed, and even as it sank beneath the dark water, one of its spidery legs jerked back, the pincer at its end grabbing hold of the Coast Guard officer across her shoulders.

Tanner screamed as the bottom half of Jefferson's body fell away, her upper half still held tight in the dying beast's pincer. She struggled to free herself, bracing her arms against the creature's claw and pushing upward. She smiled at Tanner and flopped like a marionette that's had its strings cut. Then the beast went still, and Jefferson's life left her. The pincer claw opened and her remains splashed into the river and floated downstream.

Tanner let his head fall into hands as he fought back tears, all the emotion of the chase catching up to him. How many had died? Yet he still lived. How can that be possible? It was proof there was no God, because what type of god would let him live while Jefferson died? Then he realized he had Jefferson's blood and pieces of fat and flesh splattered across his chest. He laid back in the river, water sloshing over his face.

The monster spasmed again, and this time, its tail stabbed at air and nobody got hit. A crazy memory flitted through Tanner's subconscious as he watched the scene, unable to move as he floated like a corpse on the surface of the dark water. He'd been fishing at a lake cabin, and he'd caught a nice-sized trout. He brought the fish home and decided to cook it on the barbecue whole. Ten minutes later, as he sat having a beer, the fish bucked and heaved itself off the grill, over the railing, and into the forest below.

Fire lit the night as the water reeds burned and smoldering pieces of sea scorpion floated on the river. Steam filled the air and the odor of rotting flesh and cooked fish made Tanner gag. Silva staggered across the Zodiac, searching for his men. He looked lost, and when he saw Tanner, he saluted and Tanner saluted back.

The river flattened, the fires petered out, the smoke dissipated, and the sky turned the blueish-gray of dawn.

The sea scorpion was dead.

The sound of approaching helicopters grew louder, and as the sun peeked over the Great South Bay, Tanner wept.

31

Tanner spent the day in the hospital with an IV in his arm and getting stitched up. He was released without restrictions and went home, had a stiff drink, and crashed. He slept ten hours straight but managed to get up so he could attend the memorial service for those who'd been lost. Parts of Sal had been recovered, but no remains of Officer Johnson or Officer Kipper were found. There was nothing to put in their coffins, not even scraps of clothing. The dead coasties would get a military burial with full honors, but pictures of Jefferson, Petty Officer Lance "Sharkey" Petrovich, Petty Officer 2nd Class Lester Ramone, and Seaman Yamone James would have pictures next to the cops.

Agent Silva's dead nameless soldiers disappeared without a trace, as he did, though Tanner expected him to show up at some point. Those guys always did.

He showered for an hour, but couldn't get the smell of Jefferson's blood off him. Her beautiful face haunted him, those cool eyes appraising him from the darkness. There was no malice, or regret, only resignation and loss for what could have been. Tanner thought he'd loved her, though they'd never even kissed. He still smelled the faint scent of her perfume, and remembered the way she'd curl her lips when she was surprised. He knew that people who experienced stressful and dangerous situations together often formed bonds that otherwise wouldn't have occurred. How many times had he heard of people marrying the person who saved their life? Or the Florence Nightingale Syndrome, where people fell in love with their caregivers?

Was that all Jefferson had been to him? He didn't think so, but he'd never know because she was gone. The image of her body cut in half, and the look on her face when she realized she would die would stay etched in his memory and would haunt his dreams until the day he died. Did he love her? Not in a traditional sense, that would be crazy, but he felt something for her, something major, because the burning hole of her loss left a pain in his chest worse than any injury he'd ever had.

He shut down the shower and toweled off. Physically, he felt OK, but he dreaded seeing the wives and children of the cops who'd been killed. He'd make a big deal about their roles in the killing of the sea scorpion, how their bravery saved many lives, but what did that mean to a ten-year-old-boy who would never see his father again?

He dug out his only suit, a black funeral staple he'd had since his dad passed. It was covered in a light sheen of dust, and he wiped it off with a wet cloth as he mechanically went through the process of making himself presentable. The belt buckle he'd found sat on his dresser, its shiny brass finish catching his eye. He picked it up, turning it over and over in his hand, and then placed it in his pocket.

The day was bright, and no clouds marred the endless clear blue sky. If it wasn't for the downed trees still littering the trailer park, he barely would have noticed there'd been a Category 4 hurricane almost two weeks ago. Hurricane Dan crept through the Atlantic and the thought of having to pick up after another one of Mother Nature's messes made Tanner's head ache.

He hopped in his Jeep and cranked it up. The streets and highways were back to normal, power had been restored to half the island, and fuel and food shipments had commenced. Insurance men ruled the land as they evaluated the damage and decided who would get what and when. The federal response was beyond bad, and as usual, New York State needed to bail itself out. Money and support were sent by Albany, but it wasn't enough. This pissed Tanner off in many ways, the biggest one being he didn't understand how the people who paid some of the highest taxes in the country weren't entitled to help when they needed it.

The ceremony was to be held on the ninth hole behind the marine police station. The golf course had drained, and it would be open for business in a couple of weeks, if Dan didn't have something to say about it. Much of the turf still needed to fully dry out so it wasn't ripped up and destroyed by the players.

There was already a large crowd there when Tanner arrived, and he parked in front of the old post office that had been his temporary office. He walked across the golf course, following the same path he had in the dingy the prior week. He combed his hair with his fingers and took a short pull of vodka from the stainless steel flask his father had given him. He rolled his shoulders and cracked his neck as the warm liquid slid down his throat, bringing confidence and calm. The organizers chose the perfect spot beneath a great oak tree. Tanner knew the spot well. It was the perfect place to say goodbye.

The captain saw Tanner and walked out to greet him. "How are you? Doing better?" His face was pleasant. If Tanner was in trouble, apparently it could wait for another day.

"I don't know. There are moments when I feel all right, then there are times…" He struggled to find the words. "Then there are times when I think I might shake apart, and my heart hurts and I feel like I'm having a heart attack."

Quinn's eyes narrowed and his brow furrowed. "I am sorry to hear that. It's not like you."

"Whatever me there was is gone," Tanner said.

"Don't be so glum. You made it. You killed the thing and you're a hero. All past transgressions forgotten. Even News 12 didn't run your history when they did the story. Ms. Alenso, the reporter who crucified you every chance she got, had nice things to say. Your demotion has been lifted, and if you play your cards right, I might be able to get you out of marine division."

"No. No, that's OK. If it's all right with you, I think I'll stay, at least for a while."

"Fine by me. If you change your tune, just let me know. Listen, the reason I wanted to talk to you is several of the men are asking if you will say a few words today."

"Me? Why me? Shouldn't you—?"

"Easy. Easy. You don't have to do anything you don't want to. I just thought... I don't know, that since you were there, and saw everything first hand, you would be better equipped to do this. If you don't want to, I understand, but you should try."

"Why? Why me?"

"You're their leader whether you want that or not," the captain explained. "I'm just some suit that busts your balls about overtime and procedure. How about I start and introduce you? You don't need to say much, just offer condolences."

Tanner considered this and nodded his agreement.

"Good, come on. Senator Jellison wants to meet you."

Tanner sighed.

They made their way across the sixth fairway to the crowd gathered before the elevated ninth hole tee box. Senator Jellison shook Tanner's hand vigorously, throwing platitudes at him, but Tanner hardly heard him. The podium was set right on the spot where Tanner had been drinking when he'd first encountered the sea scorpion, and pictures of the deceased stood on easels at the back to the tee box. Many of the heads in the crowd turned his way as he approached.

Randy had filled him in, so he knew the majority of the details pertaining to the creature had been kept under wraps, and the stories that spread around were exaggerated to the point of non-recognition. Randy said two kids he overheard at 7-11 said the monster was a hundred feet long and breathed fire. Tanner chuckled to himself as the crowd watched him approach with expectant eyes. They were going to be disappointed.

Tanner said hello to Tina and Randy and shared condolences with the families of the lost police officers. It broke his heart seeing the children cry, and part of him felt responsible. If he'd gotten the creature when he had the chance, Sal might still be alive, as well as many others.

"Hey, snap out it," Randy said.

Tanner was staring at the bay and the breach beyond, lost in thought. He sat next to Randy, and the crowd grew silent as Captain Quinn stepped behind the podium.

"I've given this type of soliloquy many times, and they get harder each time," Quinn said. Someone coughed, an infant cried out, and the wind gusted across Wood Point. "There are no words that will bring back our friends, fathers, and husbands. There is no reason I can give that will put your mind at ease, other than those who died did so to save others, to ensure we were all safe and protected. For that, I, and all of us, will be forever in their debt." Quinn bowed his head and paused.

The silence stretched out as Tanner fought back tears. Randy had his head down, but he was crying.

"I'd like to ask Nate Tanner to come to the podium. He knew these men better than anyone, and therefore, it's appropriate he put their memories to rest. Tanner?" Quinn stepped back, relinquishing the podium.

Tanner got up and looked around. All eyes were on him, and he fingered the brass belt buckle in his pocket. He thought of Jefferson, of Sal, of all who'd died so he could live. He felt unworthy, a cheat, a charlatan. What had he done to deserve to be here?

He settled in behind the microphone and it reverberated, sending a squeal bellowing over the crowd. He backed away from the mic, sweat rolling down his back and forehead. Tanner hadn't prepared remarks, and in that moment his heart had nothing to say. He stared out at the sea of faces, all looking to him to say words that would make everything all right, but he froze, his stomach going cold.

Silva strolled across the golf course and Tanner watched him make his way toward the crowd.

"Tanner?" the captain nudged.

"Yes," Tanner said. "I'm sorry, everyone. Please bear with me. This isn't easy, just as it's not been easy for many of you." He paused and saw Silva take a seat on a folding chair in the back row. "Salvatore Castro, Toby Hendricks, and Wes Kipper were my friends. They were brave men who put themselves between an incredible danger and all of you. They did this not because they got paid, or because it brought them fame and fortune. My friends did it for you, the folks who sit before me."

Tanner paused and wiped his brow with his jacket sleeve. "Belinda Jefferson and her crew went above and beyond the call of duty, and deserve all the honors and recompense they and their families deserve.

I'd like to thank Belinda…" he stopped, dabbing a tear from the corner of his eye. "To the families of the civilians lost, I say only, those who lead into danger save those who follow. It is with deep sorrow that I say goodbye to these fine men and women. I extend to all of you my deepest condolences." He gestured toward the large headshots of the dead policemen and coasties. "Please bow your heads in a moment of silence."

Three Suffolk County police honor guards stepped forward, raised their rifles, and pointed them at the sky. As they fired, Tanner flinched, the shots bringing back memories of the events on the river. He bowed his head and said, "Goodbye, Belinda."

32

When the honor guard finished, everyone sat in silence while Tanner collected himself. He looked to the captain, who nodded. "Father Graham will now say a few words, and afterward, please join us for refreshments at the clubhouse. Thank you for coming."

Tanner stepped away from the podium, threaded through the crowd, and sat next to Silva, who didn't look his way. He was listening intently to the father talking about how those who'd died were now in Heaven with God, and how happy they must be.

After a few minutes, Silva said, "You believe in this voodoo?"

"Where you been? You disappeared pretty fast."

"You know how it is. There was mess to cleanup. Higher-ups needed appeasement and bodies had to be sent home." Silva kept his eyes on the preacher as he went into some half-song, half-verse rift.

"Were your guys laid to rest?"

"In time. Their bodies were sent to a war zone where they'll be listed as casualties of war. That way the families will get closure, and can collect all appropriate benefits and honors."

"Kind of the truth," Tanner said.

"Kind of."

"And we must always remember that God has a plan and..." the priest went on.

"Screw your god's plan," Silva said. He tore his eyes away from the preacher and looked at Tanner, his eyes cold with anger.

"Easy. Reverend Graham's all right."

"He's a charlatan like the rest of them. Making a living off of sowing fear and division."

"Where's the sea scorpion's corpse?" Tanner asked.

Silva chuckled. "On ice."

Tanner's felt his hackles prickle.

"It's in a very safe place where nobody will ever find it except the big heads who are trying to make sense of the thing."

"Anything new to report?"

The priest was finishing up, and Silva said, "In a minute. We'll get a drink."

"So go now in peace, and peace I giveth unto you," Graham said. He lifted his arms to the heavens as if waiting for divine intervention, but when none came, he let his arms fall to his sides.

Silva got up, and the crowd dispersed, some folks making their way to the clubhouse and others heading for their cars. The captain joined Tanner and Silva as they walked.

"I don't believe we've met. Captain Quinn." The boss held out his hand.

Silva looked at it, but didn't shake it. Quinn left his hand out there for several seconds as the two men jousted with their eyes, and when it became clear Silva wasn't going to acknowledge the captain's gesture, Quinn let his hand fall. Quinn's face screwed up, and he opened his mouth to say something, but Silva beat him to it. "So you're the guy that ordered Tanner off the bay? Good call there, boss."

"Well, I—" the captain stammered. "I didn't know. I was going on slim information and I wasn't the one—"

"Yeah, OK," Silva said. "Is there something I can do for you?"

Captain Quinn glared at Silva, then at Tanner, who shrugged. Tanner was enjoying this.

"I'll speak with you later, Nate." With a sigh, the captain peeled off and went to shake hands and kiss babies.

"You didn't have to do that," Tanner said.

Silva smiled. "But I wanted to. I hate these know-it-all suits who make things way more difficult than they need to be to justify their existence. Pisses me off. Anyhow, how are you? That's really why I stopped by. I'm heading out soon and we might not see each other again."

"No offense, but that'd be fine by me."

Silva chuckled. "No offense taken. My name be trouble, and trouble be me. Not exactly the fun train." They arrived at the bar and Tanner ordered a vodka martini straight-up with olives. Silva said, "Now that's a drink. Make it two."

As the bartender made their drinks, Tanner asked, "So what's new?"

"Nothing really. The big heads say the monster shouldn't exist. Surprise surprise. The tech told me that as he was standing right next to the corpse. My brains agree with the Coast Guard brains. This thing was some kind of freak, a *Jaekelopterus* hybrid. They believe the species survived over the ages by partnering with other species, like lobsters or horseshoe crabs."

"Doesn't make sense, though, does it? I mean, how could something that big, you know, screw a small lobster?"

Silva laughed. "Part of the evolution involved fertilizing external eggs, not coitus, but thanks for putting that image in my head. Thank you very much."

"And it came from the canyons beyond the drop-off?"

"That part is more of a mystery, though that theory still makes the most sense," Silva said.

As he spoke, Tanner noticed Silva's attention shift from him to something across the room. Tanner turned to see a uniformed officer jogging across the patio toward the captain who stood laughing and yucking-it-up with Senator Jellison.

The cop interrupted the captain, who looked none too pleased. Tanner and Silva stared at the conversation, the cold moisture from their drinks dripping to the floor. Tanner took a long pull on his martini as he watched the captain's face change from annoyance to concern.

Silva downed his entire drink with one pull, placed the glass on the bar, and headed for the captain and senator. Tanner put out an arm. "Hey, whatever it is, I'd stay clear." Silva shook him off and continued on his way. "Shit," Tanner said. He downed the rest of his drink and put his empty glass next to Silva's.

When they arrived at the captain's side, his face was flush. The uniformed officer fled, and the captain excused himself from the senator's side.

"What?" Tanner said. "What's happened?"

"Someone's been killed on Carey Beach."

***

Tanner found Randy and pulled him away from his family, and with Silva, they jogged to the station at the tip of Wood Point, where a twenty-two-foot SAFE boat sat moored in the station's marina, bobbing on the gentle sea.

"Hey. Wait up." It was Captain Quinn. "I'm coming along. Wait up."

Tanner looked at Silva, who rolled his eyes.

"You want me to cast off before he gets here?" Randy asked.

Tanner looked to Silva. "Your boat. Your call," Silva said. "But if I kill him, you have to cover for me."

"Wait for him," Tanner said. "What harm can he do?"

"You don't want an answer to that question, do you?"

"No, not really."

Randy fired up the engines as Silva and Tanner undid the mooring lines. Quinn arrived just as Tanner uncleated the last rope. The captain was dressed in a suit, and he almost fell into the drink when he jumped on the bow and the slick soles of his dress shoes sent him cartwheeling across the gunnel onto the deck. Tanner and Randy restrained their laughter, Silva didn't.

They inched from their dock space and headed into open water. The bay was calm, and a light northeasterly wind pushed tiny whitecaps across the surface. It was the calm before the storm. Dan was on the way, and for now, the sky was free of rain clouds, but thin cirrus clouds stretched across the horizon like tattered clothes, and the air was crisp and salty. The reek of rot and decay had subsided.

Carey Beach was minutes from Woods Point. The boat skittered and hopped across the green water, and the captain asked, "You think we have another scorpion here?"

Tanner hadn't thought of that. "I don't know. It makes sense, though, right? Maybe our bitch had a friend, and animals always return to the site of their kills."

"Lover is more like it. I didn't tell you because I didn't want you to worry, but my big heads said there was most likely a pair, a male and a female."

The weight on Tanner's chest that lifted when the beast sank into the river returned, and his stomach ached and the pain in his neck throbbed. Tanner looked at Randy, who shrugged.

As they approached the beach, a crowd of people stood around the snack stand, huddled together like a flock of birds with no wings. The beaches were open and commercial and residential traffic was allowed on the bay, though few boats could be seen. A red streak of blood ran across the white sand and disappeared in the bay.

The SAFE boat screamed onto the beach, lights flashing, sirens chiming. Randy cut the motors and punched the tilt button, lifting the engines from the water as the boat crunched onto shore. Tanner pulled his Glock and leapt from the boat, landing in shallow bay water.

Grooves in the sand showed something had crawled from the water. Silva and Captain Quinn joined Tanner and Randy went to interview the crowd. Silva walked the beach in a grid pattern, looking for clues while Quinn stood in shock and amazement. Tanner had given everything to kill the sea scorpion, and all the time a second lurker in the bay had been waiting to strike.

"Look at this," Silva said.

Tanner arrived at Silva's side and his mouth fell open a crack when he saw what the agent pointed at. A scale, not unlike the ones they'd found inland, lay before Silva. A piece of large oval plating that had been part of a sea scorpion's tail.

Randy arrived and said, "They claim everyone was hanging out on the beach when the beast rocketed from the water toward them. Most people ran, but it got a kid who was asleep. The kids forgot about him."

Like the first few killed by the sea scorpions, there were no remains; no scraps of clothing, body parts, nothing. It was like reliving a nightmare. They'd fought and won, and it was supposed to be over. Tanner rolled his shoulders and cracked his neck. The sea breeze picked up, and a chill ran through him. He holstered his gun and sat on the sand, glaring at the Great South Bay. Silva plopped down on his right, Randy on his left. The captain stood off by himself, talking on his phone.

"You think it's smart to sit here?" Randy asked.

Tanner guffawed. "Sure. Got a blanket? Let's layout and get some rays."

"That's not funny," Randy said.

"It's a little funny," Silva said.

Tanner pulled his flask from a back pocket, twisted off the cap, and took a long pull. He handed it to Randy, who also took a deep drink. When Randy held the vodka out to Silva, the government man took it and said, "I sure need a hit." Silva took a long draft and handed the flask back to Tanner. When Tanner went to take another drink, he found the flask empty.

"What now?" Randy said.

"We get more Stolichnaya," Tanner said. Neither man laughed.

"We call the Navy," Silva said.

33

Fifth precinct headquarters had been in the same spot Tanner's entire life. The building's gray-black rough concrete facade looked like dark rain clouds, which was fitting on this day. Hurricane Dan's outer edge had rolled in and giant raindrops splattered on the Jeep's windshield. Tanner hated going to the main office. His visits usually meant he'd done something wrong, because he never got called in to get complimented for busting dirtbags taking eighteen-inch fluke. This time around, the threat posed by the sea scorpion was established without doubt, and Tanner and the rest of the locals, including the Coast Guard, had become secondary players in the blink of a Navy man's eye.

Despite this, Tanner had been summoned to a meeting at which the Navy would lay out the plan to deal with the second scorpion. Tanner still held some level of honorary status, plus the bigwigs were smart enough to understand there was value in local knowledge. Then there was Silva, who sang Tanner's praises to the higher-ups. For these reasons, Tanner and Randy would be part of the massive assault.

The Great South Bay was closed again, and the Coast Guard cutter *Vigilant* and Navy destroyer *Gridley* were anchored in the mouth of the breach, preparing to fire up their big guns. The *Gridley* was a stray from the Pacific Fleet and was equipped with the most modern weapons available. It boasted two MK41 vertical launch systems, multiple heavy guns, Tomahawk missiles, and Mark 46 torpedoes.

Tanner's head hurt. He hadn't done any heavy drinking for a few days while preoccupied with the chase, but losing Jefferson, the discovery of a second creature, and a fight with the ex-wife all sent him running to the comfort of Jack Daniel's loving embrace. Butterflies danced in his nauseous stomach, his eyes stung, and his throat was so raw it hurt when he swallowed. His right side was solid black and the bone bruises on his arms and legs hurt every time he moved.

When Tanner arrived at headquarters, he was surprised at how many people were there. It was a far cry from five short days ago, when the Navy insisted he present better proof before they'd even consider sending a ship. The alpha in charge was Navy Commander-in-Chief Drew Halphron, leader of the Atlantic Fleet. He'd arrived hours after the discovery of the second beast, and by sheer presence alone had taken over the operation. Several Coast Guard and Navy officers stood with Halphron, content to let the commander run the show. Not that any of them had any real say. Halphron was the top dog in the room by every measure.

Randy came up beside Tanner. "Quite the shit show," he said.

"More testosterone in this room than is advisable."

"You, always being the optimist."

Captain Quinn spotted them and waved, so Randy and Tanner were forced to take seats next their boss. Tanner felt the room's eyes on him. There was more brass in attendance than he'd ever seen in one place. Navy, Army, Suffolk PD, fire rescue, and harbor patrol, all waiting to learn how they could help.

The commander stepped to the lectern. He wore a light brown, casual dress uniform with all his chest candy proudly displayed. His shoes were shined and his brass belt buckle marked him as a brother of the sea. Tanner fingered the buckle in his pocket. It was most likely Sharkey's, and every time he touched it, he heard the cracking of the submersible's hull, and saw Sharkey's blood clouding the water, and the rage would rise in him.

Halphron adjusted the mike and looked out on the crowd of thirty-seven men and women. Silence fell instantly. "Thank you for being here. This briefing is highly confidential, and all information provided here, or any part of our discussion about said information, is considered confidential to anyone outside this room."

It was hot and humid, and folks fidgeted in their seats and fanned themselves with briefing papers. Halphron said, "I've been in the Navy thirty-seven years. Longer then some of you have been alive. I've seen some strange shit. Stuff that would make you wonder if you were going crazy. What we face here is such a thing. An animal out of our prehistoric past that doesn't know its environment and is frightened and hungry. We know it will attack without provocation, and this time, we must organize a preemptive strike and not wait for the beast to attack."

The commander paused, and Tanner thought his eyes flicked his way for the briefest of moments. "Our plan is simple. We'll lay a chum slick starting in the center of the bay and leading to the breach. Then I'll need PD and rescue units to work the inner waterways and canals until we locate the animal. We'll also bait Carey Beach, since the creature's familiar with that area and might return there. When we have a location for the thing, we'll pull everything back. Then, using sonic weaponry I'll go into in a moment, we'll drive the scorpion into the breach. Air support will also engage at this time. The creature will head for open water and that's when the USS *Gridley* and the USCGC *Vigilant* will be waiting to send it back to the depths."

Pain shot up Tanner's back. The Navy's plan wasn't much different than Jefferson's. Maybe if he'd listened to her, she'd still be alive. The room fidgeted and stirred, but nobody spoke. Halphron was a big dog, one of the biggest, and questioning him in front of thirty-seven brass wasn't wise unless you had a very good reason. Everybody seemed to understand this except Silva. "Ah, question here. Sonic weapons? You have these with you?"

The commander sized up Silva with an eye of recognition, and then answered the question. "I have one right here to show you." The commander motioned to someone to his left and a young seaman rolled a Long Range Acoustical Device (LRAD) to the front of the room.

It looked like an ultra-high-tech stage light. A gray round casing sat atop a tripod, and several cords snaked from the device into a large generator-like box behind it. The seaman swiveled the device up and down and side to side, showing how the weapon could be aimed. "The weapon creates a beam of extremely high-powered sound waves that can disrupt or destroy the eardrums of a target and cause severe pain or disorientation," the commander said. "This is usually sufficient to incapacitate the target. Less powerful sound waves can cause nausea or discomfort. We believe these creatures are susceptible to sound waves. That's how they know we're coming. So the sea scorpion should flee before this device, and we'll use them to drive the creature toward the slick and into the breach."

"Is there any danger to the officers operating the weapon?" Captain Quinn asked. "I'll not have my men affected by this thing." Tanner almost laughed. Maybe there was someone other than Silva in the room who didn't understand that this was a time to fly below the radar.

The Navy Commander stared at Quinn as though he were a plebe, and said, "Make no mistake, this weapon, if misused, can cause death and permanent injury. So it is with my deepest concern that I insist that you allow only Navy personnel to fire the weapons, which we must deploy on some of your vessels. In addition, as an extra precaution, ear protection will be provided and should be worn at all times."

"You plan to hit the creature while it's boxed in the breach?" a man in an expensive suit asked. Tanner wasn't sure, but he thought the man was a congressman.

"There has been discussion about the stability of the breach and what might happen if Tomahawk missiles and 130mm guns rock the area. The breach is slowly closing on its own as the tides pull sand through it. Many experts believe it will eventually close on its own. Others believe the breach is a permanent addition to the natural ecology.

Whichever be the case, it was decided that any unintentional effects wouldn't significantly affect life on Long Island."

"So…" the suit said. "You plan to attack it in the breach?"

"We feel that provides us the best opportunity for success because the animal will be contained and away from populated areas," the commander said.

"Unless it goes on land," the suit said, thinking he'd scored a point.

"If it does that, then it really has no chance against our weapons."

The room fell silent. Someone coughed and sniffled.

"As you all know, the weather is going to be a challenge. Dan is passing to the east, and we expect seventy mile-per-hour winds and wave heights of five feet on the inner bay. So be careful, go slow, and stay in contact. Now if there are no more questions…" Halphron looked at the inquisitive suit. "I'll turn the briefing over to Agent Silva, who personally grappled with the first scorpion along with members of the Suffolk County PD and Coast Guard. At the close of the briefing, please see Ensign Peters in the back there. He'll give you assignments for your boats. Any vessel outside its assigned area will be removed from service. There will be no warnings and no excuses will be accepted. Agent Silva will describe the creature for you, just in case you have to engage the beast, which I hope won't be necessary. Agent Silva." The commander stepped away from the podium.

Silva gave Tanner a sly smirk as he pushed to his feet and made his way to a folding table with a light projector on it. Silva turned the machine on, and a rectangle of white light fell on the front wall. A moment later, a picture of the sea scorpion's corpse appeared. There were several gasps and intakes of breath.

"Yeah, you should be concerned," Silva said. "It's thirty-feet long and its curved spike tail stabs randomly when it's threatened, and the two front claws move with amazing speed and accuracy." He stepped forward and pointed at the creature's back. "The carapace is hard shell plating that even armor-piercing bullets had trouble getting through, thus making small arms almost useless against it."

Silva hit a button, and the picture changed to a police artist's hand-drawn diagram showing the topside of the creature. "We think its antennas play a major role in the creature's sensory perception so if you can sever these, do so. The creature's eyes are also an area of vulnerability, as Lt. Tanner will tell you. He threw a harpoon into the first creature's eye and significantly hampered the beast."

Tanner felt all eyes on him again and he started to sweat, big drops of perspiration sliding down his back and across his forehead.

"The creature's mouth is filled with razor-sharp teeth and two fangs we believe deliver a toxin that incapacitates its prey. I made many direct shots into the creature's mouth with a heavy duty Browning fifty-caliber machine gun and the thing just kept coming on."

The room fell silent again. It was a desperate kind of silence. Everyone looked around at each other with glazed eyes, their faces full of questions. Tanner smiled. Silva sure knew how to command a room. All the agent was waiting for now was for someone to ask the question Tanner knew would be asked. Probably by some dumbass in a suit.

"So what can we do? Sounds like this thing can't be killed. How was the first one beaten?" It was the alleged congressman in the suit.

"Glad you asked," Silva said, smiling. Tanner knew he was mocking the man by the way Silva was smiling, but he and Randy were probably the only ones who recognized it. The picture on the wall changed and this time it showed a diagram of the underside of the beast.

"Aside from fire, this is where our greatest opportunity lies," Silva said. He pointed to the sea scorpion's belly. "The plating is thinner here, and it tapers off as it reaches the head. There is a gap there, by the creature's neck, for lack of a better term."

"How are we supposed to hit under there?" a Navy man asked. "Is the beast just going to roll over for us?"

"The creature breaches from the water like a whale when it attacks. That's your opportunity." Silva looked at Tanner. "Lt. Tanner, do you have anything to add?"

"Just that a strange hum and clicking sound precedes the creature, and it may be your only warning," Tanner said.

Silva nodded. "OK. If you have mission specific questions, I'll be available. Please get your assignments from Ensign Peters. Good luck and God speed to all."

34

The operation, dubbed Scorpion Strike, commenced at the end of the briefing, and as the brass received their orders, they scuttled off to put them into motion. Dan rolled in and wind tore at Long Island and the bay churned in a turbulent mess. Tanner and Randy were assigned to the vanguard that would push the creature into the breach, and a seaman was stationed on Randy's SAFE boat to operate the sonic weapon and coordinate their attack with naval command aboard the *Gridley*. The chain of command wasn't clear, as Tanner was captain of the boat, but the twenty-two-year-old skin-and-bones kid from landlocked Kansas reported to captain of the *Gridley*, Alveo Sampson. Tanner's father used to say if you have two bosses, you have none, and Tanner couldn't shake the feeling this would be a problem if things went to shit.

Tanner had considered trying to get Randy to stay behind, but had decided against it. He needed his best friend and partner by his side and it would be an insult to suggest otherwise. Plus, he didn't think Randy would listen if he was ordered to stay back. The only person who could give that order and have it followed was Tina, and she loved and respected Randy too much to ever give him that ultimatum. She'd say it was part of being a cop's wife. Worry was part of the job, and that's what she'd signed up for. She was one of the toughest people Tanner knew.

The Navy seaman was at the boat when they arrived, and he was tinkering with his toy when Tanner and Randy hopped aboard, rain pelting them and wind tearing at their rain slickers.

"Seaman Second Class Fernandez reporting for duty, sir," the spindly kid said over the roar of the wind. He wore the blue work uniform of the Navy's lowest ranks and a skinny black inflatable PFD. Two ribbons hung above his breast pocket. He looked like a Cub Scout ready to go sailing.

Tanner smiled, and worries about the chain of command faded. "Nice to meet you. What do they call you on ship?"

The kid looked at his feet.

"Can't be that bad," Randy said.

The seaman looked up. "String Bean."

Tanner and Randy laughed. "What's your first name?"

"Leonard."

"Let's go with Leo," Tanner said.

The kid's smile split his head.

Tanner stowed his gear, a container of ammo, and some food and water. Leo went back to preparing the sonic weapon, and Randy started the motors, pulled their covers, and did a thorough inspection. Last thing they needed was a breakdown when they could least afford it.

Sonic canon and gear secured, Randy piloted the SAFE boat out of the PD marina into the Great South Bay. Leo stood on the bow, his face stuck into the breeze like a bird.

"Eager beaver," Randy said.

Tanner slid open the pilothouse door and went to join Leo. The wind picked up as they entered the bay and the coastline slid behind them. When Tanner got to the bow, Leo said, "You have a wonderful home. This is an amazing body of water."

Tanner had never considered the stinky green mud-bottomed lagoon to be amazing, but he also knew familiarity bred contempt, and that he rarely saw the good things even though they were right in front of him. "Yes, it is," Tanner said. "It once supported a vibrant fishing community, but most of the sea life is gone."

The kid looked at him with the innocence of a babe. "Why was that allowed to happen?"

"That's a fantastic question I don't have a satisfactory answer to. I do, however, have a question for you. What drew a kid from the landlocked state of Kansas to the sea?"

Leo laughed. "You sound like Ma. I couldn't even swim when I signed up. She told me I was crazy."

"Why then?"

Leo gazed out across the Great South Bay. "Because of that," he said.

The motors kicked up as Randy swung the boat southeast and headed for the breach. Boats already searched the inner waterways, and several vessels of various sizes clustered together in the center of the bay. Randy adjusted course and headed for the cluster of boats. The bay pitched and heaved, and heavy wind pounded the SAFE boat.

Silva was on one of the Navy patrol boats, and he'd be at the front of the vanguard along with Coast Guard SAFE boats, Navy patrol boats, and tactical combat Zodiacs. Most of the vessels were equipped with sonic cannons, along with a myriad of small munitions.

Randy powered down as they came within a quarter mile of the cluster of ships. No sooner had his hand left the throttle than the comm channel crackled to life. "Lt. Tanner, do you copy? This is Commander Tel."

"Copy, Commander Tel, over," Tanner said.

"Do your thing then head over to Carey Beach."

"That's a 10-4. Tanner out." Randy brought the boat back up to speed.

Another reason the big boys needed Tanner and Randy was the chum slick, even though Silva had handled that chore on Carmans River. They knew what worked, what the beast liked, and could get the stuff fast, so it had been left to Tanner and Randy to create the slick that would help lure the monster into the breach.

For the job, Randy produced a nasty concoction of fish blood and entrails, decayed squirrel corpses, and a mix of rotten blue mussels, all of which had been fermented in a barrel of brine that broke down the chunks of flesh and bone.

"Tides going out right about now, yes?" Randy said.

Tanner examined his watch. "Aye. We're about a mile out. I say we start. You?"

"Do it," Randy said. He pulled back on the throttle and the boat slowed and their wake crashed against the transom, threatening to boil over the gunnel. Tanner wrapped a cloth around his face, covering his nose, before he tore off the lid to the chum barrel. As soon as he opened the container, he coughed and dry heaved, and Leo threw his head over the side, puking. Tanner didn't look in the barrel as he ladled out the liquid with a Polly-O ricotta cheese container and slowly dumped it into the bay as the SAFE boat crept north toward the mainland.

The smell spread like smoke, and the oily red-black slick floated on the surface of the bay and drifted with the current toward the breach. Pint by pint, Tanner dripped the chum into the water as the SAFE boat churned away from the breach and headed back toward the south shore of Long Island and Carey Beach. When the chum barrel was empty, Tanner washed it out and replaced the top. An oily sheen stretched across the bay and disappeared into the breach, which was now three miles off.

"That slick will attract sharks and other fishies from a hundred miles away," Randy said.

"No joke. Great white sharks can smell a drop of blood in the water from a mile away," Tanner said. "Time to head over to Carey. Make it fast."

"Aye," Randy said. "All forward," he yelled to Leo, who stood beside the sonic cannon staring across the bay. "He didn't hear me." Randy slowly dropped the throttle, being careful not to unbalance the kid.

The SAFE boat came on plane and Randy pointed it northeast. The trip didn't take long, and they ripped across the bay and were powering down before Tanner even had a chance to hit the head and take a nip of his flask. The boat came to a rocking stop a hundred yards off shore, and their wake caught up to them and crashed against the back of the boat, sending tiny rolling waves onto the beach.

A sonic cannon was set up on the concrete patio in front of the snack stand, and a chunk of rotting beef lay on the center of the beach, blood sprayed on the sand all around the carcass. Tanner sniffed the wind and caught the scent of rotting flesh. It was hard to tell if it was the rotting meat, or the slick, which seemed to stick in your nose and attach to clothing and hair like fungus despite the heavy wind. Marines assigned to the *Gridley* hid in the water reeds that separated the beach from the parking area and Svenson's Marina. Tanner could barely see them as they lay prone, gun muzzles poking through the reeds.

"They're not screwing around, are they?" Randy asked.

Tanner said nothing. The implication was clear whether Randy meant it to be or not. Would Sal and Jefferson and the others still be alive had Tanner pushed harder to get support rather than take on the beast himself? He soothed himself with the notion that it wouldn't have mattered. He had requested help and the higher-ups hadn't thought the crisis worthy of additional resources. Tristin had stretched all support services to the breaking point, and a giant prehistoric shrimp hadn't rated.

"You agree it'll come back this way?" Randy said as he settled into the bench at the rear of the pilothouse.

"Most animals return to areas where they've had success hunting in the past, and they also return to the same kill several times until they're finished with it. I can't imagine that when it gets hungry this won't be its first stop."

The pilothouse door slid open and Leo entered. "Here, take these please. Have them handy in case I need to fire up the weapon." Tanner and Randy took the ear protectors, and the kid smiled, like he'd accomplished something he'd been ordered to do, and left the pilothouse.

Tanner and Randy looked at each other and smiled. Randy said, "Oh, to be young again."

Two Navy UH-60 Blackhawks running side-by-side roared overhead, flying low as they tore across the Great South Bay. They were heading south toward the breach, and the rumble of their rotors faded as they disappeared into the raging storm clouds in the west. Soon darkness would descend.

Minutes turned into hours as they waited. Hurricane Dan tore up the bay, rolling waves coming at them from every direction, slapping the boat. It rained sideways as the swirling gale tossed and pulled at the

SAFE boat. They ate sandwiches of white bread and ham, and they offered the kid one, who took it eagerly and ate it fast and insisted on heading back out to man the sonic cannon.

Tanner flipped off the exterior light switch and the deck and surrounding sea grew dark. He killed the pilothouse house light and leaned back in his command chair, trying to steady himself as the boat pitched and heaved. The glow of the equipment panel lit the room.

Tanner's father had been a great fisherman, and to most people, he'd brag about the difficulties involved. How it required preparation, strength, smarts, and luck to catch a fish, even a simple rat like a sea robin. To Tanner, he'd been more truthful and confessed the key to fishing was simple and it only required that you have two things: good bait and patience.

Tanner already had the first one covered, and now it was time for patience.

35

Tanner dozed off, and when Randy woke him, shards of moonlight pierced the cloud cover and cast long shadows across the undulating black water. The storm still raged, but it was breaking apart as Dan's largest spiral rain band cleared the island and gave the battered land a brief respite.

"Daybreak in an hour or so," Randy said.

That meant the witching hour was approaching. Judging by the creature's past patterns, the predawn hours would bring the monster from its hiding place in search of food, and with any luck, the chase would be on by sunup. With the storm easing, the monster would be eager to leave its hiding place. A light mist hung over the bay like a blanket, and visibility was limited to five hundred yards.

Leo leaned against the deck railing, all pretenses of his vigil gone. Tanner and Randy had slept in shifts, and nothing of significance had been reported. The beef slab still stunk up the beach, untouched, and marines still hid within the reeds that swayed in the wind. Tanner saw the lights of patrol boats combing Carey Creek, and across the bay ships of all shapes and sizes waited for the guest of honor.

"Not looking too good, are we?" Randy said.

"It'll turn up. Give it time," Tanner said.

"We've given it fifteen hours."

"Then get ready to give fifteen more, or however long it takes. I'll sit here until I'm old and gray if needs be."

"That don't mean much," Randy said. "You're already old. And gray."

"Thanks, always good to have the support of a friend."

Randy laughed. "No worries. I'm always here for you."

The radio chimed, and Randy turned up the volume. Tanner slid open a pilothouse window and called out to Leo, "Kid, get in here."

Leo snapped up like a light switch had been flipped, and the rail-thin young man shot to the wheelhouse, rubbing his eyes.

"In here, kiddie," Tanner said. Leo nodded, but appeared reluctant to leave the sound cannon. Tanner sighed. "It won't go nowhere, hurry."

When Tanner returned to Randy's side, his friend said, "A Navy drone found it inside Kistover's boathouse. Right up the street from me."

"...be cautious and maintain your current position until your vessel is specifically hailed. Maintain radio silence until further notice. We want the command channel clear. All boats designated as group B, fall back to your starting positions and await further instructions. Sound cannon units in group A converge at the mouth of Stony Creek off the coast of Stones Throw. Approach with caution and check in with command onsite for your instructions. No one is to engage the creature without a direct order."

"Full speed," Tanner instructed. "Get us there fast, Randy."

Leo went back out on deck, but not before reminding Tanner and Randy to put on their ear protection. Randy dropped the hammer, and the SAFE boat leapt from the water and drove through the whitecaps. Stones Throw was only three miles east, and as Randy arced the boat toward the mouth of Stony Creek, several boats blocked their way.

Randy powered down and joined the throng blocking the canal entrance. When they got close, the lead Navy Zodiac hailed them. "Tanner, that you?" It was Silva.

"That's a 10-4. Where do you want us?"

"With me. We're going to head in and flush the thing out. You game?"

"Right as rain," Tanner said. If rain felt like acid dripping on your face, he thought. His stomach gurgled like he'd eaten a dozen bad clams and sweat dripped into his eyes. Rubber squealed on rubber as Tanner's SAFE boat rubbed against Silva's Zodiac.

Silva stood waiting, bracing himself on the Zodiac's black gunnel.

Tanner breathed deep and slid open the pilothouse door. Wind gusted as he went out on deck, and he and Silva spoke over a two-foot gap between their boats amidst the storm-ravaged bay.

"What's the plan?" Tanner asked.

"You and Randy, me and my crew, and a coastie boat will head up the canal real quiet like, and surround the creature. Then we drive it down the canal with the sonic cannons. Should be easy if we place the boats right."

Tanner nodded and turned to go back into the pilothouse.

Silva stopped him. "Be careful, yeah? You know what this thing can do. Resist the urge to attack it. This time, we'll let the big guns handle it."

Tanner nodded. Every time someone said something along those lines, his heart hammered in his chest and streaks of pain ran up and down his legs and arms. If he had only backed off when he had the chance... He wouldn't torture himself any longer. Jefferson's death wasn't his fault, nor was Sal's, or any of the others, but that didn't stop him from feeling like shit about it.

Tanner started to give Randy his marching orders and his friend cut him off. "Heard the whole thing," he said. The PD SAFE boat fell in behind Silva's command boat as it slid down the canal, and the coastie vessel trailed after. A few inches of bulkhead stood above the water, but the water was rising. Their wakes sent waves pouring across backyards, parking lots, and marinas. The tides were running higher than normal, and wind tore at the remains of the lost world that floated in the water.

Tanner saw houses he recognized as they passed like wraiths through the predawn dusk. Emergency lights cut through the gloom on the streets as police and local firemen went door to door spreading the word of a mandatory evacuation for the surrounding area. If the animal hopped onto land, they wanted no one in its way. A prudent precaution and one that might have saved the three people who were killed when the first sea scorpion had flattened Fireplace Neck.

"See it, Tanner," came a voice over the comm.

"I got it, Silva. Over," Tanner said. Then he turned to Randy and said, "Looks just like when Sal and I found the first one hiding in the house basement."

Randy said nothing as he maneuvered the SAFE boat up river, past the boathouse with the bubbles pouring out its front entrance. "Where you want me, boss?" he said.

"Full stop. Hold position until we hear from Silva."

The agent was on the bow of his boat, staring into the dusk at the boathouse, his hands on his hips. He looked back up the canal toward the SAFE boat and the coasties and held up a hand.

"What are you doing you crazy bastard?" Tanner said.

Silva's boat inched toward the dark maw of the boathouse entrance, the tip of the Zodiac disappearing within.

The bubbles stopped, and Tanner jumped on the radio. "Silva, get back. It's coming."

Silva retreated aft and the black Zodiac reversed out of the boathouse. The agent pointed toward Tanner and bent his finger in a come-to-me gesture. Randy engaged the motors and the SAFE boat slid through the turbulent water until they were north of the boathouse. The coastie boat stayed south, and Silva fell in behind Tanner.

The radio crackled to life with Silva's voice. "On my signal, engage the sonic cannons, direct them into the boathouse. When it breaches, retreat north, with cannons directed south. Everyone give me an all go, please. Over."

Tanner tapped the comm button and said, "All go." A second later, the coastie boat did the same.

The bubbles started again, and boils of whitewater rolled from within the boathouse as the beast surfaced.

"Leo, you ready out there?" Randy had patched the kid's headgear into the comm.

The boy gave a thumbs up, and said, "Ear protection, please, sir."

Randy and Tanner slipped on their earmuffs. Seconds passed, minutes, then Silva's voice boomed through the comm. "Now. All sonic cannons on."

Tanner heard nothing. The light on the cannon's power supply was on, and Leo had the round gray housing directed at the boathouse. He slipped one ear protector cuff off and heard a high-pitched screech that sounded far away. Based on their briefing, Tanner knew the ear protection was overkill because the sound waves were focused in a single direction, and due to the precision of the device damage to organisms outside the beam of the weapon saw little effect, so he pulled the ear protection off.

Bubbles and whitewater erupted from the beneath the boathouse, and Randy put the SAFE boat in reverse, moving north as Leo arced the sonic cannon over the canal. Waves pounded the boat and ran over the bow, but Leo didn't flinch as bay water rushed around his legs.

The leviathan's antennas and tail rose first, dripping with mud, then the giant claws followed by its hard black-shelled carapace. Two good eyes swiveled toward the boats, and they seemed to jiggle as the creature floated to the surface.

"Forward," Silva said over the comm. All three boats advanced toward the scorpion, sonic cannons on full power and zeroed in. The creature's hum became a wail of pain as the sound waves tormented the beast.

The leviathan breached from the canal, flopping over on its side and sending mud and debris raining down upon the boats. Then it headed south down the center of the canal, and Silva's black Zodiac jumped right on its tail. The sea scorpion dove, leaving only a mound of water and its tail behind.

"Should we hit it a few times to make sure it keeps heading south?" Randy asked.

"Negative," Tanner replied. "We're not supposed to engage. Stay behind Silva."

They drove the sea scorpion south, back the way they'd come. The sound of approaching helicopters signaled the arrival of the flyboys. A Navy drone trailed after the beast, sending video back to the command ship. Tanner considered telling Silva to call them off. So far, the scorpion had responded to the sonic cannon as expected, and the plan was working perfectly. If the helicopters came in, the beast might get spooked, as it had before, and it might risk land travel. If they needed the whirlybirds, they could call them in, but at the moment, they seemed more of a hindrance.

"Silva, this is Tanner. Over."

"Go ahead, Tanner," Silva said.

"Call off all the birds. This thing is following our playbook to the letter. Why risk it getting spooked? Like you said, let's let the big boys handle it this time."

Silva said, "I was just thinking the same thing."

The channel went dead and Tanner looked to Randy, who shrugged.

The sound of the helicopters faded, but the drone stayed.

The sea scorpion fled before them, and soon it would reach the bay. A heavy rain fell, and a harsh breeze tore at Leo, who stood by the cannon, head pressed into the wind, rain lashing him. Tanner couldn't see the boy's face, but he knew he'd be smiling. Silva gave him a thumbs up as the agent sat on his Zodiac's gunnel, talking into a radio. The coastie boat stood back, flanking Tanner's PD boat. Their little team had done its job, and now it was time to finish it.

36

The scorpion squeezed through the narrow canal mouth into the bay. It dove as soon as it hit deeper water, and its tail dipped below the surface, leaving only a swirling mass of mud, bubbles, and whitewater. Silva's boat stayed behind the creature, and Tanner and the coasties fanned out to the east and west, driving the beast south toward a knot of boats that was separating to create a path. Rain fell sideways as wind roared over the chopped surface of the bay.

Tanner took a deep breath, letting it out slowly as he rolled his shoulders and stretched his back. The ball of water rolled across the bay; every time the creature veered off course, a boat would move in close and focus the sonic cannon, and the beast would get back in line.

This went on for several minutes as the small vanguard drove the sea scorpion forward. It made no sounds as it swam, and Tanner wondered if the wind and background noise might lessen the effect of the cannons, but if it did, the beast showed no sign.

It reached the slick and slowed, the possibility of getting food overriding its flight instinct. The mound of water lessened, and the beast fully submerged. A few moments later, its tail broke the surface, then its carapace. It opened its giant jaws, sucking in the oil and rotten meat floating in the chum slick, and picked up speed as it followed the slick across the bay to the breach.

Waves broke through the breach, and the current was running fast as the tide pulled out. A solitary seagull flew next to the drone as it followed the beast toward the trap, and Tanner marveled at the bird's bravery, or ignorance. "You see this thing?" he said to Randy.

Randy looked perplexed and Tanner pointed through the front pilothouse window. "Haven't seen one of those out here in over a week," Randy said.

"What do you figure it means?"

Randy shrugged.

When they were a mile out from the breach, other vessels joined the vanguard. The Navy Freedom-class littoral combat ship *Freedom II*, captained by Hal Preston, took lead position next to Silva, and Tanner and the coastie support vessel fell in behind them. Navy, Coast Guard, SCPD, and fire rescue boats fanned out in a wide arc, fully encircling the monster except for its southern escape route. The ships with sonic weapons made up the forward team, while the rest kept a safe distance and helped keep the beast from straying off course. Drones swarmed in the air like mosquitoes now, and Tanner wondered how they weren't smashing into each other.

The tide was ripping and the current pulled bay water through the breach, creating a series of rapids and whitewater that marked the choppy surface. Sea spray covered the deck and windows, and the sound of eighteen boat engines, the faint purr of the sonic cannons, and the wind and waves created a cacophony no ear protection could ward off.

The scorpion's carapace lifted from the sea, it antennas flopped about, and it slowed. It adjusted its course to port, but was met with a PD boat, and when it adjusted to starboard, it met a Navy Zodiac.

When the vanguard reached the mouth of the breach, the creature disappeared beneath the bay, and all that remained was a swirling vortex of water. Tanner said, "Take us down a few knots." Randy eased back on the throttle and the SAFE boat slowed as the rest of the vanguard powered ahead. Tanner grabbed his field glasses and searched the horizon. There was no sign of the sea scorpion. The wind eased, and the rank stench of the beast cut through the sea air.

"It's playing possum like its buddy did," Tanner said. "Full stop."

Randy hesitated, but then complied. Tanner slid open the pilothouse door and went aft, staring across the windblown sea. Even out on deck, he heard Silva's hail. "Tanner, what the hell are you doing? We're almost there."

Tanner went back to the wheelhouse to respond. Randy was already answering Silva when he arrived on the bridge. "...it's disappeared. We've seen this before."

"It dove, that's all. Power forward," Silva said.

Tanner interjected. "You see anything on your sonar?"

Silence on the other end.

"Silva, do you copy, over?" Tanner said.

When Silva's voice came back on the channel, he sounded defeated. "You might be right, I can't see anything and there's no bubbles coming to the surface."

"So let's turn around," Tanner said.

"One minute. Let me contact Preston," Silva said. Several tense minutes passed as the entire vanguard passed them by, and soon Tanner and Randy and Leo sat alone on the torrid sea. When Silva hailed, he sounded unsure. "Tanner, Captain Preston disagrees, and the vanguard will continue on its present course."

Tanner sighed and pounded the comm console. "Silva, the creature has doubled back and is heading to the slick. I guarantee it."

"How can you know?"

"I've seen this before. Its partner tried to give us the slip the exact same way."

Silva said nothing, and only faint static crackled over the comm.

"Trust me, Silva. I'm right."

"You're willing to bet lives on that?"

"Yes," Tanner said with no hesitation. He'd taken the deaths of his friends and colleagues hard, but that last thing he wanted was for more people to die because he didn't act when he knew what needed to be done. Sitting back and letting more qualified and better-equipped professionals do the work was one thing, but sitting by when he knew those better-equipped pros were making a mistake was something altogether different.

"OK," Silva said. "Wait for me, I'm coming with you."

There was a tapping at the pilothouse door. It was Leo. The seaman's face was twisted in a frown, and he held his hand to his ear as if listening to someone speak. He knocked on the door harder, and Tanner let him in.

"What is it, sailor?"

"I have orders to continue on," Leo told him.

"From who? I'm in command here," Tanner said.

The lad looked uncomfortable. Clearly, he didn't want to go up against Tanner, but orders were orders, and Tanner watched as the young man fought with himself. Tanner knew which side would win.

Tanner stepped forward and stripped the headset from the seaman's head. "You are under arrest for mutiny. Please go down below and wait. I'll turn you over to your superior officer when this is done." Tanner hated doing it, Leo was a naïve kid, but Tanner couldn't think of any other way to protect the kid. This way all responsibility would fall on Tanner and Leo would escape discipline.

Leo looked confused, and the corners of his mouth dipped as disappointment spread over his face. He reached out and took the headset back and looked to Randy, then back at Tanner.

"You're sure?" Tanner said.

Randy said, "This isn't your fight."

"But it is," Leo said. "Brass and ass sound and mean the same thing." He smiled, tension leaving his face. "Plus, you'll need me to work the cannon if we actually find the thing."

The kid had a point. "You sure? The military don't take kindly to disobeying orders," Tanner said.

Leo nodded. "They won't miss one cannon with all that firepower, anyway." He slipped out of the pilothouse and went back to his post.

Silva arrived, and his Zodiac bumped up against the SAFE boat. He leapt aboard and was in the pilothouse in seconds. He carried a large black plastic suitcase, and he handed it to Tanner. "You might need this. Incendiaries with a short barrel launcher for close-range shots. What now?"

"I figure it'll head back to the slick looking for food."

"OK, let's do it, then," Silva said. He went back out on deck and waved for his boat to follow and returned to the pilothouse.

Randy dropped the hammer and the SAFE boat jerked from the water and was on plane in seconds, blasting through the three-foot chop. The twin Hondas buzzed as they tore through the whitecaps, shooting sea spray and seaweed over the deep green water.

"Houston, I think we have a problem," Randy said.

"What now?" Tanner said.

Randy turned aft and pointed at Silva's boat in the distance. "She's not coming."

Silva's grin disappeared, and he stabbed the comm button. "Lt. Grishel. Lt. Grishel, do you copy." Static. "Grishel, you little shit, you better answer me or you'll be piloting a rowboat in Central Park!" Nothing. "Screw you, coward." Silva closed the channel and smiled. "I didn't expect them to follow, that's why I came aboard. Those Navy tools would kill their mom before disobeying a commander's order, even if said commander told them I was in charge."

"Surprised you didn't bring in your own crew," Tanner said.

"No time. The agency is stretched thin at the moment, and this isn't the only crisis that requires attention. Then there's the matter of the crew I did have."

Tanner said nothing. Silva had lost four of his five men, and where man number five was at the moment he didn't know, but he could imagine Silva wasn't the most popular guy back wherever he called home.

The comm burst to life. "Tanner, this is Captain Quinn. You are to return to the vanguard immediately."

Tanner could only imagine the testosterone-filled command center back on land. He responded, "Terry, the creature gave the fancy Navy ship the slip, and it's back in the bay and—"

"Return to the vanguard now or you're relieved of duty," the captain said.

"Can he do that?" Randy said.

"Why not? He's the boss," Tanner said.

"Randy Vernon, do you copy?"

"Right here. Over."

"You are to take command and join the vanguard at once. Your sound cannon is needed."

"Sorry, boss, but no can do." Randy closed the channel.

Silva and Tanner stared at Randy, crooked smiles painted on their sun-burned faces.

"Proud of you, partner," Tanner said.

"You can explain it to Tina when I'm fired and I can't pay the bills," Randy said, but he was smiling, clearly pleased with himself.

The three men watched Leo as he held onto the sonic cannon, the boat bouncing and listing as it cut through the rough seas. The rain came on hard, but the kid didn't move. Lightning tore across the sky and the rumble of thunder rolled over the bay.

"You think that'll spook it?" Silva asked. "The thunder, I mean?"

"It might," Tanner told him, "but most fish like rainy weather, that's why hardcore fisherman always go out in bad weather."

A flash of lightning lit the dark water, and in the distance, a black spike cruised just above the surface. "There she blows," Silva said. He opened the large suitcase and removed the missile launcher and loaded an incendiary missile.

"That the same kind that took down the last one?" Tanner asked.

"Yup. Stingers, and this time, I plan to put it right down the thing's throat."

Somewhere above the storm clouds, the sun passed noon.

37

"Half speed," Tanner said.

Randy eased back on the throttle, and the PD SAFE boat settled as the Great South Bay roiled around it. Four hundred yards off, the sea scorpion pushed through the water, following the slick to the center of the bay. The rain stopped, but thick clouds still obscured the sun and the wind came from the north, kicking up waves and turning the bay into a churning mess. The eye of Dan, now a Category 1 hurricane, was one hundred miles to the east, but still causing severe conditions. Large patches of seaweed dotted the surface along with a covering of oil that had spread out from the chum trail.

"How do you want to do this?" Tanner asked.

Silva stared through the pilothouse window at the creature's tail as it scythed over the water, the tips of its antennas flopping about. He said nothing. Tanner figured he was thinking of the four men he'd lost fighting the last scorpion. Tanner had the same doubts and wounds, so he understood what Silva was going through. It's not an easy thing being responsible for the lives of others, and when you lose one of your people, the pain digs that much deeper.

"Silva?" Tanner said. He put a hand on the man's shoulder.

Silva turned and smiled. "I'm all right," he said. "Trying to calculate our odds."

Randy chuckled, and said, "Never tell me the odds."

"Easy, Han," Tanner said.

"We can try to lure the thing to us, or go at it head-on," Silva said. "Either way, the sonic cannon won't be much use in our attack. It'll just drive the beast away. We'll use it as a failsafe in case we need to clear the creature from the area."

"We haven't had much luck drawing the thing out," Randy told him. "We've tried that several times with little success."

"So you vote direct attack?"

"Since when is this a democracy?" Tanner said.

"Since I need you guys," Silva said. "You ever see me pull rank unless it really mattered?"

"No."

"People who are always telling you how powerful and important they are usually aren't," Silva said.

"I vote sneak attack," Tanner said. "Let's roll up on it, guns blazing, and see if we can get a solid shot with the Stinger. Randy, you pilot the boat, and I'll distract and annoy the scorpion with machine gun fire. Leo can stand by with the cannon. Silva, all you have to do is stay upright so you can fire the kill shot. All that make sense?"

Silva and Randy nodded.

"Remember, this thing hasn't been hit before that we know of," Silva said. "It's got all of its fingers and toes and is experiencing all this for the first time. We barely took down its pal who'd lost its claws, an antenna, and a poolful of blood. So be on edge, take nothing for granted, and keep your head on a swivel."

"You think we should call in backup now that we've got in it in our sights?" Randy said.

"No," Tanner and Silva said at the same time.

"By the time they get here, it could have disappeared inland," Silva said.

"They had their shot, and they blew it," Tanner added. "This thing is ours, and I'll have it for Jefferson, and Sal, and all the rest its kind has killed. Let Silva and I get into position, then ram the boat up its gut."

"Aye aye, my captain," Randy said.

Tanner checked his Glock as he and Silva went out on deck. He didn't think he'd need the handgun, but one never knew. Tanner went to the bow and braced himself against the gunnel, resting the MK18's gun barrel on his forearm.

The SAFE boat picked up speed and was on plane in seconds, even in the rough surf. The boat pounded through the waves, spraying seawater. Tanner was drenched before the boat was at top speed, and to his left, Silva covered the missile launcher beneath his jacket.

They were two hundred yards out and the sea scorpion hadn't changed course. It looked to be heading back to Carey Beach for another steak. Tanner sighted the machine gun on the creature and jacked a shell into the chamber.

The hum started when they were fifty yards out, and it quickly changed to the frantic staccato bleating that marked the beast as upset. When they were twenty yards out, Tanner opened up with his MK18, peppering the creature with bullets. The shots slapped against the water and the creature's tail. Tanner arced the gun up and concentrated fire on the antennas.

The sea scorpion breached with a massive shriek, rolling in the water and sending waves crashing into the SAFE boat and over the gunnels. For an instant, the boat swamped, but the water drained as Tanner continued to fire. Silva stood behind him, missile launcher cocked on his shoulder as he peered through the targeting sight. The beast lurched forward, slamming into the SAFE boat and sending Silva skidding over the sloping deck. He dropped the missile launcher, and it slid across the deck and came to rest against the gunnel. The scorpion's tail stabbed wildly at the water, just missing the boat.

"Back us away," Tanner yelled.

The boat didn't move.

When he looked to the pilothouse, he saw Randy working the throttle, trying to start the engines. The surge of water that swamped the boat had stalled the motors, and Tanner heard their flywheels spinning, but the motors didn't catch.

The sea scorpion's tail struck the deck three feet from where Tanner stood. Silva yelped and rolled toward the missile launcher. Tanner dove for cover as a torrent of water exploded through the hole in the deck. Tanner lost his MK18 as he was tossed around in the heaving water and he tried to keep himself from getting thrown from the sinking boat.

The scorpion wailed as Leo pointed the sound cannon. The creature's huge stinking maw peeled back as it bit down on the SAFE boat. The motors lifted from the water as the bow was crunched in the creature's massive jaws. Its teeth and fangs crushed the vessel and tore two chambers from the gunnel.

"Leo!" Tanner yelled.

The boy and his sound cannon were caught in a claw, and Tanner let loose with a guttural scream that would have scared most animals, but not the scorpion. The claw closed tight and the accompanying crunch as Leo was cut in two sent a surge of anger through Tanner.

Silva waded toward the pilothouse, the launcher over his shoulder. The SAFE boat was going down, but Randy was aft, still trying to get the boat's motors going. Silva climbed onto the roof of the pilothouse and sat with his feet braced against the roof's curved lip, the missile launcher poised on his shoulder.

"Get it to come at us again if you can," Silva yelled over the roaring and confusion.

Tanner pulled his Glock and fired from where he lay prone on the slanting deck, water rising around him. He pulled the trigger slowly, placing his shots all around the creature's head, attempting to aggravate it.

The beast launched from the water with a push that thrust the SAFE boat backward and up. The sea scorpion roared, its giant claws clamping down on the boat as it opened its jaws for a killing strike.

Silva fired the Stinger and it hissed from the tube and flew into the creature's mouth.

The beast and sea exploded and the SAFE boat rose on the tumult as the blast knocked the vessel backward. Tanner was tossed from the boat, away from the maelstrom. He spun through the air, the surrounding scene a fragmented mess of water, seaweed, burning sea scorpion parts, and boat debris. Bay water crushed him, and pieces of the creature and sections of their boat flew in every direction, slapping the bay's surface like gunshots.

Randy's bloody body cartwheeled across the sky, and Tanner felt himself crying even as he was tossed like a piece of garbage into the sea.

Tanner face-planted on the surface, and sucked in water as he tried to breathe. His eyes were open, but he saw only swirling green water filled with red and blue blood. He rolled, and the cloudy sky filled his vision. Fiery debris slapped the water around him, and pain ran through every part of his body. His inflatable PFD was on fire and he unsnapped it and let it float away. Pieces of the sea scorpion and the SAFE boat pelted him, hitting his face and arms as he sank into the brackish water.

He sucked in air and his body floated upward as oxygen filled his lungs and made him more buoyant. A black smoke cloud pushed over the water and engulfed him, and Tanner's thoughts drifted to Jefferson, Sal, Leo, and Randy. Their faces were fixed in his field of vision, floating above the water and beckoning him to join them.

The heaving sea pushed him from the tumult, and he got twisted around again. He was going under. Then his mother and father were there, the two voices in his head that kept him from falling into the abyss. They were both yelling at him, screaming for him to listen, but he could hardly hear them over the thunder of the water.

His ears popped, and he grabbed his head in pain.

"Swim, ya moron. Swim!" his parents said.

His right arm, and then his left, stroked the water, and his legs joined in, and soon he was floating on the surface, sucking in air like it was wine and he'd just crossed the desert.

"Tanner?" The voice seemed like far-off echoes coming from another place and time.

Tanner lifted his head, but couldn't see who was calling him through the smoke and rain.

Then a gust of wind drew away the smoke. Silva tread water thirty yards away, and when he saw Tanner, he yelled, "You all right?"

"I think so. You?"

"Little shaken up and I might've broken a few bones, but I'll live."

"Do you see Randy?"

Silva didn't answer.

Tanner's panicked eyes darted from side to side, searching the burning flotsam for his friend, but he couldn't find him amongst the debris and scorpion parts floating on the water. The creature's tail was still mostly intact, and its two claws floated listlessly on the surface, but the creature's head was completely blown away.

A piece of the SAFE boat exploded and fire and smoke swept across the water and scorched Tanner's face. He screamed. Randy's wife Tina filled his mind, and the children stared him with eyes that asked where their father was and why he wasn't coming home ever again. A siren wailed in the distance, but Tanner didn't care. He went limp and let himself sink below the surface. The last thing he saw before the swirling green water took him was the orange pontoons of a Coast Guard boat.

38

Blinding white light. Tanner struggled to open his eyes, but they remained pasted shut, and he realized they were bandaged. He tried to move his arms, but his right shoulder ached with the effort. His left hand found his face, and he traced coarse stitches that ran over his cheek like a forlorn railroad track. He wiggled his toes. His good hand groped downward, checking his package and sliding up his chest, and then moving over to his right arm. Needles protruded from his forearm and tubes ran away to what he imagined where bags filled with blood and other nutrients. He wasn't dead, that was for sure.

Tanner tried to remove the bandages from his eyes and a soft hand stopped him.

"Don't do that, Nate. Leave those be." It was a female voice, low and melodious.

"Tina?"

"Yes."

Tanner's stomach went cold, and he wished he was anywhere else on the planet. Tears leaked from his eyes, but she couldn't see them because of the dressings. He didn't know what to say. This was his worst nightmare come true. Had she been waiting for him to wake just so she could chastise him? Blame him for Randy's death? Would she be wrong if that's what she did?

He was responsible. He'd let the husband and father of two go into harm's way when it hadn't been necessary. They could have waited for the Navy. He could have backed off. He could have, he could have, but he didn't.

What to say? What was there to say? Randy was an adult who made his own decisions and his children would go through life knowing their father was a hero and that was some consolation, but not a very good one. There'd be nobody there to teach Fred baseball, and bring Tara to dance class on Tuesdays, where Randy used to sit and watch his daughter dance with a lopsided foolish smile on his face, pride leaking from every pore. He'd have to be the one to do those things. Tanner had always viewed Randy family as his, but now he had to step up.

"How do you feel?" Tina said.

Why she cared, he didn't know. Maybe she wanted him to recover so she could kick him in the balls herself. "Like I got run over by a truck," he said. "But I'll live." He cringed. His poor choice of words stung, and he was thankful he couldn't see Tina's face.

"That's good to know," she said.

"How long have I been here?"

"Two days. Your children and Audrey have been by your side the entire time. They went home to rest a little while and I'm covering for them."

"Covering?"

"We didn't want you to be alone when you woke up. Good thing, because you would have."

Tanner's stomach went cold when he realized he hadn't apologized. Hadn't even asked how she was, how the children were. How they were taking the loss of their father. "Are you all right, Tina? The kids?"

"A little frazzled, but OK, I guess," she said.

A little frazzled? "I'm sorry, Tina. So sorry." Beneath his bandages, he cried again, all the sorrow rushing back like the tide. He remembered getting blown off the boat, seeing Randy's mangled body cartwheel across the sky.

"Don't be. We're all just happy you're OK," Tina said.

Was it possible she didn't blame him? "How are the children taking it?"

"They're enjoying being out of school, though with things getting back to some semblance of order, the schools will be starting up again on Monday. Thanks to somebody, Dan wasn't too bad because they've already cut back winter recess and canceled spring break."

Confusion filled him and a flutter of hope. "I meant Randy, how are they taking Randy's death?"

Tina laughed. "I see. Tanner, Randy's not dead, he's two doors down."

***

After much cajoling, Tina organized a fifty-foot trek from Tanner's room to Randy's. Tanner's eyes had been burned by the blast, and he'd be wearing bandages for a few more days, but with Tina's help, he hobbled to his friend's bedside.

"I'll leave you two alone," Tina said, as she left the room.

"You look like shit." Randy's voice brought a joy Tanner had never experienced. He'd lost something special, only to discover he hadn't lost it at all.

"That's what I'm told. How the hell are you still here? What the hell are you made of? I saw you fly through the air. Thought you were gone."

Randy chuckled. "Me too, brother. It was luck, pure and simple."

"What do you mean?" Tanner said.

"The explosion blew me from the boat, just like you and Silva, but my PFD inflated. I don't remember pulling the cord, or hearing the CO2 rush into the bags. You know the sound."

He did.

"Anyway, they say I was tossed seventy feet through the air, clear of most of the wreckage. The Coast Guard boat found me. I broke my left leg in four spots and it needs surgery. It hit the Hondas as I was thrown backward. The docs say I might have a limp for the rest of my life. I asked if I could get a peg leg." Tanner laughed. "I've got a concussion, contusions and bruises all over my body, and my chest still hurts when I breathe, but other than that, everything's good."

Tanner couldn't express the joy he felt. "Man, we got lucky this time."

"Oh, and as predicted, LS is at my place until you get out of this prison," Randy said.

"Thanks." Awkward silence. "Listen, I'm sorry I..." Tanner still couldn't bring himself to say it. "Sorry I've been such a jerk. You were right to call me out on my drinking,"

"Tanner, I—"

"No. You were right. I need to make some changes and I love you for telling me so, even if you didn't use those exact words."

"You've seen Audrey?"

"Haven't seen shit, but yeah, she was around earlier," Tanner said.

"She's been here the whole time."

Tanner's stomach burned as he remembered his ex-wife's boyfriend. "What does her boyfriend think of that?"

"She dumped him when you got hurt. I think, if you go to counseling and take a few 'teach me not to be an asshole' classes, she might take you back."

"And Silva?"

"No sign of him," Randy said. "You know those guys. He's probably already halfway around the world dealing with the next crisis."

"We got real lucky this time, bud. Real lucky."

"I know," Randy said. "As I flew through the air, I thought it was over."

"Me too."

"They say when you can break out of here?"

"Naw. You?"

"Tomorrow. We're getting some kind of award for bravery or some shit when you get out."

"Award? I figured we'd be buying a deli and living off Tina's inheritance," Tanner said.

"Nope. When stuff goes right and you win, all manner of transgressions are forgotten. They're saying we were following the captain's orders. He's being praised for gutsy thinking. The kind of guy who should run things someday."

"Whatever," Tanner said. He was happy for Quinn, even if his old friend was full of shit.

"I'm gonna buzz the nurse and get something to eat. You want anything?"

"Yeah, I could eat."

***

Four days later, Hurricane Dan had passed the island by, and Tanner was released from the hospital. His vision was still blurry and overly bright, but the docs said that was normal and would fade in time. Randy needed three operations to fix his leg, but he'd gotten out of his wheelchair at the curb of Brookhaven Hospital, and hobbled the last few steps to the car.

Except for tree crumbs along the road, the island was getting back to normal. Dan hadn't added much to the existing damage from Tristin, and power had been restored to most homes. People were getting back to work and the children were starting school. The federal government sent aid and troops, and the cleanup and rebuilding was underway, though there were several areas still under review. Fireplace Neck, which probably shouldn't have been built in the first place, would not be allowed to rebuild. The Army Core of Engineers determined the likelihood of the town getting destroyed by a storm again in the next twenty years was over eighty percent, and no insurance companies would write a policy with that kind of risk. That battle had been quick, unlike many others that would drag on for years. Insurance companies didn't want to pay, they never do, and many houses along the shoreline were boarded up and would be for a long time.

The following day, the press and bigwigs gathered back at the elevated ninth hole tee box at Woods Point to honor Randy and Tanner, and all those lost fighting the sea scorpion. Medals were given, kind words were said, and when it came time for Tanner to go on stage, he waved and declined comment. The flood water had subsided, and Dan had caused little flooding, because unlike Tristin, Dan blew through at low tide.

The crowd milled about after the ceremony, and Tanner spotted Silva leaning against a tree in a small stand of thin oaks. He waved. Tanner waved back and Silva walked over. The two men shook hands, and then Silva hugged Tanner.

"Glad to see you in one piece, my friend," Silva said.

"You too. You OK?"

"Fine. I was luckier than you and Randy…well, maybe not as lucky as Randy, but pretty lucky."

Tanner nodded. "So that's it?"

"Yup. The official position of the government is that the sea scorpions were anomalies they don't expect to see again."

"What could they do, anyway?"

"A lot. They can take a picture of your asshole from space, so I imagine if we tried hard enough, we could find the things if they're out there to be found, but you're right, it would be beyond a long shot. The creatures would have to be close to the surface in order for satellite imagery to pick them up."

Lucky-shit came running up and rubbed against Tanner's leg. Silva bent and pet the animal. "This the guy you found floating in the bay?"

"Yup. We call him LS, stands for Lucky-shit."

Silva laughed. "I'm glad you made it, Tanner."

LS barked and Tanner turned to see Randy's son wheeling his father across the fairway toward him along with Audrey, Tina, and a gaggle of kids. They were waving and shouting as kids do. Pride filled him, and he realized there was no place he'd rather be.

When Tanner turned back to Silva, the agent was walking away from him into the trees. No goodbye, or farewell, or exchange of addresses for Christmas cards. Tanner never saw Silva again.

"We're heading to The Cull House for lunch," Audrey said.

"Good idea," Tanner said. "I'll meet you guys there. I need to check something first at the station."

Audrey caressed his face with the back of her hand and smiled. "Be quick."

"I will."

Tanner hobbled over the golf course, the green grass and shrubs flourishing as if Tristin and Dan had never been. He walked around the station house and waved to Beth in the tower. He sat on the beach, and six-inch waves of green water and seaweed rolled onto the sand. LS sat beside him, and they looked out on the Great South Bay and the breach beyond.

There are days that fly by in an instant and minutes that last a lifetime. Tanner leaned back onto the sand, petting LS, and shielding his eyes from the sunlight. He pulled his hipflask and twisted off the cap. As he brought it to his lips, he froze, Randy's voice echoing in his head. He stared at the stainless steel flask with the Navy logo on its side.

"Sorry, Dad," he said, and tossed the flask into the bay.

EPILOGUE

Nineteen days later…

Cindy Devero finished mixing her mimosa as she stared out the sliding glass doors at the back of her kitchen. Sunlight reflected off the Great South Bay, making the water sparkle like diamonds. She had the doors open, and the sweet scent of seawater wafted through the screens. Water lapped against the shore, and Cindy looked at her feet, remembering how her kitchen had been underwater just three weeks ago. Many of the houses along the shore were still unoccupied, but her brother was a contractor and he'd ripped out what couldn't be saved, dried out the rest with heat fans, and put everything back together for her in a week.

She took a sip of her drink, the bubbles in the champagne tickling her nose. Pounding bass came from an upstairs bedroom where her daughter Tristin blasted her latest crush band, and the thumping shook the delicate light fixture that hung in the kitchen. Tristin had had a difficult couple of weeks of being teased and mocked by just about everybody she encountered. That had mostly ended as the hurricane passed into memory, yet it would be years before "Tristin the storm" was forgotten, if ever.

The day was crisp, but warm for early October, and Cindy searched for her sunglasses so she could take her drink out onto the deck. They were in her purse, and as she grabbed them, a gust of wind pushed through the sliding glass door and she hugged herself.

She climbed the stairs to her bedroom and put on a light sweater. From the bedroom windows, the view of the bay was even more spectacular. Sailboats dotted the horizon and power crafts zigged and zagged every which way. Cindy smiled. It was good to see people back out on the water. After what happened, she'd wondered if people would ever be comfortable out there again, but people are resilient, and their memory for fear, while it may be the strongest emotion folks respond to, still had a relatively short shelf life. The monsters were gone, and no others had appeared, thus the case was closed.

Cindy hopped back down the steps and grabbed her drink. Her daughter's music had stopped and been replaced by a hollow tapping noise that sounded like something fragile banging on wood. She considered going to the steps and yelling up to Tristin and ask what she was doing, but Cindy didn't really care. The last few weeks had been hard, and she hadn't regained all her anal tendencies yet.

She slid open the screen and stepped out onto the deck. It too had been submerged in water, but it was made of a new synthetic material that could take any punishment water could throw at it. That's why she'd spent the extra money for the stuff. When you lived this close to the water, one constantly planned for the inevitable flood.

She sat in her favorite lounge chair and closed her eyes, letting the sun warm her face. She took a sip of her mimosa, and placed it on the table beside her. She was dozing when she felt the slimy kiss of her Labrador, Lester, on her face and she squealed.

The dog backed off and sat, looking up at her with expectant eyes.

"Nothing for you now," she said. "I'm not going inside. I'll give you something later."

As if the animal understood English, it laid on the deck, watching her, waiting to hold Cindy to her promise.

She drank the rest of her mimosa and the sun and the sea and the gentle breeze rocked her to sleep. She awoke to the sound of Lester barking. Not the vicious "someone bad here" bark, but a lower, more concerned bark that was half-growl, half-yip, as if the dog couldn't decide whether his alarm was warranted.

"What is it, Lester?"

The dog had his head tucked under the deck railing closest to the bay, but Cindy saw nothing that would upset the dog. Her hand darted out to pick up her drink, and when she realized she'd already finished it, she sighed.

Cindy got up from the chaise lounge and made her way across the deck to Lester. She pet the animal on the head, and said, "Quiet now. What are you barking at? Quiet."

The barking ceased, though the dog whimpered and cried.

She heard the tapping again and frowned. She'd thought it was something her daughter was doing, but the sound was stronger outside. She listened hard, walking all around the deck and trying to locate the noise.

It was coming from beneath the far corner of the deck, closest to the bay.

Her eyebrows knitted.

The bay rolled beneath the deck where it met a series of large boulders that formed a seawall along the seaward side of the property. She thought perhaps a piece of garbage had floated beneath the deck and was hitting something as the tide came in and small waves rolled into shore.

She put down her empty glass and mounted the steps down to a thin patch of grass that ran next to the deck. Lattice with square holes hid the deck supports. She worked her way toward the seawall, peering through the lattice for the source of the sound, but saw nothing.

The sound got louder and she knew she was getting close. Cindy knelt and pulled back a piece of lattice tacked to the frame with finishing nails. It was dark beneath the deck, and lines of sunlight leaked through the spaces between the deck boards, but it was hard to see.

The clicking sound had become even more pronounced, and she stuck her head through the open hole she'd made.

In the far corner, the sea pushed something against one of the deck supports. It took a moment for her eyes to adjust, but when they did, she gasped.

A large brown speckled eggshell bobbed and rolled in the bay, its remains tapping against the deck frame. It had been cracked open, and was empty.

THE END

Edward J. McFadden III juggles a full-time career as a university administrator and teacher, with his writing aspirations. His novel AWAKE was published by Severed Press in 2017, and his short story Doorways in Time recently appeared in Shadows & Reflections, an estate authorized Roger Zelazny tribute anthology with an introduction by George R.R. Martin. His first published novel, The Black Death of Babylon, was published by Post Mortem Press, followed by Our Dying Land (Padwolf Publishing, Inc..) and HOAXERS (Crossroad Press.) Ed is also the author/editor of: Anywhere But Here, Lucky 13, Jigsaw Nation, Deconstructing Tolkien: A Fundamental Analysis of The Lord of the Rings, Time Capsule, Epitaphs (W/ Tom Piccirilli), The Second Coming, Thoughts of Christmas, and The Best of Pirate Writings. He's had more than fifty short stories published, and in the 90s Ed was editor of Pirate Writings Magazine, which became Fantastic Stories of the Imagination. He also edited Cosmic SF. See The Encyclopedia of Science Fiction for full details. He lives on Long Island with his wife Dawn, their daughter Samantha, and their mutt Oli.

CHECK OUT OTHER GREAT DEEP SEA THRILLERS

HELL'S TEETH
by Paul Mannering

In the cold South Pacific waters off the coast of New Zealand, a team of divers and scientists are preparing for three days in a specially designed habitat 1300 feet below the surface.

In this alien and savage world, the mysterious great white sharks gather to hunt and to breed.

When the dive team's only link to the surface is destroyed, they find themselves in a desperate battle for survival. With the air running out, and no hope of rescue, they must use their wits to survive against sharks, each other, and a terrifying nightmare of legend.

MONSTERS IN OUR WAKE
by J.H. Moncrieff

In the idyllic waters of the South Pacific lurks a dangerous and insatiable predator; a monster whose bloodlust and greed threatens the very survival of our planet...the oil industry. Thousands of miles from the nearest human settlement, deep on the ocean floor, ancient creatures have lived peacefully for millennia. But when an oil drill bursts through their lair, Nøkken attacks, damaging the drilling ship's engine and trapping the desperate crew. The longer the humans remain in Nøkken's territory, struggling to repair their ailing ship, the more confrontations occur between the two species. When the death toll rises, the crew turns on each other, and marine geologist Flora Duchovney realizes the scariest monsters aren't below the surface.

CHECK OUT OTHER GREAT DEEP SEA THRILLERS

THEY RISE
by Hunter Shea

Some call them ghost sharks, the oldest and strangest looking creatures in the sea.

Marine biologist Brad Whitley has studied chimaera fish all his life. He thought he knew everything about them. He was wrong. Warming ocean temperatures free legions of prehistoric chimaera fish from their methane ice suspended animation. Now, in a corner of the Bermuda Triangle, the ocean waters run red. The 400 million year old massive killing machines know no mercy, destroying everything in their path. It will take Whitley, his climatologist ex-wife and the entire US Navy to stop them in the bloodiest battle ever seen on the high seas.

SERPENTINE
by Barry Napier

Clarkton Lake is a picturesque vacation spot located in rural Virginia, great for fishing, skiing, and wasting summer days away.

But this summer, something is different. When butchered bodies are discovered in the water and along the muddy banks of Clarkton Lake, what starts out as a typical summer on the lake quickly turns into a nightmare.

This summer, something new lives in the lake...something that was born in the darkest depths of the ocean and accidentally brought to these typically peaceful waters.

It's getting bigger, it's getting smarter...and it's always hungry.

CHECK OUT OTHER GREAT
DEEP SEA THRILLERS

PREHISTORIC BEASTS AND WHERE TO FIGHT THEM
by Hugo Navikov

IN THE DEPTHS, SOMETHING WAITS ...

Acclaimed film director Jake Bentneus pilots a custom submersible to the bottom of Challenger Deep in the Pacific, the deepest point of any ocean of Earth. But something lurks at the hot hydrothermal vents, a creature—a dinosaur—too big to exist.

Gigadon.

It not only exists, but it follows him, hungrily, back to the surface. Later, a barely living Bentneus offers a $1 billion prize to anyone who can find and kill the monster. His best bet is renowned ichthyopaleontologist Sean Muir, who had predicted adapted dinosaurs lived at the bottom of the ocean.

MEGALODON: APEX PREDATOR
by S.J. Larsson

English adventurer Sir Jeffery Mallory charters a ship for a top secret expedition to Antarctica. What starts out as a search and capture mission soon turns into a terrifying fight for survival as the crew come face to face with the fiercest ocean predator to have ever existed- Carcharodon Megalodon. Alone and with no hope of rescue the crew will need all their resources if they are to survive not only a 60 foot shark but also the harsh Antarctic conditions. Megalodon: Apex Predator is a deep-sea adventure filled with action, twists and savage prehistoric sharks.

www.ingramcontent.com/pod-product-compliance
Lightning Source LLC
Chambersburg PA
CBHW032010170626
46807CB00006B/2733